About the author

Lisa Cutts is the author of three police procedural novels, based on her twenty years of policing experience. She works as a detective constable for Kent Police and has spent ten years in the Serious Crime Directorate dealing mostly with murders and other serious investigations. She has been on BBC Radio 4's *Open Book* with Mariella Frostrup; part of First Fictions festival at West Dean College, Chichester; on the inaugural panel at Brighton's Dark and Stormy festival, and took part in the Chiswick Book Festival 2015. Her debut novel, *Never Forget*, won the 2014 Killer Nashville Silver Falchion Award for best thriller.

Also by Lisa Cutts

Never Forget
Remember, Remember

LISA CUTTS

MERCY KILLING

**SIMON &
SCHUSTER**

London · New York · Sydney · Toronto · New Delhi

A CBS COMPANY

First published in Great Britain by Simon & Schuster UK Ltd, 2016
A CBS COMPANY

3 5 7 9 10 8 6 4 2

Simon & Schuster UK Ltd
1st Floor
222 Gray's Inn Road
London WC1X 8HB

www.simonandschuster.co.uk

Simon & Schuster Australia, Sydney
Simon & Schuster India, New Delhi

A CIP catalogue record for this book
is available from the British Library

Paperback ISBN: 978-1-4711-5310-5
eBook ISBN: 978-1-4711-5312-9

Typeset in the UK by M Rules

Printed and bound by CPI Group (UK) Ltd, Croydon, CR0 4YY

Simon & Schuster UK Ltd are committed to sourcing paper that is made
from wood grown in sustainable forests and support the Forest Stewardship
Council, the leading international forest certification organisation. Our
books displaying the FSC logo are printed on FSC certified paper.

To Claire Finch, my oldest friend.
For being a massive part of my
own happy childhood.

MERCY
KILLING

Prologue

Few things made Dean Stillbrook happy any more but the one part of the day he really enjoyed, relished, adored, was his early morning walk through the woods from his flat to work.

The hideous experience of the last six months was only now starting to blur into the past where it belonged. He hadn't for one moment believed that he would ever look forward to the rest of his life. One stupid mistake had cost him so much but he was learning to adapt and be glad for the small things in his day-to-day existence.

As he made his way deeper into the trees, he paused for a second to tilt his face up towards the sky, the May sunshine breaking through the branches and warming his face. He stood still, eyes shut, and listened to the birds, a slight breeze rustling the leaves, and then he heard the sound of movement behind him.

It happened with such speed, Dean couldn't have reacted if he had wanted to.

His brain was finding it difficult to comprehend that

such a beautiful bright sunny morning that seemed to hold such promise could possibly result in someone tightening a noose around his neck, the rope tearing into his flesh as it pulled him straight up towards the sky he had only moments before stopped to admire.

'Please,' he tried to say, but the noose was already eating into his skin and cutting off the last breath he would take. He didn't even have time for his fingertips to attempt the futile gesture of prising themselves between the rope and his throat; let alone for the questions that would have surged through his mind before he blacked out, the most pressing of all being 'Why?'

Even though Dean Stillbrook was long past caring or knowing, it was more merciful that he couldn't feel the pain of the rope cutting into him as he was lifted up towards an overhanging branch.

He wasn't able to hear the grunts and moans of his executioner as he pulled him higher off the ground, feet left dangling in the air.

Chapter 1

Friday 5 November

Detective Inspector Harry Powell glanced at the time displayed on his computer screen. He let out a long, slow breath and refreshed the log for calls coming in throughout the county that he had somehow managed to police for over twenty-five years.

As usual, Friday-night incidents ranged from noisy children playing football in the street to violent domestics, with an unhealthy dose of traffic accidents sprinkled liberally across the towns and rural areas, not to mention the added problems that Guy Fawkes Night brought with it.

He had only been promoted a few months beforehand, so Harry was keen to make his mark and show the troops that getting to the next rank up from sergeant hadn't turned him into the sort of managerial yes-man he so despised.

Harry was the on-call senior investigating officer for the county, meaning the weekend would be spent either at work or at home waiting for the phone to ring. The last few years had turned some of his red hair grey, increased his paunch and added worry lines to his pale freckled face. None of it detracted from his formidable presence whenever he entered a room.

Many DIs would have gone home hours ago and waited for the call to shatter the peace and summon them back to work. If Harry was completely honest, there were two matters weighing heavily on his mind, preventing him from doing just that. One was the impression that he was trying to give his staff, and the second was that, with both of his teenage sons out with their girlfriends for the evening, it only left his wife at home.

He looked up at the map of the county pinned to the wall and ran an eye over the divisions he had worked on, which included the struggling ex-mining towns, the rural areas with their multimillion-pound houses and the poorer seaside towns, like East Rise, with its fair share of run-down wards and four-storey Victorian houses turned into multi-occupancy flats for those on the lowest incomes and benefit claimants.

Once more, he pressed the refresh button on his computer, almost willing for a murder or suspicious incident to flash up on the screen, saving him from a night at home and a frosty atmosphere.

His luck seemed to have run out: no one was being stabbed, or beaten to within an inch of their life.

His mobile phone rang. The single letter 'W' appeared on the screen. He'd meant to store her under

Wife when he got his new job phone, but had lost interest after the first letter.

'Hello, love,' he said.

'What time will you be home?'

'Shouldn't be much longer.' He scanned the screen again. 'There's always a chance I'll be called back in to work.'

His attempt to keep the hope from his voice wasn't convincing even to his own ears.

'You know what this town's like, love,' he felt the need to add. 'There's always something going on. Last week it was a bomb hoax that kept me late, two days ago it was a murder and who knows what tonight will bring.'

Harry turned his attention to the list on the wall of ongoing operations his incident room was currently dealing with, each with its own tale of tragedy attached.

'My knowledge of them all,' she said, 'comes from the news. I find it very informative. I won't wait up.'

He shook his head as the line went dead and ran a finger down the log of open calls in front of him.

'Be careful what you wish for,' muttered Harry to himself.

Chapter 2

Usually Friday nights were Albie Woodville's favourite part of his week. He went home to his second-floor flat, shut the door and after a simple meal purchased from the reduced section at his local Co-op, he settled down in front of his television to watch the programmes he had recorded that week.

However, something was wrong this particular Friday. He glanced around him as he walked out of the shop, passing from the harshly lit frontage to the gloomy corner of his road. Albie held his carrier bag containing half-price sausages and a dented tin of baked beans to his chest and picked up speed. Not fast enough to alert anyone watching but a quickening that meant the sanctuary of his home was all the closer.

It was somewhere he had always felt safe as soon as he shut the locking communal door behind him. When he'd rented the flat, he had chosen it partly for its video entryphone, but also because of its location. He had known immediately that this was the flat for him.

Key in his hand, Albie opened the door and he was inside the main entrance that served the twelve flats. He wasn't fond of going out after dark any more but it was the best time to save a few precious pence on his Friday-evening treat. He made his way upstairs with the whole night stretching before him, although he failed to shake off the uneasy feeling that had taken hold of him since exiting the supermarket.

The nights had got longer too, which didn't help to dispel his loneliness since his mother's death. Amongst other things, he put his jittery feelings down to the time of year combined with the anniversary of his mum's passing being almost upon him. He hadn't even been allowed to attend her funeral. Although not something that was strictly his own fault, not a day went by when he didn't loathe himself for not being there.

Thoughts of placing flowers on her grave in ten days' time occupied his mind as he unlocked his own front door, locked it behind him and punched in the code to turn off the burglar alarm.

Albie busied himself closing the curtains against the darkness, having chosen earlier in the day to leave the fading view until the sun had finally gone down. He snapped on lights, turned on the muted television and went to prepare his meal.

Once again, Albie tried to shrug off his unease, wanting to blame it on his constant worry that he would always have to look over his shoulder. The warnings had been loud and very clear. If he had been able to see the screen on the video entryphone from where he was in the kitchen area of the open-plan living room, he would have seen the dark figure as it sprinted towards the closing communal door.

Days before, residents had complained to the management company about the spring-loaded door hinge: it forced the door to slam when released and disturbed the peace of those on the ground floor. The adjustment meant that when Albie's twenty-three-year-old first-floor neighbour came home from work minutes after Albie returned, she let the door go behind her, allowing it to inch its way towards the frame. She was busy talking on her mobile phone, so she neither paid any attention to anyone behind her, nor wondered why she didn't hear the sound of the catch hitting home as she trotted up the stairs.

Behind her, a gloved hand grabbed the handle and held the door open.

He knew where he was going and made his way to the second floor, pausing on the landing both to get his breath back and to wait for his accomplice. Once the second figure had joined him, the two men stood outside the flat door, dressed head to toe in black, faces covered, listening.

They had planned for this. They knew that to stay too long was foolish but they had chosen Friday the 5th of November for a reason: Guy Fawkes Night and the loud bangs it brought with it. It wasn't the best cover they could hope for, but it was better than nothing.

As they'd discussed, the taller of the two moved closer to the door and held up his left hand. He counted off one, two, three. On three he lifted his booted foot directly beneath the handle and kicked out at the door with as much strength as he could find.

The door gave with one kick.

Chapter 3

Albie heard the noise of the wood breaking and instantly knew that today was the day. He had always known it would come and he had always assumed he would face it with a quiet dignity. Now, however, he stood shaking at his kitchen table, not entirely sure he wasn't about to soil himself, prepared to plead for his life. He held the packet of pork sausages in his hands as the two men ran into his flat, the sound of them unmistakable, and came towards him across the living room to where he was rooted to the spot in his tiny, grubby kitchen area.

The two intruders came to a stop at the other side of the rubbish-strewn table; their breath was coming fast and their hearts were pounding. Not as much as Albie's. When this was over, they knew they'd still be alive. He knew he wouldn't live to see another day.

He had been about to cook his dinner so amongst the crockery on the table was cutlery. His eyes scanned the debris, hoping to show his brain a sharp knife. He didn't doubt that it was futile. He was sixty-three years old, overweight, unfit. Despite the scarves across their faces, he knew that he was looking at two men fitter than him, about half his age.

'Please don't hurt me,' he said.

The shorter of the two moved around the table, hand pulling something out of his pocket.

'You're a worthless piece of shit,' he said, holding up a long plastic cable-tie close to Albie's face.

He felt the urge to punch Albie as he stood in front of him clutching a packet of what looked like sausages. He reminded himself that he hadn't gone to such lengths planning this moment to stoop to animal behaviour now. He had been focused on getting into the flat, doing what he needed to do, and then returning to his normal life with his sanity as intact as he could manage.

Only difficulty was, now that he was standing in front of Albie, every ounce of hatred, every night of broken sleep, and every unfulfilled dream was making him want to do more than simply kill him.

There was no point denying to themselves that the two of them had planned to cause him more harm and pain than he had ever inflicted on any of his many victims. They, however, had both sought solace in the fact that their act of retribution made them more worthy than the lowlife clutching his half-price meal with its yellow *Reduced* label showing through his short pudgy fingers. Short pudgy fingers that had been laid on terrified children's bare skins.

'Focus,' whispered the taller of the two, aware that his partner was distracted.

Albie's head snapped from the plastic tie suspended above his eye line to the one he thought was in charge.

For one moment, one cruel, misleading moment, Albie imagined that everything would be all right: he knew who this was now. The worst thing of all was that he had had no idea who was coming for him. It could have been any number of them but if this was the taller, more coherent friend, the other one was probably ...

He racked his brains to work out who it could be. He began to sweat then. Beads of perspiration started to form on his receding hairline and ran down his forehead to the end of his nose.

There had been so many of them, such sweet little boys and girls, at the home he'd run, he couldn't recall them all. If only he could, the use of just one name might save his life.

'Henry?' he asked. 'Is that you?'

All it took was a brief hesitation, while he looked across at his accomplice who in turn glanced back, for a rush of relief to flood Albie as he imagined the three of them sitting down and talking it through.

Unfortunately for him, he had guessed the wrong name.

'Who the fuck is Henry?' came the answer. 'Let's get him over here by the sofa.'

The shorter one made a grab for Albie as he let out a sob. The packet of food dropped to the floor as his hands came up in a feeble attempt to defend himself from a man half his age. Apart from being a few

12

decades younger than Albie, his assailant had also spent most of those years keeping himself very fit and strong.

With one hand still holding the plastic tie, he got the older man in a headlock and pushed his face towards the floor. His accomplice, as they had planned, ran back to the hallway, checked through the spy hole that they were still alone and helped to drag their prisoner towards the middle of the floor.

They turned him onto his front and forced his hands behind his back, he pleading with them all the while not to hurt him.

'I'll do anything,' he said, 'absolutely anything. I haven't done a thing wrong in years. It's true, it really is true. Please believe me. You've scared me now. I'm petrified and I beg you, I won't tell anyone you've been here and I won't do anything wrong again.'

'Like we fucking believe that,' came the reply.

His hands were tied behind his back, forced into plastic cable-ties.

It only left one more thing to do.

Now they had to finish what they'd started and kill him.

Chapter 4

Josh Walker, Harry Powell's uniform counterpart, sat at his shared desk in the cramped inspector's office on East Rise Police Station's second floor, typing away at a complaint report he had intended to finish for a number of days. He didn't realistically expect to get anywhere close to finishing it on a Friday night, especially a Friday night that was also Bonfire Night. It didn't stop him trying though. He knew that at some point over the weekend he would end up staying on at the end of his nightshift, running the risk of being caught up in something else. It was either that or he would have to come in on one of his days off. Neither appealed but he would have to make a decision. For now, he would get as much of it done as he could, whilst listening to the police radio which was propped on the desk beside his keyboard, wedged between overflowing cheap red plastic in-trays.

He sighed at the radio operator's voice loud and clear over his Airwave handset as it gave out details of yet another priority call.

'Nearest available patrol to Flat 12, Pleasure Lane. Call from an informant who has found her neighbour with neck injuries. Signs of a forced entry. Paramedics also en route.'

He put his hand out to pick up his Airwave. Neck injuries could mean anything but Josh knew that signs of a forced entry combined with any injury likely meant something serious. He didn't want to offer up his assistance before he knew the full circumstances but it went against his nature to stay in the office. This was especially true when he knew that the uniform sergeant was already at another scene dealing with a serious car accident.

Josh heard the call sign of a double-crewed car over the air and a voice offer to take the call to Pleasure Lane. Josh's hand moved away from the radio back to the computer. He had no doubt that the two officers were more than capable, but still he locked the keyboard, put on his police jacket and, gathering his kit, got ready to drive to the scene. His job didn't mean he had to attend every call, but for something so serious he knew he would be required, and if he was honest about it, he was curious.

He was still annoyed with himself for his earlier slight hesitation when, having driven a mile and a half from the police station, he pulled up in his marked car behind a stationary ambulance adjacent to the small block of flats, and made his way through the open communal door.

Several voices echoed down the stairwell. It was a

standard hallway, no soft furnishings to prevent any noise bouncing off the magnolia walls and across the hard-wearing carpet to where Josh now stood at the main door, propped open with a large stone from the shrubbery.

He ran up the two flights of stairs, talking into his Airwave to let the control room know where he was, making sure that his attendance was logged on the computer system.

He reached the second floor and looked into flat number 12. Two paramedics were leaning over the body of a man, whilst the two police officers stood watching. The person lying on the carpet was face up but seemed to have his hands behind him, causing his plump body to arch in an odd way.

It wasn't that that initially caught Josh's eye.

The first thing he noticed was that the man's face was purple and mottled, his tongue hanging slightly to one side. A plastic cable-tie was cutting into the flesh of his neck.

The paramedics turned him over. Josh's years of policing meant that the sight of the dead man's wrists bound together with cable-ties didn't surprise him in the least.

'Makes a change from a stabbing,' he murmured as the full realization came to him that instead of the rest of his 5th of November being spent trying to type up an outstanding complaint report, it was about to be taken up with the launch of East Rise's latest murder investigation.

Chapter 5

With the few resources he had available, Josh set about first securing the crime scene, and then finding out what the neighbours had to say about the person who used to occupy the corpse staring at him. He found out the deceased's name from paperwork and photo identification he'd glanced through on the coffee table, but left everything else undisturbed. He would wait until the crime scene investigators and the detective inspector arrived.

It looked like a straightforward crime scene to him: dead body in suspicious circumstances with boot marks on the front door of the otherwise empty flat. The foot imprints were likely to be key and on occasion had proved to be as unique as a fingerprint.

Josh knew how important boot marks could be, but it threw up a very practical problem when it came to preserving them: he needed to keep the door half-closed because the face of Albie Woodville stared at anyone as they reached the top of the stairs. He only had two officers and now one was with the initial police informant, while the other was rummaging around in the boot of her car trying to find scene tape and a scene log to record details of everyone within the crime scene.

Josh stood in the doorway, blocking anyone's view, and busied himself making sure a CSI was on their way, as well as trying to find out as much as he could about Albie Woodville. As with any Friday night, the police operators were busy asking for available patrols to deal with domestic assaults, pub fights, traffic collisions, abandoned 999 calls. It never stopped and it never would. The only difference was that modern-day policing meant that Josh now only had eleven response officers for a population of half a million.

Even though he knew the control room would make direct contact with the local area on-call detective inspector for a suspicious death, Josh was also aware that a last-minute Crown Court appearance by the person supposed to be on duty meant that all cover was being handled directly by Major Crime. He had already looked up on the roster who it was. He dialled DI Harry Powell's mobile.

'Josh,' said Harry. 'How're you doing, mate?'

'Not so bad, Harry, not so bad. Where are you?'

He heard a sigh from his plain-clothes counterpart. 'Almost made it out of the door for home, though just at the moment, there's not much to rush back to. So right now, I'm still at the nick, about to make my way over to you.'

'Things haven't improved with your missus then since we last spoke?' asked Josh, listening out for sounds of any other patrols arriving from anywhere in the county that could spare them.

'You could say that. If I didn't know better, I'd think she was having an affair. I don't think it's that: at least it would cheer her the fuck up. I'm making my way over, but based on what you've seen so far, what have we got?'

Josh lowered his voice and stepped back inside the flat, glancing down at Albie's body as he did so, mindful of where he was treading.

'I'm satisfied that we have the body of the flat's occupant. It's a male called Albie or Albert Woodville. Seems that someone broke in, tied his hands behind his back with cable-ties and then put one around his throat. Poor sod probably suffered for a couple of minutes and then knew no more.'

'Yeah, well,' said Harry. 'You may want to hold up on that "poor sod" attitude. Control room have already been on to me about this. It's why I haven't left here yet. I've spent a couple of minutes taking a look at his warning signs and he's on the Sex Offenders' Register. Albie Woodville had a thing for children, especially those he looked after in children's homes, plus he hasn't long come out of prison.'

'Well that narrows it down to only about three-quarters of the country's population wanting to kill him,' said Josh. 'I'll take a quick look around his place to make sure there's nothing obvious jumping out at me at the moment and then wait for you to get here. I'll have to go soon. I think that firearms have arrived. As usual, I've got fuck-all patrols and I've had to call them here, even though they were about fifty miles away propping up another department stripped bare in the cuts.'

Josh moved to the far side of the room to make way for the CSI who had just arrived. Conscious that he wasn't supposed to touch anything, despite the rubber gloves he wore, he pushed open the thin living-room curtains with the back of his hand.

'Give me a few minutes,' said Harry on the other end of the line. 'I'm on my way.'

'You can't miss the address,' answered Josh, shaking his head at the sight that greeted him from the other side of the window. It was weirdly comforting to know that even after all the things he had seen and the calls he had been to over the years, he could still be disgusted by the behaviour of others. It meant his job hadn't yet torn his soul out. He could make out the outline in the glow given off by the street lights of the neighbouring infant school, its playground running the length of the block of flats.

Something on the windowsill caught his eye. He was a father of three, a police officer and a man with no sexual interest in children: the large tub of K-Y Jelly pushed behind the curtain did little to change his attitude towards the dead man. Especially as the top was unscrewed and what looked like a collection of pubic hairs rested around the rim.

Josh still had a job to do but he was only human. He muttered something into the phone before he hung up that sounded very much to Harry Powell like the words, 'You dirty, dirty bastard.'

Chapter 6

Harry Powell grabbed his electronic notebook and made his way to the main door of the incident room that led to the rest of the police station. Being the last person in the office, he was about to set the internal burglar alarm when a familiar face greeted him at the entrance to the Major Crime Department.

'Detective Constable Laura Ward,' he said to her as he shook her hand. 'This is an unexpected pleasure. What can I do for you?'

'That's a very formal greeting, boss. I think you'll find it's a case of what I can do for you.'

'I'd love to stay and chat, ask about your baby. What is she – six months? A year? But I've got to rush out.'

Laura smiled at him. 'I doubt you're the slightest bit interested in how she's doing but thanks for asking and she's now thirteen months. I guess you're on your way out to Albie Woodville's?'

The remark stopped Harry in his tracks. It wasn't that he was surprised that the news had travelled so fast, but rather that it now dawned on him exactly what role Laura had chosen to take on at the end of her maternity leave. She was now a ViSOR officer, which meant spending large parts of her day visiting those on the Sex Offenders' Register.

It was one of the few times that Harry was reluctant to say what he really felt about someone else's choice of career.

'I hope you're not another of those who thought I shouldn't be doing a job like that after having a baby,' she said, leaning against the door frame, arms now crossed.

He winked at her and said, 'It's up to you what you want to do, Laura. I'm not about to warn you of the perils of bringing up a baby and working with nonces day in, day out.'

She laughed and uncrossed her arms. 'I always had you down as a bit of a dinosaur. It's refreshing to hear.'

'There's no place in the modern police service for antiquated or misogynist views.'

'I'm impressed, Harry. About both your views and the fact that you used a couple of long words there.'

'So,' he said, 'I'll ignore that if you've dropped by to tell me all about Albert Woodville and his perverted ways.'

'Now you're in danger of flirting,' she said. 'Want me to come out to the scene with you and I'll fill you in as we go?'

'That's the best offer I've had all day.'

*

Once in Harry's car, Laura said, 'I'll tell you everything I can about Woodville but I don't think it's going to really help you narrow the search down all that much. He wasn't very well liked by quite a number of people.'

'Most sex offenders aren't though, are they?' said Harry as he looked across at her, taking in the dark circles under her eyes, probably accentuated by her fair skin and blonde hair. It crossed his mind how difficult she might be finding the combination of being a single parent and working full-time, especially in such a responsible position. For a second, he almost asked her but wondered if he'd come across as a little creepy: older man, detective inspector, with a younger, very attractive woman in his car, late at night, all alone. He thought better of it, and of his pension, so he waited for her reply to his work-related question as he drove up to the security barrier of the police station rear yard.

'No, they're not on most people's Christmas card lists,' she agreed and paused before she added, 'Some of them don't continue to reoffend, but out of the sixty-six sex offenders I manage, Woodville was one of the most worrying.'

'You fucking what?' said Harry, hitting the brake as he drove through the exit. He stared across at her. 'Did you just say that you manage sixty-fucking-six sex offenders?'

'Oh yeah. We've got one hundred and thirty-three of them living in our district. Myself and the other DC split them down the middle. The odd one fell to him because we flipped a coin to see who'd end up with the extra one. He lost so I've only got sixty-six and he's got sixty-seven.'

'And how often do you see them?'

'Woodville was considered high risk so I visited him every three months, kept an eye on him when I could, but with dozens more I did my best to stop him reoffending.'

Harry approached a junction and once again glanced across at his colleague. 'You make it sound like you failed. He didn't reoffend. He was murdered.'

She moved in her seat and said, 'Perhaps you're right but I was keeping a particular eye on him because all the warning signs were there.' She let out a sigh.

'And?' said Harry.

'He'd only been out of prison for ten months. In that time, he'd moved to a flat with a school near by. There weren't many places in the area that he could afford to rent and were available. Unfortunately, this one came up and even though we didn't like the idea of him living so close to a school, he had to live somewhere. I was on maternity leave at the time but know that we managed that by giving him licence conditions not to go to the roads around the schools.'

'That's a start, a bloody poor one, but a start.'

From the corner of his eye, Harry saw Laura's head snap in his direction.

'We do the best we can, you know,' she said quietly.

'It wasn't a go at you.'

'They kept promising us another member of staff,' Laura said. 'It didn't happen. In the meantime, Woodville befriended a younger woman, a widow. She's got two children, an eight-year-old girl and a ten-year-old boy. He probably played on her vulnerability. Paedophiles are usually very manipulative, as you know.'

Harry pulled up outside Albie Woodville's block of flats. In the harsh lighting now coming from the many police and CSI vehicles in the car park, he could see Laura was biting her lip and her face was almost white.

'There's something else?' he said.

'I only told Woodville's girlfriend about his sex offending two weeks ago and she took the news very badly. It's not only that. There's something else, too. Woodville came into the nick to see me one day. He'd had death threats.'

'And you think it was the girlfriend or something to do with her?'

'I think that's highly unlikely. You see, at the time Woodville brought the threatening notes to me, saying that he was going to be strung up by his privates, that sort of thing, his girlfriend hadn't been told about his previous sexual offending.'

'Any chance she could have known before you told her?' said Harry.

'From her reaction, I would say it's only possible if she's a superb actor. I thought I was going to have to call an ambulance for her.'

'So we're narrowing this down nicely to his

26

girlfriend, her family, any of Woodville's many victims of sexual offending, and complete strangers who are vigilantes but like to warn their victims by post. This should be a piece of piss.'

'There's one more thing,' said Laura as Harry was about to open the car door.

'Of course there is. What's that?'

'Woodville also joined an amateur dramatic society. He was sorting out costumes apparently. We thought for a very long time about whether we should disclose to them his previous convictions and left the decision with the assistant chief constable. Something tipped the balance and I told the society's chairman.'

'I know I'm not going to like the answer, but what was the tipping point?'

'Their next production was *Annie*, with cast from the local primary school.'

Chapter 7

For the third time since putting her two children to bed, Millie Hanson climbed the stairs to check on them. She padded along the hallway and peeked around the door of first Sian's room and then Max's, listening to them breathe.

Her children were the most important part of her life: they were the reason she got up in the morning and made the best of the situation she had found herself in. As she stood watching her son sleep, lying on his back, mouth wide open, Spider-Man bed covers half kicked off the bed, she felt despair rising in her. How she could have been so stupid, she couldn't fathom.

She backed away from her son's bedroom, the sight of the Spider-Man covers enough to bring tears to her eyes. Max now hated them, saying he was too old for something so childish. She couldn't afford new ones and knew that was the least of her worries.

Without turning on the light, she went into her bedroom and lay on the bed. It was easier lying there in the dark: she could pretend that she wasn't on her own, wasn't so lonely and scared for herself and the children, missing her husband so much it felt like a physical pain, her chest constricting every time she breathed in, crushing the life out of her. She could so easily succumb to it but that wasn't something she usually allowed herself the luxury of. It had been six years since Clive had died, but if she concentrated, if she closed her eyes and kept very still, Millie was sure that he was there right beside her. He was there, head resting on the pillow, waiting for her to wake up so he could stroke her hair and say, 'Morning, you. Think we've got half an hour before the kids wake up?'

She could play the scene over and over in her mind. How she'd loved those stolen early mornings with him before anyone else was awake. She couldn't believe she had everything she had ever wanted – a husband, family and home.

Now the scene was gone and the same wretched feelings returned to her. She felt a sob rise in her throat but refused to allow herself to fall apart. There had been a few moments over the years where she had almost given in. For the sake of her children, she held it together and had been foolish enough to think that she could move on and put what had happened behind her, build a new life for them all.

Millie knew that she was still reasonably attractive. She had kept her slim figure, even after two children, and even she admitted to herself that her jet black hair and deep blue eyes had turned a few heads in their time. Still, she hadn't gone looking for someone for her and the children to share their lives with. Then she met Albert Woodville. An older man, but a steady influence, someone with his own flat, even if he was only renting. He hadn't even wanted to rush her into sex.

When she thought about it now, he'd seemed more interested in befriending her children. Something at the time she had found charming.

She put her hands up to her head in an unconscious effort to stop the thoughts that were now tramping through her mind. The first time she had met Albie, she'd been in the park with her children. Sian still loved to go to the pond and see the ducks and swans; Max was more reluctant these days but as long as he got to take his football, he had usually forgotten that he wasn't supposed to be enjoying himself by the time they got there.

School holidays and the warmth of the day meant that many people had brought their children out and the park was busy. She had taken drinks and snacks along in a rucksack, hoping for a picnic but knowing that neither Sian nor Max would sit still for long enough for that to happen.

Despite her awareness of people around her, she had felt perfectly safe in the park, oblivious to the horrors the world could bring to her door. There was no reason for her to be concerned. She thought that the worst had already happened to them.

Even when Albie had approached the three of them, Max sulking because he'd been told to leave his ball for five minutes and cool off with a drink, and Sian scanning the trees for squirrels, Millie squinting into the sun as she watched him puff over the hill in their direction, he'd appeared to be normal. Reassuringly normal.

He waved at her and shouted, 'Excuse me. Have you seen a Jack Russell come this way?'

She sat up straighter and shielded her eyes with her hand, saw the dog lead in his hand. 'No, I'm sorry,' she said. 'I haven't. We've been here about ten minutes.'

He stood with his hands on his hips and glanced into the trees behind them. 'The dog's not even mine,' he said, a frown creasing his forehead. 'I was looking after him for my elderly next-door neighbour.'

'Oh dear,' said Millie.

'What's his name?' said Sian.

'Charlie,' said Albie. 'I'm going to have some explaining to do when I get back. Well, thanks anyway.'

As he turned to go, Max called out, 'We'll help you look.'

'That's very kind of you,' said Albie, 'but carry on having your picnic. I'm sure he'll turn up somewhere. It's that now I think of it, he wasn't wearing a name tag or contact details.'

'Perhaps he's chipped,' offered Millie, trying to help.

'No,' said Albie as he shook his head. 'She hasn't had him long and I'm walking him because she's been ill. This will just about finish her off. I can't believe I've been so stupid.'

'Why don't you leave your number?' she said. 'In case we see him or someone finds him?'

His face lit up at this idea. 'Thank you,' he said. 'I hadn't thought of that.'

Whilst Millie scrambled in her rucksack for a pen and paper, her focus on helping a stranger, Albie Woodville nodded and smiled at her children.

Her thoughts were interrupted by the telephone ringing. She leaned over and grabbed it, hoping that one more noise on Bonfire Night wouldn't wake her children.

It took her a moment to work out who was calling her.

'Ian,' she said. 'Is that you? I can't understand you.'

Her brother's voice eventually made sense to her as he said through an alcohol-fuelled mumble, 'You don't have to worry about that dirty bastard Woodville any more.'

Chapter 8

With everyone else out of Albie Woodville's flat, senior CSI Joanna Styles got down to business. She could hear the officers and PCSOs knocking on doors in the block of flats and asking those who were living a short distance from a sex offender what they had heard on the evening of his death. From the official tone that her colleagues were adopting, she could make out that the dead man's past was not given away or discussed in any way. Whipping people into a frenzy was the job of the media, not local police officers. The latter were investigating a murder, not trying to titillate a nation for five minutes on the national news before another money-spinning vote via phone-in filled their evening television schedules.

Joanna's white paper suit and foot coverings rustled as she knelt down beside her kit bag and got out her camera. Her first task was to take dozens of photos of the body, including close-ups, before anyone disturbed him any further, seizing and exhibiting anything near or on him. She would then set about moving around the two-bedroomed flat from room to room. She knew that it wouldn't take her too long in a space as confined as this one, but Joanna was very experienced in her job, not to mention thorough.

Apart from being a very highly regarded senior crime scene investigator, Joanna also taught forensic investigation to everyone from police probationers in their first few weeks of basic training to senior investigating officers who headed up murder inquiries. It had been one of the police service's longest slogs to stop its staff from walking through a crime scene whenever they fancied, picking up items out of curiosity.

To reiterate the point, she was about to finish taking pictures of the open-plan living room and move to the kitchen area, when she heard the sound of Harry Powell on the stairs. It was usually impossible to mistake Harry for anyone else, as few people were as loud or as forthright as he was.

'Hello, Matt,' she heard him say to the officer standing outside the front door. 'I've got my paper suit on, plus these very becoming booties, and I've even picked up a face mask. Give me the scene log and I'll sign myself in.'

She zoned out of a brief exchange where the DI was warned by the young PC that he wasn't to touch the front door because of the boot marks, and then the DI, who had probably joined the police before the uniform officer's birth, asked his advice on where he could safely walk to get inside the flat without disturbing the forensic evidence.

'It's all right, Harry,' she called out. 'When you open the door, you'll see where it's safe to walk. Go to your right.'

'All right, Jo,' said Harry as his head appeared around the door.

She laughed at him and said, 'You don't need to wear the face mask in here. Not unless you intend spitting all over my crime scene.'

'I've got incredibly bad breath,' came the reply before he pulled the white card cover from his mouth and left it dangling around his neck. 'I was only trying to do you a favour.'

'These sausages go out of date today,' she said more to herself than Harry, camera poised above the kitchen table.

'Well, I've eaten, so they're all yours.'

'Very funny. They've got a Co-op *Reduced* sticker on them. It's probably that local one. He was in there today, I'd guess.'

As she spoke, Harry made a note of what she was saying and then joined her in the small kitchen area to look for obvious signs of a receipt. He saw a screwed-up carrier bag on the table top and pointed at it.

'Hang on,' she said, taking several photographs of it before allowing him to pull the bag open with his gloved fingertips.

'There's a receipt in here dated this evening,' he said, looking up at her from his position bent over the table. 'You're some sort of fucking genius. You should do this for a living.'

'I'm thinking about it,' she said, moving away from the kitchen area to the short hallway leading to the other rooms. 'These rooms have been given a quick look-over by the PC on the door but I'm going to move into the bedrooms now. Apparently one's a bit odd.'

Harry turned towards the direction of Joanna's voice although there was now a wall separating them. He thought about following her but figured he would only get in the way and had seen all that he needed to for now.

Curiosity took him towards the television and the shelf of DVDs next to it. Harry had spent many years on child protection teams when he was a detective constable and had a bet with himself that somewhere in the flat he would find a box set of *Star Trek* episodes.

He nodded his head with a sense of satisfaction as he stood in front of the shelf where a box set of DVDs sat beside another containing the latest collection of the series.

'What is it with nonces and *Star Trek*?' he said to himself, interrupted by Joanna's voice coming from the direction of the bedrooms.

'Is it right that this bloke lived alone?'

'Yeah,' he shouted back. 'Why?'

'Then I can only think of one reason why he's got this stuff in here.'

Harry wondered what new depths of depravity his day was going to take him to as he walked the short distance to join Joanna beside the bedroom door.

'Then he really was a totally sick person,' said the CSI as she pushed the door open for Harry to get a better look.

All Harry could find to say was, 'For fucking fuck's sake.'

Chapter 9

Any Friday night without either a performance of the East Rise Players or a rehearsal found Eric Samuels sitting in his study, brandy in hand, stressing over budgets, casting or ticket sales. Guy Fawkes Night was no exception as far as the worrying was concerned, but this time, although it was to do with the amateur dramatic society he had been a part of for over thirty years, chairman of for sixteen of them, what was on his mind was a meeting he had called and the fall-out from it.

Previously, two young detectives had come to see him and asked to speak to him in private, giving an even greater air of mystery to their unannounced arrival. The only times he had ever had occasion to deal with the police were when his house was broken into and when he was stopped for not wearing a seat belt, admonished and sent on his way. That had been that.

To see police at his door had been worrying, but then slightly thrilling when he realized that death messages were delivered by uniform officers. It surely couldn't be about anything that bad, he'd reasoned, whatever it was.

It merely went to show how wrong he could be.

He had just applied on behalf of the East Rise Players for Lottery funding. They wouldn't want to know now. He'd had a dream that if they could secure funding for their own premises to rehearse and store their costumes, they wouldn't have to make do with cupboards at the back of the village hall or under the stage and they'd have their own base to work from. That way they'd go on to bigger and better things.

Eric had been delighted to welcome any new member and had even approached the local schools to see if they had any up-and-coming performers.

He nursed his temples with his free hand and swilled the brandy with the other.

He realized that not only would he have some explaining to do as far as the schools went – angry parents wanting to know exactly what checks were carried out on cast and production-team members – but also he'd have to call an immediate halt to unsupervised get-togethers in members' houses. He wasn't at all sure the Players would survive.

All this was a mere bagatelle in comparison to the repercussions likely from the raised tempers caused by the emergency meeting he called a week ago. Fifteen of the members arrived within a couple of hours of his phone call to the room above the Cressy Arms.

Naturally, he didn't ask Albert Woodville to be

present, but he had asked the core people from the society, those he had known the longest and those he trusted to react calmly.

The chairman had underestimated the reaction from Jude Watson and Jonathan Tey.

He hadn't expected them to become so angry, surrounded as young people were by so much more unpleasantness than his own generation and exposed to it more frequently.

Now, as he sat in his chair in the safety of his own house, he could still remember Jude's exact words, hissed at him from across the meeting table: 'You let a bloody sex case join us?'

Jude had banged his fists on the table and Eric had heard the sound of his chair legs scraping back against the floor as he'd started to get up.

He felt himself flinch, ready for the younger man to launch at him. Fortunately for Eric, on his arrival Jonathan had taken the last empty seat next to Jude, and had the size and strength to hold him back with one hand.

'I didn't let Albert join knowing what he'd done,' Eric defended himself. 'I was as in the dark as you all were about his past.'

Eric was shaking as he spoke and hoping that no one picked up on the wobble in his voice and someone saved him from being beaten to a pulp.

'Come on,' Jonathan said to Jude. 'Let's leave and cool off.'

The two of them got up. Jude's chair knocked to

the ground as he pushed himself away from the table's edge.

Most watched the two walk towards the door leading back down to the pub, a few preferring to avert their eyes. Eric's gaze followed Jude with a kind of fascinated horror.

At the door, one hand on the handle, the other pointing at Eric, Jude said, 'Someone's got to put this right. It's sodding disgraceful. He was around our kids.'

Eric considered going to the police after Jude's outburst but what exactly was he going to tell them? He had passed on to a few members of the amateur dramatic society that one of their members had served time in prison for sex offences? A couple of them had lost their tempers and left early?

He decided that, first thing the next day, he would telephone Woodville and let him know that he was no longer one of the East Rise Players. He wouldn't even give him a reason. That wasn't something he wanted to discuss.

The only problem being, of course, that by the time Eric Samuels made his decision, Woodville had been dead for some hours.

Chapter 10

'Make that a half-pounder burger, love,' said Leon, nodding at the waitress. He thought about trying a smile at her but he knew from previous attempts that women found him creepy when he did.

The look he got in return from the young woman serving greasy food on a Friday evening to people with nowhere better to go told him she still found him repulsive. Even so, he couldn't resist winking at her.

From across the other side of the plastic table, Toby leant forwards.

Leon mirrored his actions and their faces were inches apart, chins almost touching above the glass salt and pepper pots and bucket of cheap paper napkins.

'We need people to remember us being in here,' said Toby, 'but not because you've frightened the life out of the staff.'

'I'm still not sure this was a good idea,' said Leon. He put his hands up to stop interruptions and added, 'And I know we've been through this many times about how we should appear to act normally and put ourselves a distance away around the time—'

He paused to scrape his chair nearer to the table to allow another customer to get to the empty bench behind him. He made his movements as noisy as he could and made a point of speaking to the young lad who was trying to get past. 'You all right there, mate? Got enough room there?'

A warning look from his oldest friend halted the bouncing up and down in his seat and sound of metal chair-leg studs scratching their way across the hard floor. Leon Edwards always intended to do the right thing but he had no stop button. His heart was almost constantly in the right place but he didn't know when to call it a day. It was probably his best and his worst characteristic.

The day he and Toby Carvell had met they were in a children's home, both placed there due to their misfortunes. Toby had been a skinny and nervous boy, Leon larger both in size and in heart than his contemporaries. What Leon lacked in finesse, he made up for in other ways. He picked up on the expression on his friend's face and said, 'Why are you smiling? I thought I was in for a bollocking then.'

'I was thinking about when we met and how my first thought was that you were going to beat the living daylights out of me.'

'That goes to show, Toby, how appearances can be deceptive.' As he spoke, he rubbed his hands over the front of his white shirt, stretched to capacity across his stomach, and belched. 'I'm ready for my grub now. Hope she's not too long with it. I can't even see where she's gone. You don't think she's forgotten our order, do you?'

'Trust me on this one – appearances are not that deceptive,' said Toby with a slow shake of his head. 'Going on past eating-out experiences with you, I know that you're going to regret wearing that white shirt. You asked for your burger stacked with onions, relish, sauce. You may as well ask the waitress to tip it straight down your front.'

'I'm only doing what we agreed,' said Leon. 'I'm wearing completely different stuff.'

Again, Toby pitched forward in an attempt to cut off any idle talk in the café. They had planned to use a harshly lit, town-centre, late-night eatery with a sprinkling of customers so they wouldn't stand out as odd and would mix with the regulars. For three months, every Friday, they'd made a point of dropping in at about the same time, sitting at the same table, close to the counter and near to the plate-glass windows peering out to the High Street, being served by the same waitress. Toby knew that planning was what would save them when the time came. He couldn't afford to have a careless comment give them away.

He need not have worried as the arrival of the waitress with two plates laden with food halted Leon. Little silenced him, but a half-pounder burger, chips, coleslaw and onion rings was as likely to work as anything else.

She plonked down the food without looking at either of them, concentrating on not spilling the meals. Task complete, she said, 'I've put you loads of extra pickles in yours, Dilly.'

At this point, she risked eye contact. 'Is that why you're called Dilly?'

'No, Lorraine,' Leon said, smothering his chips in vinegar. 'It's a long story but if you ever feel like hearing it, I can explain over a pint.'

Toby had read *Lorraine* on her name badge but now he read horror on her face.

'How about we let the nice lady get back to work now?' Toby looked up at her and gave her one of his smiles.

Both men watched her backside as she made her way to other customers, customers who were there to be served and not with the main intention of being noticed so that their alibi for the evening was easy to establish.

Chapter 11

Any given Friday night of the year, staffing levels could be low, but if Guy Fawkes Night fell on a Friday it was guaranteed there'd be no spare police officers on hand. Murder never took into account police availability.

Harry Powell called the control room from Flat 12, Pleasure Lane and warned East Rise's Major Crime team that a suspicious death was coming their way. Those able to postpone whatever else they were occupied with prepared themselves to work through the night.

As he said goodbye to Joanna Styles, who had finished taking photographs and was now getting ready to video every room and cupboard the flat had, Harry recognized the feeling of excitement at what was to come. Experience had taught him that most homicides were straightforward, albeit that they still needed to do a vast amount of work to get the guilty to court and ultimately to prison. It was clear to Harry that this one had something that many didn't have – no obvious suspect. Why this particular victim, however, seemed to be staring them in the face, although nothing was to be taken for granted. Harry knew the dangers of that only too well.

He wasn't going to dwell on the reason why someone had gone to the extreme of taking another's life. Motive alone didn't interest him, just as long as he got the right person. People usually killed for drugs, money or because they thought it was perfectly acceptable to pulverize a family member on a daily basis until one day they went too far. Few of the deaths he had dealt with had been pre-planned, even the most horrific ones.

Before he drove back to the police station, Harry made the decision to brief the team in the incident room rather than try to find a suitable hall or venue nearer to the scene. He didn't want to waste any more time on something that could be easily sorted out in the morning, simply so that they could have an overnight base close to Albie Woodville's flat. He knew that he only had a team of six on duty but they could cover a lot of ground between them. What was pressing most urgently on his mind was how he was going to buoy them up to investigate the murder of a paedophile.

It all started with the senior investigating officer; if he got it wrong now, the team wouldn't recover. He drove the entire way back to East Rise Police Station mulling over his tactics.

*

Faces stared at him from around the room. There were dozens of empty chairs at the enormous conference table. Only six were occupied. He was surprised to see DCI Barbara Venice taking up one of the chairs. He didn't ask her why she should be here at this time of night, and tucked away at the far unlit end of the table. She gave him the smallest of nods and he returned the gesture, making a note to ask her why she was still at the incident room six hours after her shift had ended.

Harry couldn't really make out in the gloom if Barbara was wearing the same clothes he'd seen her in earlier that day. If he was forced to guess, he'd say she had been home once and returned to work. The fact that the lights were out at her end of the table meant that she hadn't moved and tripped the sensors for some time. For reasons he couldn't give, he didn't get the feeling she was there merely to keep an eye on him, despite her outranking him.

A rattle of cups behind him alerted him to the missing member of the team as he hastened into the room behind Harry.

'I made you a brew, boss,' said Detective Constable Tom Delayhoyde, aware he was holding up the briefing but not keen to begin without a cup of tea.

'Nice one,' said Harry as he took a seat at the top of the table in front of the now dormant remote conference screen. Another of the constabulary's money-saving devices that was rarely used, its staff still driving across the county for a twenty-minute meeting.

He waited a minute for everyone to grab a mug from the tray, accepted his own as it was pushed towards him and ran an eye over everyone assembled before him. He watched each of them take a brand-new investigator's notebook from the pile, ready to record all of their notes for that day's latest incident.

'OK,' he began as he leaned back in the chair, his eyes momentarily fixing on each one of them. 'Thank you for getting here as fast as you did. We're looking at a murder investigation as you probably already know.'

Harry paused for a second and said, 'The victim is a male by the name of Albert or Albie Woodville. He has previous convictions for sexual offences against children.'

Even though some in the room already knew about the deceased's murky past, Harry sensed a change in atmosphere. He was expecting it but recognized it wasn't his imagination getting the better of him.

Detective Constable Gabrielle Royston, who sat to Harry's right, looked up from taking notes and pursed her lips. DC Sophia Ireland next to Gabrielle let out a barely audible sigh and put her pen down on the virgin page of her A4 notebook. From the corner of his eye, Harry saw one or two of the others shift from side to side in their seats.

'We're professionals,' he said, but allowed the words to hang in the air. 'Whatever our personal views and opinions, we investigate this just the same as we would any other suspicious death or murder. It's especially important that you keep your wits about you on this job because early indications from the crime scene are that we're looking for two people who broke in and murdered him.'

Once more he scanned the room.

'Fortunately for me and the people of East Rise, I know that our victim's past, and the fact that more than one person took his life, won't affect how you handle your jobs or yourselves.' Harry took a silent deep breath, looked down and said, 'This is a very emotive enquiry. It doesn't need me to tell you that.'

Now he scrutinized the expressions, trying to read them as each of them concentrated on his every word.

'Anyone who has an issue with this enquiry can speak to me after this briefing in private. I need you all, not to mention other officers in the morning, but only if you're prepared to put aside any prejudices and show the commitment you've demonstrated on so many previous occasions.'

The detective inspector gauged how his team were feeling from his chosen few words and opted to leave it there. Overdoing it would serve no useful purpose.

The end of a briefing usually signalled the start of the next step: everyone with their task to perform, targets set until the next time they came together to lay their piece of the puzzle next to their colleague's, waiting for the moment when it all made sense. This was what drove Harry and made him as committed to his job as he was.

Tonight's briefing, however, was different.

It signalled the beginning of something in complete contrast to anything that had come before.

He felt forced to go against all he believed in and enlist the help of those he despised the most. He struggled to remember a day when he felt more disgusted with what he was about to do.

Chapter 12

'What do you make of all that?' asked Sophia as she strode beside Gabrielle trying to keep up as they made their way along the department's deserted corridor through to the main part of the incident room. Their movement tripped lights as they went, illuminating the cheap blue carpet tiles. The aged floorboards squeaked mercilessly.

'How do you mean?' said the DC who was slightly younger in both years and police experience than her colleague, but somewhat taller. She ran a hand over her immaculate shoulder-length blonde hair and looked down towards Sophia.

When they reached the incident room, Gabrielle made for a desk with Sophia trailing behind her. They ended up at adjacent computer terminals and Sophia immediately leaned across Gabrielle's desk and said, 'As if we wouldn't give this job our all, the same as any other.'

She couldn't fail to register that Gabrielle kept her ice-blue eyes straight ahead, focused entirely on the screen in front of her. For several seconds she thought that she wasn't going to get a response.

'He was a nonce though,' said Gabrielle in a voice so low Sophia was now almost shoulder to shoulder with her so that she could catch her words.

'But he went to prison for what he did,' said Sophia, unable to keep her own voice as hushed.

Sophia's head snapped in Tom Delayhoyde's direction as he looked up from his seat, metres away from the two women within the rectangular room, a frown on his face.

Her view of Tom was obscured by the other three from the briefing as they moved about the room, gathered their strewn equipment and paperwork, and moved in and out of Sophia's line of vision.

The noise they made as they got ready to rush out to their allocated enquiries almost drowned out Gabrielle's muttered verbals.

'I wouldn't be quite so sure he went to prison for absolutely everything he did. There's clearly someone who thought they had unfinished business. Besides, you heard what the DI said in the briefing about the stuff in Woodville's spare bedroom. Please try to tell me how anyone finds that acceptable. And not forgetting what kind of perverted child porn we'll probably find on his phone and computer.'

Even though Sophia had known Gabrielle for a couple of years, they were nothing more than colleagues, with little attempt on Gabrielle's part at contact outside work. She had tried to be welcoming when Gabrielle had arrived on their team, but her hand of friendship had been very much slapped away.

It was then with an unsettling feeling that Sophia looked from the computer screen to Gabrielle, before staring back again.

A smile was twitching at the corner of the younger detective's mouth as she gazed upon the sight in front of her.

The terminal screen was filled with a colour crime-scene-investigator image of Albert Woodville's purple, mottled face, mouth open, eyes dead.

During her twelve years of policing, Sophia had seen a lot of unpleasantness, sometimes exhibited by those she worked closely with. A black sense of humour kept them all going from time to time, took away the pressure and relieved some of the stress, but she failed to find anything funny about the sight of the man's swollen, dead face.

Unsure which she found more fascinating, the grotesque picture on the computer screen or the look on Gabrielle's face, Sophia watched with a growing feeling of discomfort as Gabrielle enlarged the image and pitched forward in her seat to get a closer look.

Sophia was so busy staring that DI Harry Powell had to call her a third time from his office door before she realized that her name was now being shouted.

'Sorry, sir,' she said and turned one hundred and eighty degrees in her chair. 'I was completely engrossed in something.'

She hurried over to where he stood and followed

him into his office. Without being told to, she shut the door behind her. Whether he wanted to speak to her in private or not, she had something she wanted to say to him and didn't want to be overheard.

Harry leaned against the windowsill, hands in his trouser pockets, waiting for Sophia to speak.

'Everything all right?' he asked, curious as to her hesitation and why she had closed the door.

Her lip-biting silent response answered his question.

He waited again while she tucked her wavy mousey hair behind her ears, round expressionless face giving nothing away.

'I'm a bit worried about Gabrielle,' she said, taking care with her words. 'I'm not sure how she's taking to this one. Her initial reaction seems a bit odd but perhaps it's because it's been one of those weeks.'

Her detective inspector nodded at her. 'I know there's been a lot of overtime all week, plus the fortnight or so beforehand was busy for the whole department. We're all knackered.'

He could sense that there was something else that Sophia wasn't telling him. He had worked with her on and off for a while now and she had a good reputation for being hard-working and trustworthy. The same could be said of Tom Delayhoyde but Gabrielle Royston was a different matter.

'What's up with Gabrielle?'

'I'm not really sure. It's not as if it's her first murder and she's been here for some time. I get the feeling that she's ...'

Sophia really didn't want to say it. Although she had a lot of respect for Harry, and felt that as the DI he should know what was going on in his incident room, she didn't want him to think she was a grass.

She decided to keep her suspicions to herself for now. Perhaps she had overreacted. It was her sixth consecutive day on duty, she had worked over sixty hours since the start of her shift pattern and there were hours of the night still to go; that was without the thought of getting out of bed early for the next two days until her final tour of duty. She would see things differently after a day off and reflect on her bad decision to shovel more worry onto the senior investigating officer of a murder enquiry.

'Nothing, no nothing,' she said. 'I'll get her to come and see you if she says she's got a problem.'

She turned to go out of the room and then remembered that it was he who had called her into the office in the first place.

'Sorry, sir. What was it you wanted?'

'I wanted to make sure that you were OK before I leave the nick to see someone. You had me worried in the briefing. It's acceptable if you're not on board with this one.'

'Worried?' she said, starting to feel that the DI was losing his touch: it was another member of his team he should be concerned about, not her. 'I admit to finding what Albert Woodville had in his spare bedroom a bit unsettling, but I'm OK.'

'Apologies, Soph. I know that child protection

wasn't something you were ever involved in before you came to Major Crime, so I wanted to make sure you were OK. I don't want to be criticized for being one of those DIs who doesn't go in for all that touchy-feely bollocks and forgets about his staff. Although I do mean it when I say don't stay too late tonight – there'll be loads to do over the weekend.'

She nodded and left, annoyed that he had got the whole thing so wrong, and almost changed her mind about telling him her fears over Gabrielle's attitude.

One thing she did know as she made her way back across the incident room, was that Detective Inspector Harry Powell wasn't as good as he thought he was at getting the measure of people.

Chapter 13

Millie was on the verge of hanging up on her brother, but she knew how he had reacted to bad news in the past; even the death a few years ago of his beloved boxer dog, Digby, had sent him off into depression. Ian had packed a bag and disappeared. He hadn't contacted anyone for months and then only turned up again because he had been living in Crete, working in a bar, and the holiday season had come to an end. With nowhere else to go, he had come back to England.

Getting a taxi to his house this time of night was out of the question for Millie: she wasn't about to wake the children and take them with her and she didn't have anyone to watch them.

Another new feeling of hopelessness came over her, this time mixed with anger at her brother who had given her something else to fret about.

'Please,' she said into the receiver, 'don't tell me that you've done something stupid.'

Tears formed in the corner of her eyes. She'd promised herself that she wouldn't cry, not again. Her life was slowly unravelling and everything she'd done over the past six years to get it back on track was feeling like a waste of time. She'd worked so hard to lighten the blanket of grief she'd carried on her shoulders since the death of her husband.

It had started small, with a trip somewhere familiar on her own, then a trip somewhere new, a visit to a place she and Clive had thought about going to. After what felt like forever but which was in reality only twelve months, each little task hadn't seemed so daunting. The heavy blanket weighing her down became lighter and lighter until she was only aware of its presence on particularly low days.

Now her brother was scaring her into thinking something even worse was about to happen to her family.

She sat on the edge of the bed, eyes closed, waiting for her brother to say something, hoping that he hadn't passed out.

'Hello, Millie,' said a different but familiar voice. She opened her eyes, couldn't place who it was. 'It's Dave.'

'Oh Dave,' she said. 'Stupid of me. Of course it's you. I'm glad you're with him. I can't make head nor tail of what he's on about. What's happened?'

'Your brother's very upset about all you've been going through, Mills, that's all.'

'Oh, he told you?' She missed the absence of a cord on the end of the phone to twirl around her fingers. Something to occupy her spare hand would have distracted her from the embarrassment of someone else now knowing her business. Worst of all was that that someone was David Lyle, her brother's best friend, a man she had spent years nurturing a crush on until she met Clive.

'Is there anyone who doesn't know about the fool I've made of myself and more importantly the danger I've put my children in?'

She heard him let out a slow breath.

'Do you want me to get a taxi over?' he asked. 'We've both been drinking so I can't drive. I can be there in about twenty minutes.'

She thought of Dave, tall, muscular, reliable, handsome. There was little doubt that the worst thing she could do right now was to ask a man to her house so late on a Friday night. She didn't like the idea of being alone again after the companionship she'd shared with Albie, but look how badly that had gone. If nothing else, Millie recognized the peril of feeling more vulnerable and desperate than she ever had. She couldn't afford to make another mistake.

Albie was the first man to show any interest in her after her husband's death, and in truth, the first man she had looked at twice. Even now, she wasn't entirely sure why she had given Albie so much as a second look. Clive had been everything that Albie wasn't.

Perhaps that was the reason, or maybe it was because he'd seemed so unlikely to be a threat to her or to leave her for someone else. She couldn't bear the thought of more heartache. He might even have been grateful that a younger woman was paying him attention, especially one who already had a family and responsibilities. She saw so clearly now that this was why he'd picked her out of the crowd – she had children.

'I think you should stay and look after Ian,' Millie answered. 'He sounds as though he's in no fit state to be left alone.'

She bit her lip, desperate for company, but the need to keep her children safer than she had so far managed outweighed her own desire for someone to talk to.

'Well, if you're sure?' he said, oblivious to the fact that she was shaking her head at the answer she was about to give.

'Positive. Stay with Ian, but, Dave—'

'What is it?'

'He hasn't gone and done anything stupid, has he?'

'Don't worry about him. Where he goes, I go. The two of us will look after you, Sian and Max. Get some sleep. We'll talk more in the morning.'

She listened to the sound of the disconnected tone and gazed at the phone's display in the gloom.

In some ways, it would have been better if Dave hadn't been with her brother. Ian often did impetuous and thoughtless things but they were usually on a small scale. The only reason he had taken off to Crete was because Dave had booked him the flight and driven him to the airport. It had always been the same throughout their childhood: every ridiculous and reckless thing the two of them had ever undertaken had Dave behind it.

The worst worry of all was that, on the day Millie married Clive, Dave had told her that he would always look out for her and be there if she needed him. At the time, it had given her a tiny thrill to know that someone who had meant so much to her was on her side. He had repeated his promise to her on the day that Clive had died, too.

His words were so vivid that even now she could remember them.

'If anyone ever harms you, I'll come for them.'

Chapter 14

Even as Harry Powell slowed his car and turned off the headlights, he wondered if he was doing the right thing. It was one thing to go out on enquiries – usually met by whispers of, 'Doesn't he know he's the DI and supposed to stay indoors?' – but it was another to take himself off in the middle of the night and meet up with people who didn't always stay on the right side of the law.

He sat in his car, engine idling, and wondered, not for the first time, if the back of an out-of-town industrial estate was really the best place for him to meet anyone, let alone two people he despised.

A couple of minutes went by until he saw car headlights bouncing their way along the rutted, potholed tarmac of the track that led from the main road to the rear of the wholesaler's.

He fought the urge to drive away but knew that the enquiry was a necessary evil. He would do almost anything to detect a murder.

This crossed a line.

The car pulled up next to him. As he looked across to his right, he was aware of a movement to his left. A dark figure appeared at the passenger window and tugged at the door handle. Harry had had the foresight to lock the doors. He also had his personal protective equipment, complete with PAVA spray and ASP, under his seat. He glanced across at the face at the window, hesitating for only a second before reaching for the button to let the glass drop a few centimetres so he could be heard by the crouching individual, desperate to be let inside his car.

'Didn't have you down for the nervous type, Harry,' said the man, mouth now to the gap between the pane and door frame.

'You're such a slippery bastard, Greg, I wasn't sure if I was about to be mugged.'

'Are you going to let me in?'

Harry jerked his thumb in the direction of the VW Golf. 'What about her? I assume it's your trusty side-kick Martha Lipton.'

'She'll join us in a second. That's if you ever open the door.'

Against his better judgement, Harry unlocked the doors and watched Greg Webster as he nodded towards the car and gave a thumbs-up to the driver.

He waited for him to get inside, and tried not to think of his acceptance of Webster's company, or the idea of Martha Lipton climbing onto the back seat. He was grateful he'd brought a police car and not his own. It would be bad enough being in the same space as the two of them, never mind having to drive his family around on the same upholstery.

'Well then,' said Greg. 'It's been a while.'

Harry nodded slowly, reminding himself that he might need the help of these two and he was the one who'd initiated the contact.

He watched the woman as she got out of the car, the interior light briefly showing off her curves. Her tight leggings and sky-blue jumper were snug against her slim body. The fact that Martha was one of the most attractive women he had ever set eyes on made the situation all the more miserable. Harry gave an involuntary shudder of shame.

'You getting a chill there, old man?' laughed Greg.

'It's the cold air you two bring with you.' He kept his eyes facing in front as he heard the sound of the car door behind him opening and its soft click shut.

He felt a hand touch him on the left shoulder, out of the corner of his eye glimpsed long painted fingernails and the sparkle of a diamond ring.

'Good to see you, Harry,' said Martha.

The fingers squeezed his shoulder. He kept his breathing calm, fought the urge to get out of the car and walk away from what he was about to do.

'Martha.' He nodded, confident of his attempt at measured congeniality.

She removed her hand and snuggled back against the seat. 'Before Greg got your call, I said to him I knew it wouldn't be long before our old friend, Detective Inspector Powell, was on the blower, wanting

65

a favour and to know everything we know about Albert Woodville.'

Harry's hand went up to the rear-view mirror. He adjusted it so he could watch her face, unlined, beautiful, cold. 'I didn't say anything about Albert Woodville. I just said I wanted to meet up.'

She laughed and looked out of the window into the gloom. 'Except it was on the news that a man was murdered, the TV showed the block of flats where it happened, and we know that Woodville was a pae-dophile, on the register, visited regularly by your lot.'

'You'd know all about that,' said Harry.

She shot forward in her seat, an action so quick her breath was on the side of his face before he could react.

'Don't fucking come it, Harry. You want our help or not?'

It was Greg's turn to speak up. 'It was you who contacted us. I never thought I'd see the day that you sought out the Volunteer Army.'

Harry closed his eyes and shook his head. 'The Volunteer Army. That's what you're calling yourselves, is it? Aren't you worried that people will confuse you with the Salvation Army and wonder where the brass band is at Christmas?'

'Your piss-taking is all very well,' said Martha, 'but we've got better places to be on a Friday night than sitting here in a police car at the back of Wholesale King, being asked to grass up a murderer.'

The sound of the door opening behind him forced Harry to turn round and face Martha straight on. She was not only the brightest of the pair by far, but for reasons that he had never fully grasped, she was the one in charge. She might have been the one who had driven them to the meeting point, but it had been Greg who had been sent out into the cold November night to sneak around the industrial estate on foot, creeping through the shadows to appear at Harry's window as her car pulled up, checking out the enemy in the dead of night.

One day, he would find out exactly what hold she had over Greg. The important thing for now was that Harry had something on Martha, and it was probably the only reason they were all huddled inside the ageing Skoda with over one hundred thousand miles on the clock.

'Close the door, Martha,' Harry said. 'This is important. If someone's going around killing paedophiles, it impacts on you too.'

They stared at each other for several seconds, Harry safe in the knowledge that she wouldn't get out of the car and drive off into the night, all the while willing her to tell him what she knew.

'OK,' she said.

He let out a breath.

'Despite your mickey taking,' she said as he held up his hands, 'we're trying to make people feel as safe as they can about living with sex offenders around them, and we want to work with the police.'

Martha gripped the back of the headrest of Harry's seat. 'We have meetings, open meetings, so anyone can see what it is we're doing. We have a website and a newsletter, but most of all, when we find someone online grooming children, we turn them in to the police. We're not taking the law into our own hands, you know that. We're trying to do our bit to help.'

He mulled this over for a moment before he said, 'You, Martha, I get why, in a twisted way, why you do it. What I don't understand is your involvement, Greg.'

Harry turned to Greg as he spoke, catching him unawares. The look of complete adoration on his acne-marked face as he gazed at his fellow vigilante gave Harry some sort of insight into how Martha Lipton had the ability to lead grown men astray.

'Because it's the right thing to do,' said Greg, not taking his eyes off her.

'Greg,' she said, 'why don't you wait in our car for me?'

He opened his mouth to say something. Martha made a pre-emptive strike by thrusting the car keys at him.

He took them, glared at them for a moment and then threw a similar look in Harry's direction before he got out of the police car and into the driver's seat of the VW Golf.

'Nice lad,' said Harry when Greg was out of earshot. 'You've got him well trained.'

'You too,' she replied. 'Thought you might tell him then for a moment.'

'What would be the fun in that? It wouldn't give me any leverage, would it?'

'No,' she said, head on one side, 'although it would move us off your area. I wouldn't be able to stay in the gorgeous seaside town of East Rise if Greg knew the truth. I think that you like having me around.'

'I'm talking to you now simply because you may be able to help me, as much as it grieves me to say it. You have the ear of the part of the community I can't always get to, and as things currently stand, they trust you.'

She chewed her bottom lip.

'I'll pass back to you what I find out,' she said, 'on the condition that no one knows about my past.'

Harry sensed this was the end of the conversation for the time being, confirmed by Martha's hand pushing open the door. A cold gust of air invaded the car. Up until this point, Harry hadn't noticed the raindrops hitting the window.

'Do I have your guarantee on that?' she said, one foot on the tarmac, the other still inside the Skoda.

'Of course you do. And you're right: as things currently stand, your band of merry men trust you. They find out the truth, we all lose.'

Chapter 15

'Oh great,' said DC Tom Delayhoyde. 'To finish our very long night at work off nicely, it's teeming down.'

Sophia, sitting beside him in the driver's seat of the unmarked Skoda, zipped up her jacket and peered through the windscreen.

'My favourite,' she said, 'house-to-house enquiries in the rain, and only a stone's throw away from the home of a murdered paedophile.'

She switched the engine off and scrambled behind her for her handbag and worn leather file.

No sooner had she turned off the wipers than the inside glass began to mist as the rain pelted down on the car.

'Someone's already calling at the flats in Pleasure Lane,' said Tom. 'That's typical of my luck to get the houses with the big driveways along from the bloody crime scene.'

'Stop moaning,' she said as she leafed through her paperwork to pluck a handful of forms and place them on top of all the others within the file.

'I've got the house-to-house forms and the questionnaires ready so you don't have to worry that your hair'll get wet and make all that gel run down from your boyband foppish hair to your pretty choirboy face and get in your eyes.'

'And you won't have to worry that the rain will wash out the dye in yours and show all of your grey.'

She turned sideways to face him as fully as the seats would allow.

'Tom, can I ask you something?'

'Yeah, Soph. At your age, I think you're a natural brunette. Honest.'

'No, not that. It's about Gabrielle.'

'Go on.'

She listened for a few seconds to the sound of the rain as it drummed on the car roof. Eventually she said, 'Do you get the impression that she's a bit odd?'

Tom rubbed his chin and thought about the question before he said, 'Ye-es. But I think it's only that – she's a bit odd and possibly aloof. Maybe she's got personal problems at the moment, stuff that's nothing to do with work. What exactly is your concern about her?'

'It's something I can't quite put my finger on. I watched her tonight when she was looking at the CSI photos of the scene and Albie Woodville's body. She reminded me of what was in that sick sod's spare room too. Not that I needed telling again.'

Her colleague shifted in his seat, let out a slow breath and said, 'I get little joy myself from working all hours to find the murderers of a man who spent most of his adult life sexually abusing children, especially one who thought it was perfectly acceptable to fill a room with dolls and mannequins of children, dress them in hospital gowns and have his own children's ward for kids with sexually transmitted diseases. He was a sick bastard, but Soph, murder is murder.'

She sat and thought about Tom's words for a moment.

She hated to criticize a colleague, even in the confines of a tatty police Skoda on a rainy Friday night with only Tom for company. Frequently tempers were raised on enquiries and within the team. They'd sound off at each other, or behind each others' backs, say their piece and move on. Each others' integrity was never an issue, which meant that Sophia recognized when she was speaking out of turn.

'Well,' she continued, 'I know you won't tell anyone what I'm about to say, but the reason I'm reluctant to get this off my chest is because it involves her suitability to be on this enquiry.'

'OK,' said Tom after a minute, and waited for Sophia to say more.

'You don't think that she'd deliberately do anything to mess up the investigation, do you? Such as not feeding information back that could point towards a suspect? No one likes a sex offender, probably not even other sex offenders, but we can't live in a society that thinks it's OK to kill them off without so much as a trial.'

'Albert Woodville was a paedophile but you're absolutely right. What if whoever killed him thinks they've got away with it? Who do they murder next? An innocent person maybe. It means if you've any concerns about Gabrielle, you have to do something about it. I get that you don't want to seem to bitch about her but you're not saying that she shouldn't be on the department, are you? All you're saying is that she shouldn't be investigating the murder of Albie Woodville.'

'I suppose you're right,' she said after weighing up his words for a second or two. 'Shall we get out of the car now? We've managed to steam up every window and the rain's easing off a bit.'

'If you're worried, at least talk to her.'

Tom twisted back round in his seat. With one hand on the door release, he said, 'And let's be honest, it's all hands to the pump on this one, but there's always another murder around the corner that Gabrielle can get her teeth into. I worked on three different murders in as many days. I keep track of the jobs I work on. In the last two months, I've been on two rapes, an attempted rape, three murders, a kidnap, a blackmail and Greenpeace taking over a power plant. Never a dull moment.'

Chapter 16

Following burgers and chips to line their stomachs, Leon Edwards and Toby Carvell made their way to a pub several streets away, each pausing to get money out from a different cash point along the route.

Toby chose a bank he didn't have an account with because it had a cash machine within its foyer. The foyer had a camera and he was keen to be on its footage.

'Dilly,' he said as he turned from taking his beer tokens from the slot in the wall, 'the booze is on me tonight.' He fanned the twenty-pound notes out and waved them at his friend. 'Give me a minute though; I need to ring the wife. It'll save the moaning later.'

He took his phone from his jeans pocket and made a point of waving it in his hand at Leon. Toby had his reasons for using his mobile on camera. He wasn't the brains of the outfit for nothing.

Leon took his cue and waited in the street outside, pacing up and down as they had planned, well within the town centre's CCTV capture.

He was joined a couple of minutes later by Toby, whose face showed only the signs of someone with no cares in the world, about to enjoy many libations with his best mate.

'Where are we starting, Tobe?' said Leon as they strolled along the High Street past its many pound and discount stores, charity shops and fast-food outlets.

'I thought we'd try the Blue Bar to begin with.'

'Bit wanky in there, isn't it?'

'Wanky but quiet this time of the night. We can sit at the bar and you can stare at that barmaid with the big tits.'

'She thinks I'm creepy.'

'You are creepy. You keep staring at her chest. Once she gets to know you, she'll change her mind and be putty in your hands.'

Toby carried on walking, feeling as though a weight had been lifted from his shoulders, before he realized that Leon was not beside him. He slowed and looked back over his shoulder to see that his friend had drawn to a stop and was being swallowed up by a hen party wearing little except for pink-fur-trimmed cowboy hats and their underwear on a chilly November evening.

Toby stood rooted to the spot, worried that he had underestimated the toughest, most resilient person he knew. Leon's expression was a blank, although that was usually the first sign of trouble.

He gave the twenty or so scantily clad women time to walk past as they whooped and shouted before he made his way back to his stationary friend.

'Something is definitely wrong,' Toby said. 'You didn't even glance at those girls and most of them weren't wearing skirts.'

Leon looked down at his feet, or in that direction as his eyes probably only got as far as his burger-sauce-stained belly.

'That's the problem, you see,' he mumbled.

'What's the problem? No skirts?'

'No, no, you don't get it, do you?' he said, looking up. 'You've got a wife and two fantastic kids. I don't have anyone.'

It had been a difficult day and Toby usually had time for his friend's maudlin attitude towards being single, but tonight should be the night of all nights that they let their hair down and didn't get depressed about anything.

Toby stopped short of sighing and put a reassuring hand on his friend's arm.

'There'll be someone for you one day, Dill. I promise.'

'It's not that,' Leon said, shaking his head. 'You've got a wife who will probably forgive you for just about anything. How do I ever meet someone who'll understand and accept everything that's happened to me?'

'I don't know, mate, I'm sorry. I really don't know but let's at least go and get a drink and talk inside.'

Toby watched Leon lumber towards the Blue Bar, worried more than ever about his friend and how life would be for him from now on.

Chapter 17

One thing Harry knew only too well was that with every year that passed it was more of a struggle to recover from a missed night's sleep. Even though he enjoyed what he did, arriving at a crime scene, a dead body, sometimes more than one, trying to fit the pieces together and work out who thought they had the God-given right to take another's life, it took its toll. If he was honest, the groundwork was all done by the detective constables and civilian investigators anyway. Now that he'd been promoted, he managed and oversaw the investigation. He was more than capable of nicking someone, but beyond that he only had a basic idea of how to put the paperwork together and get the investigation towards the court system. He always left that bit to the DCs. Most of the time, it was for the best.

He pushed this thought from his mind as he turned off the engine and looked up at the front of his house. He could make out the dim light of his wife's bedside lamp through a crack in the curtains. That immediately annoyed him.

The memory of their row in the department store was engraved on his mind, despite it being over five years ago: she had insisted on ordering the most expensive made-to-measure curtains, fully lined with blackout material to ensure eight hours' shut-eye. And she never closed them properly.

'Two bloody grand,' he murmured to himself as he got out of the car and fumbled in his pockets for his door keys.

He tried to keep as quiet as possible, but he was clumsy and usually made more noise when he attempted to creep around the house. All too often, he was chided for not putting something back when he had finished with it. Some of his wife's complaints were well founded.

Harry glanced up at the kitchen clock, saw with surprise that it was after three in the morning and wavered between putting the kettle on and pouring himself a whisky. The trouble with whisky was that one was never enough, and he was in need of sleep, so he opted for a glass of milk.

He stood leaning against the kitchen cupboard, eyes closed, thoughts turned to decades before when a glass of milk was a childhood comfort, no space in his head then for mutilated bodies, raped children, sexually exploited young girls, paedophiles and their murderers.

He downed the rest of the milk, wiped his hand across his mouth and felt his way in the darkness of the hall to the stairs.

Three steps from the bottom, he was able to make

out a sliver of light from under the master bedroom's door. He hoped that by now his wife had realized that he was home and at least done the decent thing and was pretending to be asleep. Luck clearly wasn't with him tonight. He was going to have to talk to her.

'Hello, sweetheart,' he said as he pushed the door open. She was lying on her side, long blonde hair swept back, a book about the partition of India and Pakistan held in front of her face. 'You look both beautiful and intelligent, as ever.'

Her features hardened as she dropped the book and glared at him.

'What's made you late this time?' she said.

'Murder,' he answered as he hung his jacket up.

The conversations always went like this when he got home in the middle of the night. She knew what his job as detective inspector involved, and so he couldn't for the life of him work out what it was she expected him to talk about.

Trying his best to avoid a row, he sat on his side of the bed, his back to her, as he removed his shoes, socks and tie. Harry dawdled deliberately, hoping that by some miracle by the time he was ready to stand up and take his trousers off she would have lost interest in his day and would want to talk about something else. Or if the gods really were picking him as their favourite, would even want sex. That last bit was too much to hope for, but avoiding a row still had a slim chance.

'And don't roll your bloody socks into a ball.'

Her words were accompanied by the sound of her turning over, then the click of the light switch.

Harry stood in the darkness next to the bed, the trousers he had already undone now around his ankles.

Sex was certainly off.

Chapter 18

Saturday 6 November

The following morning's briefing took some time. Both police officers and civilian investigators had been called in on their days off to supplement the meagre number of staff on weekend cover. There was a time when the senior investigating officer would have had his or her pick of the entire department, but as the overtime rate was now slashed by twenty-five per cent most preferred to keep their days off. So the conference room was made up of the usual people who never turned down a bit of extra pay and those who felt too guilty to ignore their ringing phones when off duty.

Eventually the DI said, 'We've covered all we need to and everyone's had a chance to raise issues. Has anyone got anything else they want to say?'

Harry looked around the room at each member of staff in turn. Each of them shook their head at him.

Once again, DCI Barbara Venice had been in the

conference room with them. It wasn't unusual for someone of a higher rank to attend another officer's briefing, but it was a little odd for her to arrive after it had started, sit at the back, say nothing and then leave without a word.

'If that's it,' he said, 'you all know what you're doing and I'd like to talk about staffing with the DS.'

He remained in his seat at the top of the table with Sandra Beckinsale, his stony-faced detective sergeant, next to him.

Once they were alone in the conference room, the noise of stampeding staff making for the toilets and kitchen in the background, Harry started with, 'We need more staff. Six would do it.'

'No,' she said with a shake of her head that made her jowl wobble, 'we won't get six.'

'Well, let's ask for six and we'll probably get four. We ask for four, we'll get two.'

'Fine.' She made a note in her book and looked at Harry with a blank expression.

'How are you settling in to Major Crime?' he said.

'Fine.'

'Any problems?'

'No.'

For the couple of weeks she had been working in Major Crime, Sandra Beckinsale's force-wide reputation for being professional and hard-working had already shone right through, unlike her personality. No one so far had got a glimpse of that.

'I'll ask for more staff,' she said as she closed her

notebook. 'I'll get on to that as soon as I've given out these other enquiries. And DC Rainer's back from his holiday on Monday. I'll earmark Pierre for outside enquiries and we've the new DC, Hazel Hamilton, starting then too.'

She paused.

'That's if you've finished, sir?'

Harry nodded as he wondered why some people were such hard work.

'Yeah, of course,' he said as she got up to leave the room.

Within minutes Sandra Beckinsale had almost finished giving out the work she wanted completed; that was all except two enquiries.

She found DC Delayhoyde at his desk searching through his notebook for something.

'I've run out of staff so I'd like you to take a look at both of these, please,' she said as she handed him the relevant paperwork.

He glanced down at the sheets she was holding, inches from his grasp, and tried in vain to read the names on the pages.

'One is one from Albie Woodville's past,' she explained. 'The other, very much his present.'

'Have you got one from his future?' asked Tom. 'You know, like Scrooge?'

Beckinsale ignored his remark and said, 'I know you'll do your homework on them both before you go, but one was originally part of the trial against

Woodville years ago and the other is his girlfriend, Millie Hanson. Take a look at this lot and get back to me if you need to.'

The DS started to walk away from him and called over her shoulder, 'You never know how they're going to react; potentially you'll be sitting on the sofa in a murderer's house so take someone with you and keep your eyes open.'

Chapter 19

The street where Toby Carvell and his family lived was on the outskirts of East Rise and filled with neatly kept semi-detached homes. It was the sort of area sought after by those with decent incomes who wanted the convenience of a town centre, a railway station and a beach near by, but didn't want traffic and noise. The road was devoid of both people and vehicles when they arrived.

As Tom pulled the unmarked Peugeot over to a stop outside number 34, he nodded appreciatively.

'Toby Carvell is doing OK,' he said as much to himself as to Sophia sitting beside him.

'So we got his name from the original trial against Woodville in the 1990s?' she asked. 'That was bloody fast work. Why wasn't the paperwork archived or destroyed?'

'It was archived,' said Tom as he checked the facts from his file, wedged beside his seat. He tapped his finger on the page as he read. 'Woodville was on trial for sexual abuse against five children. He was found guilty in 1991 of several offences of indecency against three children but acquitted on all counts against another two of them. Toby Carvell was one of the two victims he didn't go to prison for. Someone dug this out from the original operation on the HOLMES system and printed off statements, reports and other stuff.'

'Right, well, let's see what he's got to say about where he was last night,' said Sophia as she gathered her own stuff from the footwell.

The two of them stood next to their unmarked car which was covered in seagull droppings – one hazard of working so close to the coast – and made their way along the driveway to the Carvell family home.

It didn't escape Tom's notice that the dark blue Ford Focus registered to Toby was missing from the front of the house.

The door was answered a couple of moments later by a woman dressed in a purple onesie. Her long dark hair hung loose but was stuck to one side of her face. She looked from Tom to Sophia as they stood on her doorstep, warrant cards in hands.

Concern ran across her features at the unexpected visitors on a Saturday morning.

She opened her mouth to say something as the hand gripping the door frame tightened, turning her knuckles white. The other hand flew up to her chest.

'No, Mrs Carvell,' said Sophia as she recognized the look of a panicked mother when she saw one. 'Please, it's your husband we've come to see.'

The relief exploded within her and forced a nervous, high-pitched laugh.

'Thank God,' she said and stepped aside. 'The kids were at a bonfire display last night and stayed at their cousin's house.'

Although Mrs Carvell moved out of their way, as if to let them in, it wasn't until the realization sank in that they weren't about to deliver a death message that she pulled the door behind her.

She stood almost six feet tall, a ferocious Amazon of a woman despite being clad only in her nightwear.

'What do you want to speak to him about?' she said, arms crossed.

'It's best that we tell him ourselves,' explained Tom in a tone intended to placate rather than provoke.

A movement behind her on the stairs caught Tom's eye, and he witnessed two bare, hairy legs descending towards them.

The officer really hoped that Toby Carvell was clothed and just as important that his attitude didn't match his wife's. This thought was interrupted by the person they had come to see as he shouted from the staircase, 'Let them in, woman. And why are you standing there like Barney the fucking Dinosaur?'

Chapter 20

Once the four of them were seated in the Carvells' living room, Toby insisted his wife put the kettle on.

'You're sure you don't want me here?' she asked him over her shoulder as she got up from the two-seater sofa she'd been sharing with her husband.

'Absolutely, Shirley,' he replied, raising his eyebrows at the two officers on opposite ends of a larger leather sofa. 'I'm gasping for a cuppa. I had a couple of beers last night and my breath's as rough as crap.'

He aimed the last remark at Tom, as if to band together with the other man in the room, somehow implying this was how their entire gender began its Saturday mornings.

Sophia took her opportunity to give Toby Carvell the once-over and drew her opinion that he was a good-looking middle-aged man who kept himself in shape. She then found herself shifting self-consciously in her seat because his loosely tied, mid-thigh-length dressing gown was beginning to gape in the middle.

One awkward aspect of police enquiries was at what point the officers informed their witnesses that their genitals were on display.

'Shirley,' he called out towards the kitchen, 'put some toast on as well. I'm starving.'

'The reason we're here, Mr Carvell,' began Tom, 'is that we're investigating a murder.'

He looked closely at Toby's face for any sign of anxiety or the tiniest indication that he had any idea what he was going to say next.

Not one facial muscle moved.

Tom edged forward on his seat, the squeak of the leather loud in the otherwise silent room.

'The victim's name is Albie Woodville.'

Tom Delayhoyde saw something pass across Toby's face. The detective had a feeling that he was hiding something from him. The problem being, he wasn't sure what that something was.

Toby Carvell might have been hiding his part in a murder, but he equally might have been hiding the secrets of his childhood. Tom was willing to give him the benefit of the doubt, but not to the extent of letting a murderer go free, whatever the circumstances.

As soon as the sound of the kettle boiling could be heard, and Toby was safe in the knowledge that its hum obscured their conversation, he leaned forward and said, 'So what exactly brings you to my door?'

'We know that you knew Albie Woodville,' answered Tom as he held the older man's stare.

'Knew?' said Toby, as he ran a hand over his shaven head. 'I more than knew him, the dirty, fucking bastard. You'll know all this anyway.'

His last remark was made with a glance across to Sophia.

'Are you comfortable talking in front of both of us?' asked Tom, not wanting to be left alone without a colleague for back-up but wondering if it would be a better idea if Sophia wasn't in the room.

'Ah, the police at their best,' said Toby with a wry laugh. 'I had all this, you see, the first time round, when I gave evidence against the scum that is Albert Woodville. The police came round to see me, a nice couple of blokes they were. They gave it all the spiel: Was I all right talking about it? Did I prefer to speak to fellas or women? Did I care? How was I feeling? Don't upset yourself, Toby. We believe you, we really do. They took me to a house somewhere, made me tea, bought me a sandwich, put me in touch with support groups.'

He stopped talking and wriggled in his seat, fingernails on the sofa either side of him. He was almost digging them into the material, trying his best not to tear the cover.

'Worst thing of all, worse in some ways than the abuse I suffered at the sick fuck's hands, was the way I was treated in court. That horrible sod probably couldn't help it, but here was a courtroom chock full of legally trained professionals, intent on ripping me up for arse paper. And the fucking judge let them.'

The two officers watched in silence as the person they had come to talk to about his whereabouts on the night of the murder of a convicted sex offender seemed to melt into the furniture.

'I got into that witness box,' he said, voice full of horrors never quite forgotten, 'and I was made to feel like a lying piece of crap. I was accused of making it up for compensation. I didn't want money, I wanted justice. Except, justice is a bloody joke.'

He seemed to remember where he was and that there were two detectives sitting in his front room on a Saturday morning whilst he poured out his heart over his second degrading assault, this one in a court in front of a judge, jury, legal teams and spectators in the public gallery.

'So, in answer to your question,' he said, voice louder now, 'I'm fine talking in front of you both. I've been laid bare in a court, so why should I object to you two?'

The kitchen door opened and Shirley walked in with three mugs of tea.

'Do me a favour, love?' said Toby as she plonked the last of the three mugs down.

'I know,' she sighed, 'make you some toast.'

'No,' he said, as he reached for his tea, 'go and get dressed. You're offending my eyes.'

On her way out, she called a few choice words in her husband's direction, which made him grin as he watched her leave the room.

The problem for him was that his brash way of

LISA CUTTS

dealing with people wasn't fooling Sophia and Tom for one moment.

They had seen the real, vulnerable Toby Carvell and they had a growing feeling that he was involved in Albie Woodville's murder. Their problem was going to be how they proved it.

Chapter 21

Try as hard as he could, DI Harry Powell could only summon feelings of hatred towards Albert Woodville. Yes, he saw him as a victim of murder, the worst crime imaginable, but he had also handed out his own death sentences. One of his victims of sexual abuse had attempted suicide following the end of Woodville's lengthy trial, and another had an impressive criminal record, beginning around the time he was placed into Woodville's care, when, presumably, the abuse started.

Harry knew that however the enquiry went, there would be no winners, certainly not amongst his staff.

He hadn't failed to recognize what Sophia was trying to tell him about Gabrielle Royston but as ever, it was what he did with the information. He could call Gabrielle into his office and ask her for her opinion of perverts, but even if for one minute she didn't jump to the conclusion that her senior officer was trying to come on to her, she would hardly tell him if she had a secret longing to annihilate everyone convicted of sexual offences. Nothing in life was ever that simple.

This particular Saturday was likely to turn into a very long one. Harry gave a brief thought to the hours he worked and the strain it had put on his marriage over the years, something that for so long he hadn't considered to be a problem. His domestic instructions were now very clear: unless he fancied the idea of being divorced, he wasn't to 'hide at the sodding police station'. Even he knew that the threats weren't idle and that their marriage was on the rocks. He could either pay Mrs Powell more attention or she would leave him, obliterating everything he had aimed for and built. He simply didn't want to risk it.

Not that he would ever tell anyone that. He made excuses that he was getting on a bit and didn't have the staying power of his younger years. The truth was that he hated the idea of his marriage going wrong and was petrified of being alone after being a husband with children around. He was sure that life had the potential to go the right way for him and he wasn't going to let a dead paedophile spoil things.

Or so he thought.

'Hi there, Harry,' said a voice from the office doorway.

He smiled before he looked up from his computer screen.

'Don't be too pleased to see me yet,' said DCI Barbara Venice. 'You don't know why I'm here.'

'Babs, I'm always pleased to see you. What can I do for you?'

'Don't call me Babs, for a start.'

'I've been calling you that for decades.'

'And I've been asking you not to, you cantankerous old bugger.'

By now, the two old friends were sitting opposite each other, like grey-haired bookends, bitter at the world for the crap it had thrown their way, but still determined to do the best job they could, despite the ever-growing difficulties that accompanied any investigation.

'There was a time,' said Harry, 'when you and I would have cracked open a bottle of Scotch and sat talking bollocks.'

'I don't drink,' she replied. 'But go ahead with the talking bollocks. You've always done enough of that for two.'

'As much as I'm loving the verbal sparring, Babs, what did you want?'

'The murder we had on Friday possibly wasn't a one-off.'

Harry threw himself back in his chair, head tilted, eyes on the cracked and blistered ceiling paint, hands going up to his face. He rubbed at his stubble, something he always fought a losing battle with. As a new recruit, he was berated for not shaving properly, so one morning, to his then sergeant's astonishment, he brought his shaving gear to work with him and shaved in the parade room in front of the entire shift. Three hours later the stubble was back and no one questioned his standards ever again.

'Where and when?' he said eventually.

'Someone's been looking into suspicious deaths in the last year,' she said. 'I'm amazed they linked these two so quickly, especially as the one I'm going to tell you about happened several months ago in another force's county.'

'If there are other departments with so many staff on at a weekend, perhaps they can send me some. I'm scratching around here for an outside enquiry team. I'm only grateful I've got Pierre coming back from his annual leave on Monday and a new DC, Hazel Hamilton, starting. Pierre I can vouch for, but she better be as good as her reputation. I'm up shit creek here.'

'From what I've learned so far,' said the DCI, ignoring the comments, 'it was a male, aged thirty-three years, found in the woods with a noose around his neck, hanging from a tree.'

'Not suicide then?'

She paused, leaned back in her chair and said, 'That was the first thought. Especially as there was a note, and he had no family, well, none that were speaking to him.'

Harry raised an eyebrow.

'The victim was called Dean Stillbrook. His family had severed all ties with him after he was arrested and charged with the attempted rape of a young girl who lived in his street.'

'Oh fuck,' said Harry, the realization of what was coming next about to hit him full pelt.

'The case went to trial but the jury acquitted him.

He left the court a free man, went into the woods two weeks later and was found hanging by his neck.'

'That doesn't make any sense,' said the DI, lurching forward in his chair to tap the words 'Dean Stillbrook' into his keyboard.

'It wouldn't have made any sense if it actually was suicide,' agreed Barbara. 'Only, the chances are that he didn't take his own life.'

'What makes anyone think that?' said Harry, but already knowing that there was much more to it, or he wouldn't have a DCI sitting in his office on her day off telling him about it. He wondered if this was the reason that Barbara had been turning up at his briefings. He was on the cusp of asking her outright when it struck him that she had only just found out about the possibility of the two deaths being linked, so it didn't explain her presence on Friday night. The time wasn't right to ask her, and besides, he knew that she would tell him if there was something else bothering her. Their relationship had never been more than a comfortable working one, but nevertheless it was solid.

'Well, for starters,' she continued, 'it was only two hours' drive from here to where he died. The cause of death was strangulation and both Woodville and Stillbrook are alleged sex offenders, although one was found innocent and one found guilty at court.'

'There must be more than that?' said Harry, trying to keep the hope from his voice.

'Take a look at Dean Stillbrook's suicide note and then I'll tell you something really interesting about it.'

Chapter 22

By the time DC Tom Delayhoyde and DC Sophia Ireland left Toby Carvell, they both felt their energy levels had dropped. They walked out to their car, not entirely convinced they had made any progress.

Once inside the confines of the battered green Peugeot, complete with approximately twenty scratches and paintwork scrapes that no one had ever admitted to, the pair exchanged a look.

'What do you think?' asked Tom.

Sophia pulled a face and turned in the direction of the house they had spent the last three hours in. 'We've at least got a signed statement from him saying where he was on Friday night, but didn't you get a feeling that he wasn't telling us everything?'

'I'm honestly not sure. I felt truly uncomfortable listening to what happened to him as a kid so perhaps it clouded my judgement a little. He certainly gave us lots of detail about where he was and who he was with, including where he left his Ford Focus overnight. That shouldn't be too difficult to confirm.'

For a few seconds Sophia thought this over before she added, 'Didn't you think it was a little too detailed?'

'We were only asking him about as recently as yesterday, although I get your point. Do you reckon he was expecting us?'

'He could only have been expecting us if he actually murdered Woodville.' She let out a long slow breath and said, 'In which case, if he reckoned he was with Leon Edwards, they did it together. Not very friend-like, is it?'

'We either make a decision that we now go and see Leon Edwards, check out Toby Carvell's alibi, which is what we really should do, or complete the other task given us, and we go and see our murder victim's girlfriend, Millie Hanson. What do you want to do?'

'I want to keep my job, so I'll let someone else make the decision, because whatever we do we'll no doubt be wrong.'

The sound of a phone ringing filled the car via the hands-free before DS Sandra Beckinsale answered her mobile.

'Beckinsale,' was all she said.

Tom raised his eyes at Sophia who smiled and shook her head.

'Er, Sandra. Hello, it's Tom.'

When she didn't reply, he shrugged and continued. 'We spoke to Carvell and got a statement from him about where he was on Friday night. He said he was with his mate, a bloke called Leon Edwards. What do you want us to do now? See Edwards, follow up on where Carvell said he was and finish this enquiry properly, or go to Millie Hanson's?'

There were several seconds of silence.

Sophia and Tom exchanged a look.

'What do you both think about Carvell?' she asked at last. 'Do you reckon he's telling the truth or not?'

'It's difficult to say,' said Tom, giving a hunch of his shoulders that his detective sergeant couldn't see. 'We've talked about this and both Sophia and I feel that it's a tough call to separate out how much of what Carvell might be keeping from us is because of his past sexual abuse, or because he knows more about Woodville's murder than he's letting on.'

He paused but then felt compelled to fill the silence when once again the DS on the other end of the line kept quiet.

'I'd prefer to go and see the girlfriend now, even though we haven't strictly speaking finished this enquiry,' he said.

'As long as we don't lose anything evidentially,' said Beckinsale, 'go with your instinct and see Millie Hanson next. Make a note that I've told you to do it so it doesn't come back on you if the proverbial hits the fan.'

'OK,' he said, as he nodded his head in agreement, 'will do. And thanks. See you later.'

Tom leaned across and pressed the disconnect button. 'Some people think she's a bit of an old bag, but I quite like her.'

'Tom,' said Beckinsale's voice. 'I'm still here. You didn't end the call.'

'I can't believe you did that,' said Sophia half an hour later as they pulled up outside Millie Hanson's house. 'Beckinsale's going to have your guts for garters.'

'There's no need to find it quite so funny,' said Tom. 'You can do the talking on this one.'

'I don't mind. And if it's supposed to be a punishment, you can't keep quiet for long enough to make me ask all of the questions anyway.'

As they stood at the front door, both of them were already aware of what kind of person Millie Hanson was from what they could see of her house. It was clean and tidy, a smattering of children's books and toys strewn across the living-room floor, visible through the window. The front lawn needed a cut and the flower beds were neglected, but the absence of bags of rubbish all over the front garden or broken or boarded-up windows pointed towards her being civil towards them at the very least.

Neither of them voiced their prejudice that a mother of two young children couldn't possibly be a murderer.

When she opened the front door, her face didn't register surprise, but almost relief that at last the police had come. Without one word, she stood back to let them in. Sophia still felt that introductions were needed but from the flitting of Millie's bloodshot eyes from her to Tom, she wasn't entirely sure she was listening.

'Come in,' said Millie, eyes in the direction of the staircase.

'Is this a bad time?' asked Sophia, felling a little uneasy that Millie seemed so conscious of her surroundings in her own house.

'I know why you're here,' she said as she closed the front door. 'My children are upstairs. I don't want them to hear what you're going to tell me.'

She walked into the depths of the house, the two detectives exchanging a glance before following her into the lounge.

Without asking, Sophia and Tom took a seat on the sofa opposite her.

'You said to us in the hallway, "I know why you're here,"' began Sophia. 'Why do you think we're here?'

'Albie,' she muttered, and then louder said, 'Albie. You're here about Albie.' Millie waited for the officers to speak and then said, 'Because of his past and what he did. I've already been told this by DC Laura Ward. I've got her card here somewhere.'

She made to get up.

'Millie, please don't worry about that now,' said Sophia, watching her closely. 'When did you last see Albie?'

'It was a month ago, the same day that Laura came round here and told me what he'd done.' She put a hand up to her mouth, a nervy shaking hand, and then put it back down in her lap. 'What sort of a mother lets a man like that anywhere near her children?'

'Do you know what's happened to Albie?' Sophia

said, wondering how she was going to give a death message to a woman who was likely to have very mixed feelings about the imminent news.

The widow shook her head and peered out through tear-filled eyes.

'This is so hideous. Has he done it again? Please don't say he's done it again.'

'No, no, it's not that. Millie, Albie Woodville was found dead last night.'

Her eyes widened and this time the tears cascaded down her face. All she said was, 'Dead. Oh God, he didn't?'

Chapter 23

It wasn't long before Eric Samuels' Saturday ritual of catching up with East Rise Players' business and correspondence was behind him. Lunch, as usual when his wife was out, was taken on a tray in the sitting room.

He tried to put any unpleasant thoughts about the future of his full-time hobby – some might call it an obsession – out of his mind and focus on the homemade pea-and-ham soup that Belinda had left for him before going off to start her weekend round of visiting elderly folk in hospital and at home. It was something that his wife was as passionate about as he was about his productions. She, however, didn't have all the worries he faced, especially the more pressing one of the success of his upcoming musical, *Annie*. Four of the teenage girls had dropped out already, one with a particularly angry father who thought it was acceptable to shout abuse down the phone at Eric.

He lifted a spoon of steaming soup from the bowl to his mouth, and willed himself to concentrate on the television lunchtime news. He waited for the soup to

cool before taking a sip and lost himself in the international disasters unfolding in front of him.

Several times he tutted and shook his head at the
atrocities in the world and marvelled at how people
could blow each other up, shoot and kill their neighbours, all because of religion, land or money. He still
went on enjoying the soup, now and again a too-hot
spoonful taking him by surprise.

He enjoyed his lunch so much, he decided to get
himself some French bread to go with it and mop up
the remains in the bottom of the bowl. Having placed
his tray on the side table and pressed the mute button
on the remote control, he wandered into the kitchen
to find the loaf he had seen that morning. As he did
so, he began to hum to himself, wondering, not for the
first time, whether he was overreacting to the whole
Albert Woodville interfering-with-children episode.
He was even wondering where his daft idea of tele-
phoning Albie to tell him he was no longer welcome
at the Players had come from.

After all, he only had two police detectives' word
for it. They might have been embellishing the truth.
Now he came to think of it, he wasn't entirely sure
that they'd told him how many children Albie had been
convicted of touching. If it was only one, surely it was
the child's word against that of the adult? How times
had changed.

Once Eric had cut a single piece of bread, he decided
that he would have a second. He was feeling much
better and now he'd had time to ruminate on the

Albert Woodville affair, he put it down to no more than a storm in a teacup. Apart from not having all the facts in front of him, he really liked the man. He had always turned up on time, been courteous and well presented. These weren't the signs of someone who had a tendency to interfere with children. Once he started to reflect on the legal system he couldn't help concluding that juries got things wrong all the time. That idiot woman who lived four doors away was recently on a jury and she didn't have the brains to know which way was up.

That was Eric's mind made up: the legal system couldn't be trusted and there was no way one small, impressionable child, who couldn't have known wrong from right and was no doubt coaxed by her parents and the police, could understand what she was accusing a fully grown man of.

He put the bread on a small plate, as he didn't want Belinda scolding him for dropping crumbs everywhere again, and almost felt sorry for the image he was conjuring up in his head of a scared seven-year-old girl who was encouraged to tell lies about a grown-up.

'Pitiful,' he mumbled to himself as he sat back down in his leather chair to catch the local news.

The screen filled with a miserable-looking news reporter, raincoat pulled tight around her, long blonde hair flapping in the wind, rain hitting her face from time to time and forcing her to blink rapidly. Behind her were police cars, vans with *CSI* on the side of them, people in sodden white paper suits and a uniform officer standing in front of some blue-and-white tape to keep the public out.

What caught Eric's eye was what the police officer was guarding. If he wasn't very much mistaken, it was the front door of a block of flats that he had been to on more than one occasion. For some reason, it seemed that the entrance to Albie Woodville's home was being protected.

He had an awful feeling that word had got out that somewhere a young foolish girl had told a pack of lies about a man Eric would be happy to call a friend. Perhaps the police had been called to keep the angry mob out; after all there could only be one person accused of such an atrocious crime in the seaside town of East Rise.

Eric fumbled for the remote control, unable to take his eyes from the screen. He watched the news reporter turn, glance over her shoulder and thumb in the direction of the block of flats. At that moment he hit the correct button, releasing the words ... *murder investigation of a sixty-three-year-old man, as yet unnamed by the police ...*

The rest of the words were lost on Eric as he sat stunned and not fully grasping what he had heard. In spite of the warmth of the room and the hot meal he had eaten only moments ago, he couldn't help feeling a chill.

Someone had killed his good friend Albert.

With shaking hands, he picked up the phone and

dialled the incident-room number that had been shown on the television screen.

It wasn't long before someone answered and clearing his throat he said, 'I've just seen on the news that a man's been murdered. I know someone who lives in those flats and if Albert Woodville's been killed, I know who's done it.'

Chapter 24

'So, come on then,' said Jude Watson as he looked around the dingy back-street pub they had agreed to meet in. 'What exactly are we going to do now?'

He scrutinized Jonathan's hands as he picked up a beer mat and began to tap it on the edge of the table. He couldn't remember ever examining the back of another man's hands before and was surprised to see that one had a red welt across it.

'How did that happen?' he asked, pointing at the mark.

'Very funny,' said Jonathan. 'Don't pretend that you don't know.'

Jude pulled a face and said, 'Do you want another beer?'

'No thanks. I'd better get going after this one. I've got to pick my daughter up from some swimming gala, so one bottle's my limit.'

'OK then,' said Jude after the man nearby got up to go to the bar, 'what exactly are we supposed to do now? What's the plan?'

Before he gave his answer, he ran an eye over the few other customers, making sure they were out of earshot. 'For now, I'd suggest that we do nothing.'

'Genius. Wish I'd thought of that.'

Jonathan sat back in his chair, holding the stare of the other man. He wouldn't exactly call him a friend, more of a passing acquaintance. He'd never wanted to join the amateur dramatic society but had been talked into it by his wife; bullied into it was more like it. He used to spend a lot of time playing golf and cricket but owing to a busted ankle and a dive in finances, one was now physically impossible and the other barely affordable. She had been telling him for ages that cricket was seasonal and he couldn't play as much golf in the winter as he used to so he should do something else, indoors and cheap. Gone were the days when he got away with giving her a right-hander. She told him if he touched her again, he wouldn't see a penny of the inheritance that was coming her way.

Although he wasn't in a hurry to admit it, Jonathan Tey, accountant, knew he would miss being on stage and the centre of attention. It suited him and even if it was something he would never credit his wife with, he was glad he had been forced into it.

He hadn't been able to work out exactly what made Jude Watson tick but they got on all right and found they had the same views on several things – politics, sport and paedophiles.

'I still can't get over that bloody idiot Eric allowing

Woodville to join,' said Jude as he tore at the label on his beer bottle.

'Keep your voice down,' said Jonathan as the man who'd been sitting nearby returned to his seat with a pint of something dark brown in a glass with a handle.

Jude followed his accomplice's line of vision towards the elderly man as he placed his drink on the cigarette-burned table.

'Has he got a pint of mild?' said Jude. 'I didn't think they still made it.'

'And in a jug? You've brought me to the pub that time forgot. And my shoes are sticking to the carpet.'

'I thought it was the best place for us to talk in private,' said Jude.

'The only other people likely to see us are other sad bastards who look like they're up to no good,' said Jonathan, regretting not being able to have another beer. That would at least have made the experience of being in such a dump with someone he didn't entirely trust, talking about a sex offender, slightly more palatable. 'We need to lie low. It's too soon for us to do anything without it being obvious.'

'But how long do you think we should keep quiet?'

'I don't know, Jude. What am I? The Sage of Old East Rise Town? Have you come across anything like this before? Ever worried yourself to sleep about what you could have exposed your kids to? I worry about mine every day as it is, without feeling like a giant piece of crap for encouraging my daughter to audition for poxy *Annie*. I'm only grateful that she's so much better at the front crawl than she is at singing "It's The Hard Knock Life".'

For some reason this struck Jude as extremely amusing and he battled to keep a smirk from his face. He wasn't entirely sure that he'd managed it until he caught Jonathan staring at him. He was cautious of his accomplice who clearly had the brains and the brawn. He didn't want to get on the wrong side of him.

He let out a long, slow breath when Jonathan said, 'I can see how cut up all of this is making you too.'

Chapter 25

As soon as Albert Woodville's post-mortem was completed, Harry left the mortuary, annoyed that the pathologist had been so delayed. He left behind the smell of clinical bodies and climbed into the sanctity of his own car, shook off his exasperation and made a phone call.

Martha Lipton answered on the third ring.

'Hello to you,' she breathed in his ear. 'Give me a second. There are a few people here.'

'It sounds like you're in the street,' he said.

'Very astute, Inspector. We're in the good part of town, handing out leaflets. I can drop you one in to the police station if you like. It's only a short walk over to you at the rougher end of town.'

There was a pause as he made up his mind whether he wanted to see her in person, or if a chat on the phone and a leaflet drop would suffice. She still made his flesh crawl and he had just watched a pathologist peel the face off a paedophile. He preferred the dead; they gave him less to worry about.

'I don't think it's necessary to meet up,' he said, hearing what sounded like a chuckle in his ear, although he might have been mistaken over the traffic noise and sounds of East Rise's shoppers on a Saturday afternoon. 'Anything new to tell me?'

'I've been thinking about this. If I tell you what I know, what's in it for me?'

He let out a sigh. 'Martha, I thought you founded the Volunteer Army so that you could help people feel safe in their own homes, send their kiddies to school without the big, mean pervert waiting for them by the swings on the way home. The rousing speech bullshit you gave me yesterday in front of your stooge wasn't only for effect, surely? You had me believing you and now you're asking for money?'

'I didn't say I wanted money.' It was Martha's turn to sigh. 'I want some sort of public recognition for the work of the VA.'

This was the part that Harry had to stop himself laughing at. He wanted to shout down the phone line that these imbeciles were nothing more than glory-hunting prats, but thought better of it.

His mind ran over what he had to be careful of telling her. She was a dangerous woman and he wouldn't put it past her to record their conversation. If he made her any promises, it might cause him complications down the line. She was a potential witness, so entice her with anything other than the reward of justice, as soon as they had their murderer on trial Harry knew he'd be in the witness box waiting for the defence

114

barrister to make a meal out of him for encouraging her to give information, whether it was true or not.

'You know full well, Martha, that I want to find out who killed Albert Woodville, but I'm not prepared to jeopardize a potential conviction for murder by offering you anything I can't give you.

'I'm treating you the same as any other witness and asking you if you know anything. Don't mess me around on this and after it's all over we'll meet and talk things through. It's the best I can offer you, you know that.'

'When you say talk things through—'

'That's exactly what I mean. Come on, Martha. Help me out on this. We want the same thing at the end of the day. People murdering paedophiles can't be doing your business much good either. It's certainly killing mine, pardon the pun.'

Harry heard the sound of footsteps and when she spoke next she was breathing faster.

'Tell you what I'll do,' she said, 'I'm on my way to the police station now. I'll leave you a copy of our newsletter, you read it and tell me what you think and by the time you've got back to me, I should have some news.'

The sound of the disconnected tone told him that his conversation with her was over.

He scratched the stubble on his chin and contemplated what he found more abhorrent: working so hard to identify a paedophile's murderer, or that he had just sweet-talked the most depraved of all human beings.

He prayed to a God he didn't believe in that hell had a special place for Martha Lipton and her kind. The last bastion of all that was good was finally breached when Harry discovered that mothers who sexually abused their own children were allowed to walk the earth.

Now he had found himself placating her.

It was this kind of horror that stopped him from going home and telling his wife what he'd done at work all day. Some things were better left unsaid. Harry knew that if his untainted wife got even a hint from him of the daily crap that came his way he would probably repel her for good.

It wasn't only the thought of that on top of the issues Martha had brought to his door that was bringing on a headache. Despite rubbing his fingertips against the base of his neck, he couldn't quell the invisible band that was tightening across his forehead.

He now had another very real problem to contend with: the post-mortem had showed up old, healing injuries to Albert Woodville's face.

Prior to his murder, someone had given him a beating, and Harry had no way of knowing if both attacks had been carried out by the same people.

Chapter 26

Evening of Saturday 6 November

Leon Edwards was eating his way through a half-pounder burger, fries, coleslaw and extra-large side of pickles at his new favourite diner. The only disappointment of the day, apart from getting to the late-night eatery and finding that the waitress he had taken a shine to was not working, was that when he had phoned Toby that afternoon, his friend had sounded a little distracted. He was feeling a bit down that his oldest, most trusted friend hadn't even called him by either his Christian name or his nickname.

As he chomped, open-mouthed, on the hamburger, Leon thought that perhaps he had got it wrong and the two of them were supposed to remain incommunicado for a couple of days.

He was so puzzled by the turn of events that the large crease on his forehead drew the attention of the waitress who hurried over to ask if everything was OK.

'Blinding, love,' he replied, spraying relish across the Formica table and giving her a thumbs-up in case she couldn't understand him. At least the menus were wipe- clean, he thought, as a chunk of tomato hit the chef's-special section.

There had been few times in their thirty-or-so-year friendship when Toby had excluded him and it always worried Leon more than it would most people.

He really had had very little in his life for starters but despite his bulk giving him a tough exterior he was someone who cared more about others than himself. Though he cared about his food.

Leon ate out more than he should; once a week he ate at Toby's, Shirley always asking in advance what he wanted. Sometimes she even cooked it too. Eating out on Fridays had become a ritual for him and Toby, and he had been cheered to hear his friend say that they would have to keep going to the same place every Friday for a few more months to come. Once a week he ate in his local pub, but it was dreadful, everyone said so, including the cook.

Whatever his life had become, and it wasn't much, Leon was determined to make use of his time on the planet, but because he had no family of his own it was taken up with work and the Carvells.

He knew how much he owed them and thought about how, if things had been different, he could have had a smasher of a family like Toby's. He mulled it over as he slurped at his milkshake, rammed chips into his mouth in handfuls and tried to see how far he could open his mouth to push food inside without actually dislocating his jaw.

It wasn't long before he was finished and, as he had already paid, he threw a couple of coins on the table for the waitress when she finally waddled over to him to clear his table. She wasn't as fast on her feet as Lorraine, his favourite, but he spared a thought for the woman who, on the wrong side of fifty, arse like a waterbed squeezed inside her leggings, probably didn't want to be working anywhere on a Saturday night, least of all at the Waterside Late Night Diner.

Feeling a little less satisfied with life than he should have done after one of his favourite meals, Leon made his way outside and towards the High Street. The noise of late-night drinkers, screeching women and men goading each other on in loud voices reached his ears as soon as he turned the corner into the main drag of the town. He thought back to the previous evening when he had told Toby how he was feeling about not having anyone in his life. Then the full realization of why he had been experiencing such melancholy emotions hit him.

He and Toby had turned a corner with what they'd done.

The thought stopped him in his tracks as he paused mid-stride at the junction of Duke Street and the High Street, several people having to move out of his way. A smaller, less visible presence coming to a sudden stop on the pavement might have got a few comments or even some abuse. Not Leon with his size. The tide of drinkers parted around him, like a human stream navigating a twenty-three-stone island.

He didn't know that he could live with himself now. The panic started to rise up to his throat, making its way to his brain. How could he look people in the eye, talk to them, act normal? Act like anything other than what he was – a criminal?

Leon tried to catch his breath, but his mind was telling him that he didn't deserve to take a breath. That was something he didn't have the right to do. Surely, if you did wrong and harmed someone, you were forced to carry the guilt for eternity. He felt the weight of something that common sense told him wasn't there. He knew it was in his imagination but he couldn't stop the pull of his head towards the ground as he doubled up, there and then on the broken paving stones that East Rise Council hadn't even had the decency to fix.

He couldn't stop himself as his face got closer and closer to the pavement adorned with a white greasy wrapper housing half a doner kebab. Leon felt his own meal coming up and marvelled at how he had managed to keep it together for so long.

There was an easy answer to that of course: this was the first time he had allowed his thoughts to sneak up on him and hijack his sanity. It was also the first time that he hadn't merely turned to Toby and got the answers and reassurance he needed from him.

His head was now only inches from the discarded takeaway. The smell of the chilli sauce was making its way to his nose, climbing inside his nostrils, telling his brain that his stomach ought to reject his own late-night meal.

It was the image of food on the ground that brought Leon to his senses. He found himself drooling, the juices in his mouth reminding him how close he had come to vomiting over the pavement and probably his own shoes.

Food shouldn't be wasted and if it was there on the ground it should be eaten.

He pushed himself away from the rancid kebab, the fat from the meat white and congealed. He leaned back against the wall for support, knees still at an angle, palms resting on his thighs.

He closed his eyes and the blackness was filled with a memory, a terrible memory of being eight years old and made to eat food from the floor, Albert Woodville standing over him, pushing his head down.

Chapter 27

Early hours of Sunday 7 November

The black-clad figure kept to the shadows and shied away from the road side of the pavement. Anyone driving past or looking out of their window would see a dark shape hurrying to its destination, probably away from the coldness of the night. Although a cloudless sky meant that the temperature had dropped by a degree or two, he was sweating as he made his way to the outskirts of East Rise, away from the clubs and late-night drinking dens. Partly this was due to nerves, partly to the weight of the rucksack over his shoulders.

Previous experience meant that he knew where the CCTV cameras were, and his chosen calling of stealing other people's property in the dead of night had taught him well how to hide from the police. It wasn't all that difficult as most of them drove diesel cars – he could hear them coming a mile away – and he was a local, knew all the alleyways. It wasn't the first time he had needed his wits about him, moments before breaking the law.

Unusually, tonight, it wasn't what he was going to be carrying off from the scene of the crime, but what he was bringing to the party.

He really was upping his game, but they deserved what they got.

Fifty metres or so shy of his destination, he ducked behind a tree and ensured that his face was still covered, his gloves still on and no one was watching him. Breathing more heavily now, he shrugged the rucksack from his shoulders, worked the drawstring around the opening loose and removed the one item he had transported with so much care.

He contemplated leaving the rucksack behind but dismissed the idea almost as soon as it had formed. He had learnt about DNA evidence the hard way: it was going home with him until he could safely get rid of it.

This left only one thing to do.

He ran towards Norman Husband House, covering the distance in no time. He opened the letterbox, lifted the pesticide-sprayer nozzle and began pumping the petrol inside.

Twice his resolve to empty the five-litre container almost gave way. Driven by a desire to finish the job, he carried on, oblivious to all around him.

He was so carried away by the task in hand, he forgot why he was about to burn a building down with people asleep inside.

A noise in the street jolted him back to reality.

He froze.

The sound of a car coming around the one-way system made his heart beat faster than he thought possible. He could hear his own breath, raspy and uneven.

If he didn't do it now, he never would.

He dropped the pesticide sprayer and pulled a cheap plastic cigarette lighter from his pocket along with a copy of that morning's local newspaper. His hands were shaking as he lit the corner of the front page. With some difficulty he pushed the paper inside the letterbox, not having thought through how he was going to get a burning wad of paper as thick as the opening itself to the other side of the door. He definitely hadn't taken into account that his own gloves, some of his clothing and the porch entrance he was standing in had petrol splattered all over them too.

Panic began to set in and he turned from the front door and hurried away.

He stopped at the corner and looked back over his shoulder as the flames were beginning to rise up above the solid bottom half of the door to the frosted reinforced glass part.

With a satisfied smile, he ran off into the nearest alleyway, the smell of petrol and smoke chasing him.

Chapter 28

Sunday 7 November

'Are we the only two bloody detectives on this enquiry?' complained Tom as he and Sophia made their way to their unmarked car for the day. 'There weren't even many people at this morning's briefing because of the arson at Norman Husband House.'

'How about you stop moaning and we go and see these two blokes from the am-dram society?' said Sophia as she threw her file onto the back seat.

'OK, Soph, but the first "lovie darling" we run into, I'm off home.'

Once they were in the car, Tom produced a coin. 'Heads we see Jonathan Tey first, tails we see Jude Watson.'

'I must have been absent the day that was taught on the CID course,' said Sophia as she reversed the car out of its space and made for the security gate. 'Have you got anything a little more professional that we could use to decide who to drop in on first?'

'Tails it is. I'll put Watson's address in the satnav. So these two have come to light after the chairman of East Rise Players called the incident room yesterday and thought they were possibly up to no good.'

'He thought more than that,' said Sophia pausing at a red light. 'According to his call, Eric Samuels said that he knew who was responsible for killing Woodville, after he saw the police at his flat on the news and it was Tey and Watson.'

She pulled away as the light turned green, then added, 'You know what my problem is with what Samuels said?'

'Let me guess,' said Tom, 'it came from Gabrielle who went out to see Eric Samuels last night and you don't trust her to do a good job.'

'It's not so much that I don't trust her to get it right, she's a good detective, but she makes me feel uneasy.'

'Whatever you think about her, Gabrielle wouldn't deliberately lie about something a witness said. Besides, if she hates paedophiles as much as you think she does, then surely what she'd do is underplay any information that was forthcoming from members of the public, and not take a twelve-page statement from them, then come along to this morning's briefing and talk about it at great length.'

'So you're another one of the blokes in the office who've fallen for her long legs and piercing blue eyes, not to mention her short skirts.'

'Don't get touchy. You still look OK for a woman

of your age with wavy hair and a face shaped like a balloon.'

'I'm younger than you.'

'Really?'

'Lucky for you, Delayhoyde, we're here.'

She pulled up next to a row of modest mid-terraced houses, three doors down from Jude Watson's home. The windows were closed, curtains drawn and a car was parked on the street close to the front door.

The information shared at that morning's briefing was that Jude, East Rise Planning Department employee, was married with two young daughters, so neither of the DCs about to knock on his door were under any illusions that calling on a Sunday morning was likely to result in anything other than a houseful of people wanting to know what was going on.

They stood shoulder to shoulder on the pavement and Tom rang the bell.

Before too long, they heard movement and a man of about thirty years of age opened the door. His brown hair was dishevelled but his handsome face showed genuine surprise at seeing two people on his doorstep at 9 a.m. on a Sunday morning.

Not wanting to be mistaken for anyone other than a police officer, Tom showed his warrant card and said, 'Mr Watson? Can we come in and talk to you about the East Rise Players?'

'Some of our performances were a bit pitiful, but I don't think they're actually a crime,' he said as he let them in.

Two blonde-haired girls peered out at them round the kitchen door. 'Finish your breakfast, you two,' Jude said to them, 'then we'll get over the park in a bit.'

He shut the door on his family scene of wife and two daughters eating their cereal and showed the two police officers to the privacy of the front room.

'I take it,' he said, making himself comfortable in the armchair, 'that this is about Albert Woodville?'

'What have you heard about him?' said Tom.

Both Sophia and Tom watched his face for any sign of guilt, a flicker that meant he was holding something back, or even a hint that he knew more than he should about their murder victim's demise.

Jude Watson leaned forward towards Tom. 'You should know what he is – a kiddie fiddler. What are you doing about him being near kids in the first place? It's disgraceful. Fucking country's going down the pan faster than bog roll. He better not have touched my daughter or I'll fucking kill him.' He rubbed the spittle from his bottom lip and ran a hand through his hair. 'Sorry, sorry, it's that I love my girls so much I—'

He was interrupted by the door opening and one of the children put her face in the gap and said, 'Daddy, we—'

'For God's sake, Charlie,' he shouted, 'bugger off and eat your bloody breakfast.'

The door slammed shut and Jude continued. 'Yeah, I love my girls to bits, don't know what I'd do without them. So what do you want to know about Woodville?

I'm guessing it's urgent if it's brought you here on a Sunday morning.'

Sophia and Tom didn't want to miss a thing. They both knew that there was never a second chance to gauge Watson's real reaction.

'When did you last see Albert Woodville?' Tom asked.

Watson let out a breath, glanced down to his left, eyes on the worn pink carpet. 'Don't know. About two or three weeks ago at rehearsals. Why? What's happened?'

'He's dead,' said Tom. 'He's been murdered.'

'Oh.'

'You don't sound very surprised.'

This was met with a shrug and raised eyebrows. 'He was a horrible bastard. If you do that sort of thing, you've got to expect people to come for you. Parents especially.'

'Parents especially?' echoed Tom with a glance in the direction of the children in the kitchen who could be heard squabbling over Coco Pops.

'I'd do anything for my kids,' said Jude, fixing his stare on the detective constable, 'but I didn't kill Woodville. You want to arrest me, go right ahead but the last time I saw him was long before he died.'

'How do you know when he died?' said Tom, his tone so soft and casual, he sounded nothing like a murder detective stalking his prey.

'What?' His mouth hung open and he seemed to run out of air. His lips smacked shut and then he smiled. 'Nice one, nice one. When I last saw Woodville, he was still very much alive. That was some time ago and since then, you've come round here asking about his murder. Well, I'm assuming you two' – he waved his index finger back and forth at them – 'haven't left it two weeks to come and see me. If I was a gambling man, I'd say that he's only recently been murdered.' There was a somewhat smug look on his face.

All the while Tom sat, impassive, with only one thought in his head: he didn't believe what Jude Watson was telling him.

It was some hours later that Sophia and Tom had finished talking to Jude and finding out exactly where he had been over the last few days, who he had seen and what had happened the last time he was in close proximity to Albert Woodville.

When at last they had everything in writing, Sophia took a DNA mouth swab from Watson and Tom took his fingerprints.

'It's standard in an investigation like this,' she said as she tried to lighten the mood that had got distinctly heavy over the last twenty minutes. It had seemed to go downhill after she'd read out the declaration at the top of his statement that told him he might go to prison if he had misled them in anyway. He didn't seem to appreciate getting ink all over his hands from the mobile fingerprinting kit either.

The pair of them stood up with their paperwork, fingerprints and DNA sample and Tom said, 'Thanks for your time.'

'I didn't really have much choice, did I?'

Tom stopped at the living-room door and considered his response. 'To be honest, no you didn't, but we're grateful to have done it this way and not at the police station.' He opened the door and called over his shoulder, 'We'll be in touch.'

From the living-room window, tucked behind the curtain, Jude Watson stood looking out onto the street, down the road to where the two detectives got into a tatty Citroën. In one hand he held the edge of the curtain, and in the other his mobile phone.

'Jonathan, we've got a problem.'

Chapter 29

Afternoon of Sunday 7 November

'Harry,' said Martha Lipton, head resting against the front door's frame. 'How nice of you to come and see me at home.'

He held a piece of paper up to her face.

'Well, I can't read it properly as it's only a couple of centimetres from my eye, but I recognize my own newsletter when I see it.'

Harry took a deep breath and resolved to keep the promise to himself that he'd made on the journey over: he wasn't going to show this woman how much she wound him up.

'Have you any idea what you and your mucky little bunch have done?' he said, aware that he was over-enunciating every syllable.

'What's up? Spelling mistakes in an article?'

She leaned into the frame, arms crossed over the front of an impossibly tight T-shirt, one long leg in front of the other, bare toes tapping at the concrete step which separated them.

'You printed this vile shit and then handed it out in the street, the day after a sex offender was murdered.'

Harry stopped waving the piece of paper around his head. He knew that he appeared to be slightly demented and he had, after all, knocked on the door of her ground-floor flat. It was one of only two in the large converted Georgian house that had its own entrance. The other four flats on the next two floors were reached via a communal door but it didn't stop everyone within the street or neighbouring buildings seeing and hearing the spectacle he was making of himself.

'Do you want to come in?' she said. 'We can stand out here and discuss this if you like.'

What got to him most was that she came across as so reasonable, so rational and was so beautiful.

It made it all the worse for Harry.

'I don't have to tell you what's on the front page of your own sheet of spite.'

He held the page out in front of him with one hand and jabbed at the article with the other.

'Right here,' he said, 'under the main piece about Albert Woodville being murdered and your helpful top ten of how to spot a nonce, immediately below that, you print the address of Norman Husband House and list the likely sex offences those housed there might have served time for before their release into East Rise.'

'Listen,' she said, standing tall, the height of the doorstep making her head and shoulders over the policeman, 'everyone around here knows where Norman Husband House is anyway. Most people know it's a hostel for those released from prison with nowhere else to go. The only thing they wouldn't necessarily know is what kind of crimes those people have served time for.'

Harry stared at her for several seconds. He saw that it unnerved her. That made him smile.

He took a step forward. He took a step upwards, bulled toecaps touching her bare toes.

She inched backwards.

'It's lucky for you that the fire didn't spread.'

Her jaw dropped open.

'Fire . . .'

'There are only two reasons,' he said, face closer to Martha's than he would have liked, 'that I haven't nicked you. The first is that I don't at this point think you had anything directly to do with it, and the second is that you're coming down the police station in the next five minutes to make a statement to one of my officers, telling them everything you know about Woodville and the fire.'

He moved his head back.

'Got that?'

'Yes,' she said, unable to make eye contact. 'I'll get some shoes on and my coat.'

'No,' he said. 'We're not leaving together. I don't want to be seen with the likes of you.'

Head held high and chin thrust forward, she said,
'How do you know I'll turn up?'
Harry looked her up and down.
'You'll turn up all right.'
He turned and walked away.

Chapter 30

Jonathan Tey was a man with a lot on his mind. He sat in front of the television with his wife curled up beside him, daughter on the floor doing her usual last-minute homework before school the next day.

It was a scene that should have shown domestic Sunday-evening bliss but he couldn't help feeling restless. He couldn't stop his foot from tapping, a nervous sign that gave him away.

His wife glanced at him a couple of times, distracted from the drama she was watching on the screen. He knew that she wouldn't ask him what the matter was. That was a comfort.

Everything probably would have been all right if he hadn't decided it would be a good idea to go along to a vigilante meeting. That was probably a dumb mistake to have made.

He hadn't been all that interested in finding anything to replace the void left by his exit from the East Rise Players, an unusual mixture of individuals, all in all a decent albeit clueless bunch of people. On joining them Jonathan had immediately gained a self-importance he hadn't expected. Other than his enjoyment at being on stage, they asked his advice, got him to settle squabbles between them. That was what he missed – not having something to occupy his time and his already overcrowded mind, but the sense of purpose and belonging.

How was he to know that the day after he walked out of the Cressy Arms, livid with Eric Samuels for his stupidity, he was going to watch one of the most beautiful women he had ever seen stride towards him on the High Street?

He had barely regained his composure when she handed him a leaflet and smiled.

Jonathan had found himself smiling back, unable to drag his eyes away to look at the news-sheet he was gripping on to as if his life depended on it.

'We could do with some new members,' she said, unbuttoning her jacket.

Rather than stare at her chest, he concentrated on the words in front of him.

'I don't want to join a cult,' he said, a frown on his face.

'We're not a cult,' she said. 'It's all very out in the open what we do. Have a read of that, and here—' She opened her jacket to remove a pen from the inside pocket and taking the leaflet back scribbled her mobile number on it. As she handed it over she looked up at him, eyelashes fluttering, and added, 'And my name's Martha.'

It was some time later that Jonathan got the creased-up newsletter out of his overcoat pocket and read through it. His interest was piqued at what the Volunteer Army were trying to do, although that alone wouldn't have been enough to ensure his attendance at their meeting. What tilted the balance was the smile and wink Martha had cast over her shoulder before the throng of dreary shoppers swallowed her up.

Smile still playing on his lips, Jonathan realized that he was back in his own living room, wife watching some brain-numbing period drama on the box and his daughter whingeing under her breath that she didn't understand the point of learning about the industrial revolution, it wasn't as if it would happen again.

Elaine turned towards him at the point where he was recalling the full details of Martha's backside, skin-tight leggings moulded to her buttocks as she sashayed away from him.

'I knew that a night at home with us would cheer you up, love,' said his wife.

'Something like that,' said Jonathan as it crossed his mind that even in her heyday Elaine was no Martha. And especially not recently.

She'd let herself go quite a bit. He might even reward himself with an affair.

Chapter 31

Hazel's phone bleeped somewhere in the living room, jolting her from her thoughts. Still full of nervous energy, she jumped up to find it, moving magazines, cushions and handbags, finally locating it under a couple of old blankets she had fished out of the back of the airing cupboard and added to the heap of bedding on the floor.

As she unlocked the phone and opened the text, she was half hopeful that it would be another message from work, cancelling the request that she get in at the crack of dawn the next day. She was nervous enough as it was at the thought of having to be there before most of the other DCs were on duty, and then being sent off to carry out enquiries on a murder she knew nothing about. At least the old familiar practice of putting the staff's welfare at the bottom of the list made her feel as if she had never left. Nothing had changed in that respect.

It was also doing little to make her think she had made the right decision to rejoin Major Crime and that she could pick up from where she had left off. The problem was, she had missed the work more than she imagined she would. Hazel had battled against choosing an easier but less fulfilling option over the biggest buzz a career was capable of giving her, though it gave room for little else.

The one other thing she did make time for outside work was now messaging her on her phone.

Hazel, she read from her phone's screen, *is there any chance you're free for an overnight emergency? Wouldn't ask but I've tried everyone else* ...

She held the phone to her chest and let out a long sigh. She couldn't say yes when she was starting a new job so early the next day. Any other time, she would have requested a last-minute day off, but there was no way she could ask her detective inspector she hadn't yet met for a favour. Not before she had a chance to set foot inside the department's door.

After a few seconds, with heavy heart, she tapped out a reply.

Really sorry but off to work at 5 a.m. Call me tomorrow morning if you're still stuck. Hazel xx

She hated to say no when someone needed her and couldn't help but wonder if getting the blankets and spare sheets out of the various storage places around her home had triggered the call. This was something that she knew was nonsense and Hazel was by no means a superstitious person, but it had been several weeks since she'd been contacted out of the blue asking if she would take in a last-minute lodger.

Hazel didn't expect a reply to her text and turned her concentration to what she was going to wear to work for her first day and packing the correct stuff in her bag. Uniform officers had the advantage of not having to pick an outfit – one less thing to worry about. At least she wasn't going to have the added bother of picking stray dog hairs from her clothes.

She stacked the bedding into a neat pile and left it at the end of the sofa. Something told her that before the week was out she would have use for it.

Chapter 32

Monday 8 November

Monday morning had started a little earlier than usual for Detective Constable Pierre Rainer. He and his other half had been away for a week, soaking up the sunshine in the Canary Islands, and he wasn't officially due back on duty until 8 a.m.

He had a reputation for being very conscientious and keen, always ready to help out even after twenty years as a police officer. Harry Powell had immediately thought of Pierre when he had to pick someone who would not only answer their phone on a Sunday when off duty, but also be prepared to spend a long day on a very sensitive and important enquiry, possibly being required to stay overnight.

Pierre knew he had been picked for those reasons and Harry knew that Pierre was aware he was one of the most reliable on the team. It was something that Pierre took for granted with no hint of arrogance or self-importance, despite usually landing the best roles on the most interesting enquiries.

As he got ready for whatever was about to be heaped upon his workload, Pierre swiped his access card through the security door and headed for his desk. He took a good look around the incident room, ran an eye over the wire post trays screwed to the wall, the box files and heaps of paperwork strewn over the desks, and checked the whiteboards for the latest official and unofficial updates. It was reassuring to see that nothing had changed. It was its normal, messy, chaotic, familiar jumble of evidence with a hint of policing's human side, borne out by the mock-up photographs of members of the team stuck to the whiteboards complete with sarcastic comments underneath each one.

Usually, he would spend the first hour or so back at work checking through his emails and any post that had made its way to him. Today, he knew that he didn't have the time.

Despite it being 5.30 in the morning, Harry Powell was in his office, waiting for Pierre's arrival.

He heard the door swing shut as Pierre made his way out of the incident room, the computers in idle mode, hardly a light on in the entire area.

'Morning, boss,' said Pierre as he leaned one of his broad shoulders against the door frame of his detective inspector's office. 'Don't see you here very often before even the cleaners have put in an appearance.'

'Morning, P. How was the holiday?'

'We had a brilliant time, thanks. And it's always great to be back at work.'

'Did you miss us?'

'No.'

'Got to admire your honesty. Look, get yourself a coffee or something, grab a notebook and I'll give you the heads-up about this enquiry.'

'Well, you've certainly got me intrigued,' said Pierre as he walked off in the direction of the kitchen, putting caffeine before making notes.

'Very much a need-to-know basis,' called Harry after Pierre.

Once Pierre was back in Harry's office, he glanced up at the open door. He thought briefly about shutting it but knew that anyone coming into the incident room through the only entrance would make enough noise for him to be able to hear them long before they heard one word of what he was about to say.

'I take it that this has something to do with last week's murder?' guessed Pierre.

'In a roundabout way,' said Harry. 'You're aware that a male called Albert Woodville was murdered in his own home? Found with a plastic cable-tie around his neck and another bound around his wrists, hands behind his back.'

'Suicide was out then,' said Pierre as he looked up from his notebook.

'It's funny that you should say that,' replied Harry. 'Actually, it's not fucking funny at all.'

'Oh, I'm sorry. I—'

'No, no,' said Harry. "I'm not giving you a bollocking. It's that there's been another couple of deaths that looked like suicide, but one or two aspects of them appeared a little bit odd.'

'Odd?'

Harry broke eye contact to scratch the stubble on his cheek, and to give himself a few extra seconds to get the words out in the correct order. He wasn't a man who struggled to find the right thing to say, but his bluntness wasn't one of his best characteristics.

'One was so badly decomposed, it was difficult to tell. The pathologist couldn't even give a definitive cause of death. Nothing had been stolen and there was no other DNA, fingerprints or sign of anyone else having been inside the flat. That wouldn't have been so unusual had it not been for the neighbours saying he had a lot of visitors. I won't go into lots of details about that one at the moment but you get the idea. It'll be looked at again and we'll see if it's linked to these latest ones. For now, you only need to get the gist of it.'

This was the point where Pierre knew to keep quiet and contemplate what was coming his way.

'I want you to deal with this,' said Harry as he pushed a folder across the desk to him.

Pierre raised an eyebrow at him.

'Yeah, yeah. All right, I know it's like a bad detective series to pass you a file or an envelope rather than pointing you in the direction of the computer database, but there's a reason. I can't get you access to it until the rest of the HOLMES staff come in so I've printed you off what you need to know.'

He watched as Pierre opened the file, ran a manicured fingernail down the front page and once again raised an eyebrow.

After leafing through several sheets of paper, he sat staring for some time before he placed the open file on the desk. Both men looked at the full-page colour photograph of the corpse hanging from a tree.

'This one's not suicide either?' said Pierre.

'You've got it in one,' said Harry. 'You've got the bare bones there of the murder investigation into Dean Stillbrook's death.'

'Why do we say it wasn't suicide after all?'

'This is Dean Stillbrook,' said Harry. 'He was found in the woods, hanged two weeks after he was acquitted in Crown Court of the rape of an eleven-year-old girl.'

The eyebrow-raisings were now replaced by a look of cynicism from beneath a fringe of black hair, smatterings of grey all the more prominent against his tan.

Harry gave a sigh and said, 'It's a bit sensitive. It happened in Sussex and there's no criticism of them. For all intents and purposes, this looked like a suicide. The thing is, if the offenders are the same as Albert Woodville's killers, we need to take the lead. The decomposing body was found on us too. It'll have to be a cross-county investigation and I know I can rely on you to go to another county and be discreet. You know, not upset them. I've told them that you'll be on your way today and to expect you.'

Pierre stared straight at him with a look that Harry interpreted as that of an over-worked detective, used to having tasks piled upon him merely because he was capable and competent.

'I reckon, P,' said Harry, not missing a beat, 'that your money's on the little girl's family. Mine was too to begin with. It didn't take very long to rule them out completely, but I still want you to go and see them again. Find out anything you can, especially as we now know that it could no longer be a suicide.'

Harry paused to make sure he had his colleague's undivided attention.

'Go on.'

'Next page,' said Harry pointing at the file. He gave Pierre a few moments to register what was on the sheet of paper.

'It's a suicide note,' said Pierre. 'What's unusual about that?'

'It was another reason the little girl's family were ruled out. They were well aware that Dean Stillbrook couldn't read or write a single word.'

Chapter 33

Someone was causing Toby Carvell a great deal of anxiety, and that someone was his best friend, Leon Edwards.

There had been occasions too numerous to count over the last few years when Leon had told him of a desire to hunt down Albert Woodville and teach him a lesson; each time Leon's hatred spilled out and seeped into Toby's very core.

Once Toby had prepared himself for Monday morning and what his working week would bring, he got out of bed, kissed his sleeping wife on the side of the head and crept out of the pitch-black bedroom to the bathroom.

Habit meant that despite knowing he would be sweaty and grimy in a few hours, he stepped into the shower and began his morning ritual. He needed to rid himself of a layer of dirt invisible to the naked eye: it was cathartic more than anything. He tried to give very little thought to the death of Albert Woodville as his life was worth next to nothing. He justified what had happened by telling himself that there was not a soul alive who would lament Woodville's death; Toby had nothing to feel bad about.

That was what he kept telling himself.

He picked up the bottle of shower gel from the corner of the bath and squeezed some of the contents into the palm of his hand before rubbing the blue gloop over his body. Despite the warmth of the water and his need to scrub away an invisible dirtiness, he shuddered. He could never help the involuntary reaction that getting clean brought out in him. He knew that he could avoid showering in the mornings by waiting until he finished his window-cleaning round in the afternoons, so why didn't he?

Eyes screwed shut under the stream of water, he wondered, not for the first time, whether it was some sort of self-flagellation he put himself through in an attempt to atone for what he had allowed Woodville to do to him all those years ago.

Rational thought told him that a child couldn't stop a fully grown man from stroking him and caressing him, but still he couldn't shower without having his back to the wall. The buggery might have stopped decades ago, but the darkness hadn't gone away.

Now, Toby was happily married with two fantastic children, he had a job and a comfortable lifestyle, but not a day went by when he wasn't aware of how much lighter his mind would feel without the burden, the pressure, of knowing he was dirty.

He had only been seven years old when it happened

the first time. Cornered and alone in the bedroom he shared with Leon, Toby had returned to get the marble collection hidden underneath his bed. He hadn't wanted the other boys in the home to know where he kept it so he had practically crawled under his single wooden bed frame to dig it out from behind his suitcase. His marble collection was one of the few possessions he had been allowed to bring with him, and one of the few that hadn't been stolen since his arrival.

No sooner had his fingers gripped the coarse brown twine knotted around the cloth bag than he was aware that someone was in the room with him.

At first, as he wiggled out from under the bed, moving backwards on his belly, he thought it was Leon come to see what he was doing.

Something made him freeze and the hairs on the back of his neck stood up. Perhaps it was the noise of the door being locked. Perhaps it was a trick of his mind.

Most seven-year-olds wouldn't have been as astute as Toby, but most seven-year-olds didn't dread their father coming into the room. He had become attuned over his very short existence to the change in the air, the anticipation of a hiding, meted out according to his dad's mood.

One too many times Toby had appeared at school with a black eye, bruising around his throat, finger marks on his arms. Eventually he was admitted to hospital with a broken wrist.

Social services saw fit to remove Toby from harm.
So they placed him with a paedophile.

Toby turned off the shower and stepped out onto
the mat to dry himself. He rubbed vigorously with the
towel and tried as hard as he could to park thoughts
of his tragic childhood, something he wouldn't wish
on anyone.

It was how he had justified to himself what he and
Leon had planned to do to Woodville and how he had
managed to get to sleep over the last three nights.

If no one else was prepared to hand out justice, he
had no hesitation about doing it himself.

He rubbed the bathroom mirror with the towel and
looked at his reflection, complete with reddened eyes
underlined with heavy dark rings.

The death of Albert Woodville had been a necessity.
It was all that was standing between Toby and mad-
ness. Over the years he had tried to imagine what he
would say to him if he ever saw him, how he would
react. His tortured mind played scenes out where
he was driving his van and saw Woodville cross the
road, his own face pressed up against the windscreen
as he mowed him down. Or he would be waiting for
a train and see Woodville at the edge of the platform,
minding his own perverted, disgusting thoughts, and
Toby would time it to perfection and push him under
the train.

He knew he would never do any of those things, and
that was for one reason only – he would get caught. So
instead, he bided his time and planned. He was good

at waiting for the right moment to strike.

Now Woodville was dead, Toby felt an emptiness that he couldn't explain. It certainly wasn't sadness at his murder, it was something stranger and more complex than he could begin to understand.

There had been times when he was in the children's home when, despite the terrible things that he did to him, Woodville had paid him some attention and been good to him.

The reasons why were now blatantly obvious to Toby as a full-grown man. It was nothing short of grooming.

It still gave him goosebumps when he thought of the storm of emotions that had raged inside him, his confusion at how he could feel warmth towards the person who was sexually abusing him.

Now when he thought of him lying dead, the storm was replaced by sheer exaltation.

Chapter 34

It only took DC Pierre Rainer about half an hour to read through the file he had been given and get himself up to speed. He carried out the necessary intelligence checks to make sure he wasn't walking into anything unprepared, and waited for the newest member of the team to arrive to accompany him.

Thirty minutes later, the incident-room door opened to reveal DC Hazel Hamilton.

Pierre watched her stride in, a long gracious entrance that made her appear to belong there, or at least to give the impression of belonging.

She wore a navy trouser suit and had her blonde hair loose to her shoulders.

'Morning,' she said with a smile after running an eye over the room, empty but for Pierre.

'Hello,' he said as he got up and met her halfway across the worn grey carpet, brown masking tape holding it down to stop the staff breaking their necks on the torn segments. 'You must be Hazel. I'm Pierre.'

They shook hands and Pierre felt a firm hand-grip

from the woman standing several inches taller than himself.

'You've either got incredible detective skills or no one else would get here this early.'

'Both of those are true, and also you've been issued with a security pass,' said Pierre as he finished shaking her hand. 'That kind of gave it away. Welcome to Major Crime. Do you want a coffee or anything before we leave?'

He gave a glance up at the clock on the wall above her head.

'If we're pushed for time, I can make do until the services,' she said. 'I was told that I'm in your hands and to crack on with whatever you tell me to do.'

Pierre laughed. 'I take that to mean that you've been briefed on the phone by our very direct detective inspector, Harry Powell?'

She closed her eyes and smiled. 'He didn't waste many words on me.'

Harry's voice boomed out from his office, sparing Pierre the dilemma of whether or not to tell their newest detective that the person she was talking about was within spitting distance, sitting in a ten-foot-by-ten-foot room, and could easily hear them through the thin partition walls.

'So Hazel's arrived?' he hollered, although there was no need to be so loud.

Pierre raised an eyebrow and said, 'Let's say hi and then get on the road.'

*

Harry had been on holiday when the interviews for a new detective in the department had taken place, having a thoroughly miserable fortnight with his wife in the Maldives. It was somewhere he hadn't wanted to go and he hated the sun. His pale freckled skin and red hair meant he usually burnt. And because he had a five o'clock shadow by eleven in the morning he had the extra problem of catching the sun on only half of his face.

He had spent most of the holiday in the shade reading military-history books, and managing to annoy his wife whatever he did.

There had been no way of finding out what Hazel Hamilton looked like, although he had heard the rumours. He had rarely paid any interest to the women around him, especially other police officers. Despite the volatile relationship he had with his wife, he had never strayed. He knew in his heart that this was because he adored his children and couldn't bear the idea of her taking them away from him, rather than because he loved her. The boys were older now and would soon leave of their own accord, off to university or travelling the world; then there'd be something missing in his life.

None of this raced through Harry's mind as Hazel appeared. At that particular moment, he was incapable of thought.

'All right?' he said after an awkward short pause.

'Yes, thanks, sir,' she said.

'Pierre looking after you?' Harry pointed

unnecessarily at the other detective in the room. He saw the look Pierre was giving him and realized that he must have been staring at Hazel.

'He certainly is,' she said, and glanced across at Pierre, a smile taking hold of her face.

For some inexplicable reason, Harry felt jealous. He knew it was ridiculous to have such feelings over a woman he had only known for seconds, especially because he kept telling himself that he was happily married; and most of all because Pierre was gay.

Harry dealt with it as he usually dealt with anything uncomfortable, covering it with bluster and a façade of indifference.

'Well, best you two get out of here and on the road,' he said as he looked back to his computer screen and feigned concentration. 'Call if you get any problems.'

He gave them a dismissive wave in case his verbals weren't entirely clear.

He couldn't resist another look at Hazel as she eased her way from his office back through to the main part of the incident room.

Harry wondered how long the thermostat in his office had been malfunctioning as he loosened his tie and opened the window to the November morning.

Chapter 35

Monday mornings had become a traditional part of Toby Carvell and Leon Edwards's eating ritual. In summer, they went to a takeaway stand on the seafront overlooking the Channel, bought teas and egg-and-bacon foot-long French sticks, and then Toby watched Leon drop the egg and bacon down his shirt. In winter, they went to a café a couple of streets inland, ordered teas and full English fry-ups, sat at their regular table, and Toby watched Leon drop the fry-up down his shirt.

As Leon drove to Toby's house to pick him up, he ran through in his mind what he'd really like to get off his chest and tell his friend. There was so much he needed to say but he wasn't the most eloquent of people. He was more raw emotion, rather than collected orator. He had a vulnerability beneath his very large surface; few ever really saw it, but many took advantage of it.

Toby had done that very thing, only he had no idea what he had done.

They had been friends for so many years and trusted each other with every aspect of their lives. Leon had no remaining family of his own and little in his life that didn't involve his friend and business partner Toby.

The sound of the diesel van alerted Toby to Leon's presence at the top of the driveway, and Toby appeared at the passenger's side.

'Right then,' said Toby once he had shut the door, 'Scabby Larry's for breakfast?'

When he got no answer from Leon, he glanced across and saw in the faint light of the winter morning, signs that his friend had hardly slept all weekend.

'You want me to drive, Dilly? Would you rather pull over and talk?'

The reply came as a nod of the head.

They continued along in silence. Leon indicated left and drove them to the dead end at the local park's entrance. As he pulled the van to a halt over the stones and pebbles of the dirt track, he avoided stopping too close to the few early-morning dog walkers getting out of their cars. Not one of them seemed to pay any attention to the window-cleaning van with ladders atop. Their attention was taken with wrapping up against the chill and getting their overexcited canines out for their exercise.

Toby sat and waited.

Once or twice Leon released his grip on the steering wheel and splayed his fingers, palms resting at ten to two.

Eventually, above the soft thud of the engine, he said, 'Can we ever justify what we've done?'

'We spoke about how we—'

Leon's hands were now off the wheel and in front of Toby's face.

'Do you know how hard I have to concentrate to stop my hands shaking?'

Toby placed one of his own hands across his friend's. 'You don't think that for one minute I'm doing absolutely fine after all this, do you?'

Leon gave a sad little shake of his head and made eye contact with Toby for the first time that morning.

What Leon saw there unnerved him more than the hatred he'd glimpsed when they'd first talked about what they were going to do to Woodville. His eyes held an emptiness that hadn't been there before. If Leon now felt even marginally better, it was because he at least regretted what he'd done: Toby had long since left that emotion behind. That was clear to Leon now and that he found almost as sad as his own remorse.

When it got to the point where Leon felt he couldn't sit in silence any longer, he steeled himself to say what he had spent all of Sunday practising. He had no idea how his friend was going to react but he wanted to get it off his chest so much that he felt a physical pain deep inside him. He didn't know what else it could be other than the damning of his soul as it turned black.

He opened his mouth to speak, he licked his lips, he put his hands back on the wheel.

He fought the urge to say nothing.

'I need to tell you—'

'Stop this, Dilly. You're going to tell me how bad you feel, how you can't sleep and what it's doing to your mind. You won't be telling me about anything that I'm not experiencing myself. But this is why you've got to stop.'

Toby turned in his seat so that he was side on to his friend.

'Stop fucking feeling sorry for yourself and remember why we wanted to do this. You saw along with me where that dirty fucker chose to live. Next to a primary school. My son goes to that school and that bastard's window overlooks his playground. It's not simply because it's my son. There are over a hundred kids in that school. If you ever close your eyes and picture Woodville's dead face, instead of feeling sorry for the piece of shit, what you do is you replace that image with what he made you do. If that still doesn't do it for you, then think about how you'd feel reading in the paper that he'd buggered another child.'

Leon watched Toby, spittle at the side of his mouth, eyes vacant.

After a short silence, he put the van into gear and headed in the direction of the café. His confession would have to wait for another day.

He couldn't bring himself to speak. Not just yet anyway.

Chapter 36

Once Pierre and Hazel had put their overnight luggage in their allocated car, Pierre offered to drive. Hazel didn't take it as being a gallant offer, but more of a practical one: he'd had a head start on reading the file and gleaning what he could on the enquiry they were driving towards.

'Ask away with any questions you've got,' he said as they pulled out of the yard.

She was silent for a long time, head bent over as she read page after page from the file. Occasionally she would pick up her notebook from the footwell and scribble a couple of words.

She absorbed the information along with the pitiful human element that entwined the police facts of the sexual assault of a child with heart-tugging sorrow.

Several times she paused in her reading and glanced out of the window at the morning struggling to come to life. The darkness not entirely replaced by a weak November sun.

A couple of things in the paperwork bothered her but she couldn't put her finger on why. It was perhaps her mind playing tricks on her. She had been wrong once before and the feeling still niggled. No one had actually blamed her but it had been enough for her to leave Major Crime two years ago, thinking that she would never be back. It wasn't merely a case of time being a healer; if she was perfectly honest the role she had found herself in after she had left wasn't one she'd particularly enjoyed.

She became aware of Pierre saying something to her.

'Sorry,' she said. 'I was miles away and thinking about this little girl we're about to see.'

'I thought you might want to stop for a coffee in a bit and take a turn driving.'

'Yes to both.'

She yawned and stretched out her legs as far as the space in front of her seat would allow.

'I've been told this is your second time in Major Crime,' said Pierre.

Hazel had known that this was coming and was relieved to get it out of the way. 'That's right,' she answered. 'I was here for about four years but it was time to move on and try other stuff. The department was changing too and I'd had a relationship with someone on the nick and felt the need to leave. Give myself a bit of space.'

It wasn't the entire reason she had gone but she guessed that Pierre wouldn't want to pry too much on her first day. In her experience, most men usually gave the topic of bad break-ups a wide berth. Hazel hadn't reckoned on Pierre.

'Is he anyone I know?'

'How do you know it wasn't a she?'

'Because I'm gay and statistically it's highly unlikely that we both are.'

She laughed and said, 'OK. It was a he and it was Gordon Letchford.' She watched his face for a reaction and was rewarded with an open-eyed, forward-facing stare.

At last he said, 'Oh.'

'Your face is a picture,' she said. 'Don't worry, most people react like that but he isn't a bad bloke. He's just—'

'The most boring man on the planet?'

'You've certainly met him then,' she said. 'I seem to attract very sensible men. Sensible usually goes hand in hand with dull. Anyway, after him, I thought that's my lot for a while, and certainly as far as policemen go. I'll find myself a nice biker or ex-con.'

He risked another glance and another question.

'What was the final straw if you don't mind me asking?'

For a moment, she wasn't entirely sure whether she did mind him asking her or not. She chewed on the inside of her mouth for a second and said, 'For my birthday, he bought me screen wash and antifreeze. I couldn't take it any more.'

'It's practical,' laughed Pierre. 'Nothing else? Just that?'

'Just that.'

'I don't want to make it a competition,' said Pierre, 'but I can probably beat that.'

'If you win,' she said, pointing at the sign for the service station, 'the coffees are on me.'

'An ex once bought me a set of bathroom scales and a defibrillator.'

'That deserves a latte.'

Chapter 37

A bad night's sleep was something that DCI Barbara Venice rarely had to contend with. She was sometimes woken in the night by her police mobile phone ringing, but those occasions were limited to when she was on call. Now though it was four o'clock on Monday morning and she couldn't shake off the despair she felt about a mistake made many years ago that was about to pull her incident room apart.

Something a lot more unpleasant than choosing table arrangements and the seating plan for her daughter's wedding had been niggling her all weekend. She had tried to put it aside to deal with which members of the family wanted to sit nearest the bar and which wanted to be closest to the top table. During the daytime, she'd been able to focus and her mind hadn't wandered too far but at night when she shut her eyes the familiar stomach-dropping dread would return.

It was stealing into her dreams and bringing about a restlessness that she finally succumbed to, making her way downstairs.

She sat in the dark, head back against the armchair. Eyes open or shut, she could see it playing out in her mind, how years ago she had taken Albie Woodville from his police station cell and walked him to the interview room.

Barbara hadn't really wanted to interview him. He was a nonce. A dirty, revolting child abuser. But she was police and she did what she was told.

Along with doing her job went professionalism. She had to be nice to him, not make him feel like the revolting piece of shit he was. She had always wanted children of her own, and long before either her son or her daughter was born she struggled to see how anyone could allow themselves to hurt or rape children. How could a person do such a thing and then carry on existing? How could they walk amongst the normal people? How could they look at themselves in the mirror?

These were questions she asked herself over and over again and then forced to the back of her mind before she opened the cell door and looked at Albert Woodville for the very first time.

Sitting in the comfort and safety of her own living room, she felt goosebumps on her arms as she recalled the large metal key on a metal ring with several other keys, the noise as they jangled together whilst she found the right one to unlock the heavy solid door. The smell of the custody block assaulting her senses with body odour and dead air. The worn brown leather shoes next to the cell wall that she stepped around as she swung the door open. Her feelings at staring evil straight in the face.

Albert Woodville looked so ordinary. That was what was so frightening.

He looked like any other man, not a pervert and a paedophile. Barbara had thought she would be able to spot one, but it hit her hard that it was impossible to tell. There were probably times she had sat next to a child abuser on the train, stood behind one in a supermarket queue; perhaps there was even one amongst the police officers she worked with.

Their eyes locked. He was perched on the edge of his bed, cross-legged, dirty white socks, brown trousers and a beige jumper. He appeared insipid in his dull clothing, unremarkable in his features.

Perhaps they had the wrong man in custody, she thought as she stood in the doorway, unable to speak. Briefly she even hoped that they had arrested an innocent man. That would at least explain her lack of gut instinct.

It was only when she thought about it later, and then countless times over the following years, that she realised she didn't want Woodville to have raped and buggered children when she had sat and spoken to the man as if he was human. She had tarnished herself by spending time in his company and putting him at ease, checking he wasn't too cold in the interview room, making sure he had breaks when he needed them, even joking with him about the weather. What exactly did that make her?

And when the interviews were finally over, she had asked him if he wanted something to eat and he had laughed and said, 'I don't think much of the food in this place. I hope I'm not here much longer.'

Her only thought was that she wanted to put an end to his laughing and joking but she was totally powerless to do anything but her job. Her own feelings were the price she had paid for investigating child abuse.

Detective Chief Inspector Venice allowed herself the luxury of one solitary tear. By the time it had run down her face and reached her chin, she would stop dragging up the past and her first child-sex-offender interview. She would get ready for her day at work and deal with the murder of Albert Woodville. The man she had despised for so many years and had never completely forgotten about, despite being one of hundreds she had interviewed over the years and one of thousands she had loathed for the misery they inflicted on other human beings.

She had made a single and honest mistake and now she couldn't help but feel that it was time she fully paid for it. One error as a detective constable shouldn't stand in the way of how she handled the investigation into the death of Woodville. Someone had murdered him and she had more than a feeling who might be responsible. In the meantime, she had her own demons to contend with and there was one person she could rely on to give her any help she needed.

Chapter 38

Try as he might, Harry failed to concentrate. The tactic he had up his sleeve for those of equal or lower rank was to tell them to come back later.

The appearance of DCI Barbara Venice at his door meant a different approach. He decided to annoy her away.

'Babs,' he said as he leaned back in his chair, hands behind his head. 'Don't see you for ages then here you are twice in only a few days.'

'You haven't become less aggravating over the weekend then?'

'Do you have time for a coffee?' he said as she sat down.

'No thanks. I wanted to speak to you about a couple of things to do with the Woodville murder.'

He waited for her to get to the point as he wondered what it was that she hadn't mentioned when they'd last spoken.

She took a deep breath and said, 'I know you've read

169

the file. You must have seen my name on the original investigation. I was the DC who interviewed Albert Woodville. I remembered his name, and of course the allegations of child sex abuse.'

Harry waited a few seconds for her to continue and when she kept quiet, he said, 'The interviews were fine. Of course I've read them. What's the problem, Barbara?'

'At the time, he pretty much confessed what he did to Toby Carvell.'

'There you go then,' said Harry, not clear where she was going with this information.

He watched her wind her wedding ring around and around her finger.

'I wasn't Barbara Venice then,' she said. 'I was Barbara Jones, a few years younger, but I really should have known better.'

Harry found himself wondering if his friend was going to admit some kind of years-old police corruption and hoping that he was wrong.

'From the look on your face, you think I'm about to say that I stitched him up.'

'Fucking Nora, Babs. Not in a million years would I think such a thing about you.'

Nevertheless, he saw her raise an eyebrow at him.

'The interview was fine. He was cautioned and asked if he wanted a brief. You know, the usual. He declined a solicitor and I went through everything I was legally obliged to tell him. It all went a bit wrong though later on down the line.'

The glare of the overhead strip light showed the lines and wrinkles in Barbara's face with little mercy. Harry was still able to remember the beautiful fresh-faced young woman he met years ago at training school as Barbara sat before him now.

He had already abandoned his idea of trying to get her out of his office; it was clear she needed someone to talk to.

Barbara breathed through pursed lips. 'It was the usual pressure of get the job done and move on to the next thing. It seemed as though it was going to be a straightforward investigation, especially when he admitted to what he'd done.

'I remember it very clearly although it was so long ago. Partly because it was one of those jobs that got to me. We came out of the interview room, me, Woodville and the other DC I was working with, Jon Newton. Jon went off to get Woodville a coffee and update the custody record that we'd finished.'

Harry watched her pinch the top of her nose with her thumb and forefinger and take a pause.

'We walked around the corner to his cell and Woodville said to me, 'I won't go to prison for all of this.' He had such an arrogance about him. I hated him all over again. What he'd done to those children was bad enough and now he was telling me he wouldn't go to prison. The fucking audacity.'

Harry sat and watched her, unaware that she was replaying in her mind the same scene that had kept her awake and up long before the sun.

Whatever the struggle going on in her head, he could tell it was eating at her.

Over the years, few things had got to Barbara so much that she made a point of speaking to anyone, least of all Harry. Most police officers were terrible gossips and Harry had an ear to the ground at all times. He thrived on the gossip and the speculation about others' reputations. This was something different though: he was watching an old friend fall apart and that wasn't something he relished. She needed a confidant, not a fishwife.

'So what happened?' he asked.

Her eyes snapped open and she peered out through a watery gaze. For a moment Harry worried she might lose it. He had never been one for crying women. If he was honest, they petrified him. He'd rather face a drunk armed with a blade or broken bottle than deal with an emotional female. They were uncharted territory for him and possibly part of the reason that his marriage was going so wrong.

Unlike his wife's stony tantrums, he really wanted to find out what the issue was for Barbara. Only he didn't know how to.

He tried the only option he could think of – he sat and listened.

'I hated Woodville,' she said. 'I hated him before I met him. He represented everything I despised, I simply didn't know it yet. When I joined the police, and I expect it's the same for most people, I had this starry-eyed notion that I'd impact on the world, get it in a headlock and make it behave. Exactly how long is it before someone pisses on that idea? The first day you put on your uniform, walk outside and someone assaults you and the court hands them a fine that they never pay? Or is it the first time you see a decomposing corpse that's been there for weeks with no one to care that the flesh and skin have melted into the carpet? Or perhaps it's the first time that someone with HIV bites you? Remember that time I was stabbed with a used needle and I was off sick for weeks until I was cleared to come back to work? That was fun.'

Harry watched as it all moved across her features, some of it fleeting and some of it etching itself into the creases of her face and attaching itself to her very being. His own visage was full of cynicism and distrust. Some would call it character. He would call it horror.

Before his eyes, Barbara's face hardened.

'He surely couldn't have known what he was doing, what he was orchestrating, but Woodville stopped me just around the corner from the interview room and he leaned forward to whisper in my ear.'

A hand went up to her throat, toying with the thin gold chain there adorned with a small cross.

'Stupidly, I didn't think further than don't make direct contact with his head. I'd already had head lice twice since joining up. I moved back and he cackled at me. "I won't go to prison for Toby Carvell," he said.' She slowly shook her head. 'I didn't get it, Harry. We'd spoken in interview about five children who had

173

accused him of sexually abusing them and he only denied touching one of them.'

'But he admitted to what he'd done to Toby Carvell,' said Harry.

'Exactly. He admitted it all. It was one of the gut-wrenching things he seemed glad to get off his chest. He was adamant that he wouldn't go to prison for it. I didn't understand at first.

'It was the look on his face, you know. He said to me—' She broke off and shook her head. '"He liked it. Toby liked it." I wanted to punch him but I stood motionless, completely stock-still. Never before or since have I wanted to hit anyone, prisoner or otherwise. And he deserved it, but I didn't.'

There was something about the way Barbara leaned forward and placed her hands palms down on the desk that made Harry push himself back in his seat, suddenly unsure how he was going to handle the fallout of whatever she was about to tell him.

Seconds later, he let out a breath. 'What's really the matter?'

'Later on, he made out that I'd lured him round a corner out of earshot of Jon and out of the gaze of the custody staff so I could speak to him in private.'

Other than telling her that she was talking nonsense, Harry was short on words. There were so many questions going through his head.

The first was, 'What about the cameras?'

'This was before the days of digital recording and everything being centralized at Police Standards

Department. In those days, as you know, if you needed the custody footage, you took the tape.'

'And?'

'And I seized it and didn't look at it until three weeks later. It was the wrong bloody date.'

He watched as Barbara hung her head as she made her confession.

'Oh fuck,' he said. 'You lost the footage of what he'd actually said to you?'

His question was met with a miserable look and a weak nod of the head.

'We went to court some months later,' she said. 'He pleaded not guilty and then his defence barrister ripped me up for arse paper in the witness box. She made out that I'd threatened him and even told him that if he confessed he wouldn't go to prison but be let off with community service and some behaviour therapy. Well, I couldn't say under oath that I'd never been alone with him because I'd been in the custody block. The only thing that could have backed me up was the custody CCTV and it was gone. It was my word against his and the jury believed him. He was acquitted of some of the allegations because of something I'd done. I have to live with that.'

She continued to slide the cross on her chain from left to right.

'What if my mistake all those years ago has propelled someone to murder him? What if that someone is Toby Carvell? That means that this is all my fault.'

For once, Harry didn't have an answer.

Chapter 39

When DC Gabrielle Royston arrived for work and made her way across the incident room to her desk, she noticed that her DI Harry Powell was deep in conversation with DCI Barbara Venice. Both had seemed pleasant enough when Gabrielle had started in the department and she had no particular problem with either of them. However, now she watched the two of them talking, heads together in Harry's cramped office space, she felt the old familiar feelings of paranoia that they were talking about her.

There was no rational explanation for why they should be doing such a thing, but Gabrielle felt that, wherever she worked, her colleagues spoke about her behind her back. She knew that she could sometimes come across as a little odd but that was mainly because she was a little odd. She never really fitted in anywhere and she had never been able to work out why that was. No one had ever explained it to her either which only made her worry all the more. She had joined the police at the age of twenty-one and had few friends to speak of. There seemed to be something about the other police officers that gelled them as one, but however much of an effort she made she still felt as though she was an outsider.

By the time two years of not being welcomed into the fold had passed, she had decided that it would no longer bother her. She had long since looked on the bright side and now she had been a police officer for eight years she considered it a blessing. She wasn't part of or privy to the gossip and rumours that she found childish, she wasn't part of the office nights out where certain individuals were embarrassed about their antics the next morning, and she didn't have to put up with endless questions about her private life and background. There wasn't very much to tell but what there was, she held back for a reason. She didn't like people very much and she didn't trust them.

She positioned herself at her desk so that she could see the outline of Barbara Venice as she leaned across to talk to Harry. She found herself inching forward in her seat so that she could see Harry's face a little more easily and felt her stomach lurch as he looked up and caught her eye.

It was a weird sensation for the young officer to experience, especially in a working environment. It momentarily confused her as to what it might actually mean. She might have been a bit strange but she wasn't daft and realized that it wasn't likely to do her career much good if she mooned about all day over her inspector.

On the other hand, so many of her peers were having affairs with their colleagues perhaps that was why they thought of her as peculiar. Maybe she was the only one not sleeping with someone else's spouse.

These obscure thoughts ran through her head as she sat absent-mindedly in front of her computer screen, tapping her pen against the side of her head.

Gabrielle wasn't sure how long she had sat pondering having sex with her detective inspector, but it was long enough for Harry and Barbara to finish talking and for him to make an appearance and say her name more than once.

'Sorry, sir,' she stammered, dropping the pen to the desk. 'I was miles away then. What can I help you with?'

She blushed at her own words even though Harry couldn't possibly guess what it was that she had just been fantasizing about assisting him with.

'Can you come into my office and speak to me for a few minutes whenever you've finished doing what you're doing?'

She saw him look down at the pen on the desk which had come to rest next to her blank computer screen, still switched off from the night before. She was not about to impress him with her work ethic if she got to work half an hour before everyone else but then sat daydreaming.

Gabrielle was aware that without intending to she was behaving a little differently from the way a detective constable should, especially when her superior was standing a couple of feet away, waiting for her to answer.

'Of course I can. I'm free now,' she said.

Harry nodded at her and walked back to his office.

She closed her eyes and shook her head at her stupidity in front of the man she had been trying hard to impress with her professionalism, and now had a crush on.

As he made his way back to his office, Harry regretted asking Gabrielle to speak to him before anyone else arrived. The girl was odd and had gone almost as red in the face as Harry's hair when he spoke to her. He put it down to being caught by the inspector staring into the distance and banging a biro against her head. He had worked with some weirdos in the past but he hadn't thought of Gabrielle as anything other than quiet and reserved up until now. The reservations that Sophia Ireland had brought to him about Gabrielle's attitude hadn't caused him much concern at the time, although he would be the first to admit to himself that he had been wrong before.

He considered calling Barbara back to sit with him while he spoke to Gabrielle and then ruled it out. Apart from the DCI having enough on her plate at the moment, if he couldn't handle one woman detective constable, he didn't deserve to be the rank he was.

As he reached his chair, Harry turned to sit down and saw Gabrielle standing in the doorway.

'What are you, a cat? I didn't hear you move.'

He saw her smile and shift her weight from one foot to the other.

'Have a seat but don't worry about closing the door. This will only take a few minutes.'

She sat in the chair opposite him, crossed her legs and he had to try hard not to look at them, short skirt riding up over her thighs. With sadness, he realized how old he was getting as his initial thought was that she should wrap up a bit warmer at this time of year. Perhaps that was why his wife had had enough of him: he was past his prime.

'How are you getting on here, Gabrielle?'

'Good. Really good. I've enjoyed it so far. It's very different from child protection, but that's one of the reasons I wanted to come here.'

He risked a smile, wary of coming across as a lecherous old pervert who had called the new, young, attractive member of staff into his office so he could stare at her.

'I'm pleased to hear it. I wanted to check with you that the murder of Albert Woodville was something that you're all right working on.'

He paused to gauge her reaction. Her expression didn't change. In fact, he noticed that there seemed to be little behind her eyes at all. She had an empty look and then slowly she moved her head to nod at him.

'It's fine.'

'That's it?' he asked, wanting to hear more. 'It's fine?'

'Yep.'

'OK then, Gabrielle. I'll check in with you again, but in the meantime, if this gets too much for you, there's always another murder, or rape, or kidnap along any time soon, or even the arson at Norman Husband House. The chances are that at some point, probably this week, I could end up having to put you on another investigation anyway. The point I'm making is, don't be afraid to say if the murder of a paedophile is something that you're uncomfortable with. I'm sure one of the reasons you decided to leave child protection was to get away from child rapists.'

Once again, he examined her face but failed to find a single spark behind her eyes.

'Thanks for your time, sir,' she said as she got up to leave. 'I'll let you know if I run into difficulties.'

He focused on his computer screen as she left, not wanting to watch the retreating backside of a beautiful but very weird young woman.

Chapter 40

As soon as Jonathan Tey heard his wife leave the house to take their daughter to school, he threw back the bed covers and padded over to the window to make sure the car drove away with both of them inside.

Working from home two days per week had its advantages, especially today when he wanted no one else to know what he was about to spend his morning doing.

Jonathan reckoned on having about an hour to himself before his wife got back from the school run and the supermarket, giving him just about enough time.

He put on clothes dropped on the floor from the day before and then went out to the landing where he pulled down the loft ladder. Barely waiting for the ladder to come to a stop, he rushed up the first few rungs, head level with the opening, feeling into blackness until his hands sought out and found what he was after. He grabbed the holdall and flung it onto the landing below. He knew that his wife wouldn't miss it. Besides, she was always on at him to throw more junk away and that was exactly what he was about to do. He then continued to grope in the darkness, not wanting to waste time getting a torch.

Finally, his hand touched the laces of the training shoes he had dumped in the loft in a fit of panic days beforehand, only too eager at the time to hide them from view. Now, he carried the cheap white trainers back down to the landing and placed them inside the holdall. He pushed the ladder back to its original place, closed the hatch and checked the landing for any sign of cobwebs or other debris that would give him away to his fastidious wife.

Satisfied that he had covered his rapid ascent and descent, he opened the airing-cupboard and took out the newly washed black socks, black jogging bottoms and black hooded top.

He added them to the bag, ran downstairs and opened the back door.

Jonathan listened for sounds of a car and made sure that his neighbours weren't about to look over the fence before he took three bricks from a pile stacked feet from his kitchen waiting to be made into a barbecue.

He added them to the bag, put on his jacket, locked the back door, made a point of making sure that his mobile phone was on the work surface in the kitchen and walked to the front door, holdall in hand.

Before he stepped outside, he listened again for sounds of a car or anyone about to knock on the door. The previous day it had been hard work keeping his wife and daughter out of the house until late afternoon, and it had cost him a fortune in food, drink, new clothes and cinema tickets. He wasn't about to walk straight into the police wanting to ask him questions about where he had been over the last few days.

Satisfied that the street was empty of detectives, he left the house, attempting to adopt a walk that was somewhere between brisk and purposeful. He had timed it often over the last week and knew that without a holdall weighed down with bricks it took him eight minutes to get to the seafront.

He stretched his legs out, partly to see if he could knock thirty seconds or so off his time. He told himself that he wanted to see how invigorating the walk could be in the blustery weather, whereas in truth he wanted to get it over with.

The strength of the wind forced him to keep his jacket done up so as not to catch a chill from the sweat he was breaking into as he strode down one street after another. He knew the route so well he could do it with his eyes shut, but he was on full alert this morning. The last thing he wanted was to bump into someone he had gone to school with or who was a parent of one of his daughter's classmates. He had no time to stop and chat. It would throw his schedule out and, worst of all, they might remember he was walking the streets with a holdall on his way to the seafront.

The relief hit him when he finally saw the swell of the Channel, heard it rushing up the beach towards him and tasted the salt on his lips.

It was only another two minutes now until he got to the part of the harbour wall he knew would give him the best chance of not being seen.

He dabbed at the perspiration on his forehead, trying to avoid looking as though he was nervous, wanting to give the impression he was simply a man out for a morning stroll.

The nearer he got to his final destination, the more relieved he felt. Soon it would all be over, and he could see grey columns of rain making their way across the water towards him. An impending downpour would mean fewer people in the harbour, fewer people to remember him or what he was carrying.

After all, it wasn't every day that someone stood on East Rise's harbour wall and threw a bag of clothes into the sea.

Jonathan knew that careful planning would be his salvation when the police did knock on his door, and if he was anything, he was careful.

Or so he thought.

Chapter 41

Even though Monday should have been DC Sophia Ireland's day off, she chose to work. She was tired and fancied a lie-in but not only would the money come in handy, but also she felt guilty about taking her day off when there was so much to do.

She also wanted to keep an eye on Gabrielle.

It wasn't her responsibility to do so, that fell to the sergeants and ranks above, but they weren't always aware of what was going on in their incident room, and some decided to ignore it. Doing nothing was always the easy way out of a problem. It didn't make it go away.

Sophia had promised Tom that she would go with him to track down Jonathan Tey whom they had been unable to find on the previous day. Several trips to his house and attempts to call him had failed, so it was their priority today.

Before they went out on their enquiry, Sophia had one or two other things to take care of but she didn't want anyone to see what she was up to.

She bided her time until everyone was either out

on enquiries or had left the incident room to grab a last-minute late breakfast at the canteen. Once she was satisfied she was alone, she made her way over to Gabrielle's desk amongst the banks of other empty workspaces.

Seated, she started to feel foolish and that her snooping around another officer's paperwork was a really low thing to do. She hadn't got very far when she heard the sound of someone walking along the corridor to the incident room. Doing the only thing she could think of, she picked the phone up and held the receiver to her ear.

Tom appeared in the doorway and stopped short when he saw where she was sitting.

'Really?' was all he said.

She put the phone down and brushed her skirt, her eyes following her hands so she could avoid looking at him.

'The phone was ringing,' she said as she walked in the direction of her own desk.

'I'm not sure whether to find your behaviour amusing or worrying. It's certainly not normal.'

'Enough of the psychoanalysing. Shall we find Jonathan Tey?'

They left in silence, Tom wondering if his colleague should have taken the day off and put some distance between herself and the problems that seemed to only exist in her head.

'It's not healthy,' he said to her when they were in the car.

'I know it's not, but I can't sit and do nothing if I feel something's wrong.'

'I've told you what you should do, speak to someone about it.'

'I tried to talk to Harry,' she said. 'I didn't want him to think that I was telling tales on a colleague, so I told him half of what I feel. I've got no proof of anything.'

'That's the thing, Soph, you've got no proof of anything, so leave it alone.'

'You're right, let's go and see the elusive Tey.'

Within twenty minutes they pulled up outside a semi-detached house, far enough away from the seafront that parking wasn't a problem, but close enough for a walk to the restaurants and bars dotted along the front.

A dark-haired woman in her late thirties was heading from the car on the driveway towards the front door. She glanced round at the diesel car as it came to a stop in front of her house but walked on towards the property.

It was only as she put the key in the door that she realized the occupants of the green Skoda were following her down her driveway.

With a puzzled look, she stopped and turned towards them.

'Mrs Tey,' said Sophia as she held her ID out for inspection. 'We're from Major Crime and wondered if we could come in for a minute.'

Elaine Tey's face had a kind of fascinated horror

creeping across it, but all she said was, 'Is everything all right? I'm not sure what this is about.'

'It's really your husband, Jonathan, we wanted to see,' said Tom. 'Can we come in and speak to him?'

Her face brightened momentarily as she realized that their business wasn't with her. She then added, 'He should be working from home today. Come in and I'll get him from his office.'

Many minutes later, the three of them sat at the kitchen table, notepads in front of Tom and Sophia, and her husband's mobile phone in front of a worried Mrs Tey.

'I don't know where he would have gone without his phone,' she said. 'It's very unlike him. I hope everything's OK. He would have left a note if it was an emergency. I only went out an hour ago.'

For the fourth time since taking a seat opposite Sophia, Elaine Tey glanced up at the kitchen clock on the wall above the officer's head.

'I'm starting to get worried now. Can't you tell me what you want to see him about?'

Sophia opened her mouth to answer the question but was interrupted by the sound of the front door opening.

Six foot two Jonathan Tey walked into his own kitchen and didn't look especially pleased to see any of the three people waiting to talk to him.

Chapter 42

No sooner had Elaine Tey shown Detective Constable Sophia Ireland and Detective Constable Tom Delayhoyde out of the front door, she turned to her husband with a look that he knew meant she wasn't about to be fobbed off with any answer he cared to give.

'Explain,' was all she said.

She might have been a foot shorter than him and a slight, petite woman who was normally so placid she bordered on boring, but today she recognized the look of a guilty husband when she saw it.

'Laine,' he said, all open-palmed gestures and head held high, 'I've—'

'Cut the crap and tell me where you were this morning. I'm not the police. I won't fall for your lies. What have you been up to?'

'We need to sit down.'

In truth, he was stalling for time. Jonathan might not always portray the most dedicated husband and father but he knew that his family was the reason he got out of bed in the morning and kept on going throughout the week, despite what he might have put his wife through in the past.

He walked towards the kitchen table where the police officers had sat for the last three hours, asking all sorts of questions about his whereabouts since Friday, the woman scribbling his answers down by hand, the other one taking his DNA and fingerprints. All the while, his wife had looked on and said nothing.

By the time he reached the table and pulled out a chair, Jonathan had managed to adopt a neutral expression, or so he thought. He wasn't kidding his wife of fifteen years.

'And you can wipe that look off your face too,' she said as she pulled out a chair for herself in full inter-rogation mode.

He opened his mouth to say something but she silenced him with a withering look.

'Talk, Jonathan. Start with why the police were here asking about a murdered sex offender.'

His eyes tried to search out anything in the room that wasn't his wife's expression. He was used to being the one in charge, although he recognized that he was only the figurehead until something went wrong. That was the moment he would claim he shouldn't be expected to deal with so much on top of his work. Often, it was a mess he had created, such as the time he insisted it was a good idea to de-ice the back of the fridge-freezer with a carving knife and wouldn't hear of any other plan. As soon as he pierced the refrigeration unit, he remembered he had to drop some accounts off at a client's house and returned home a little after midnight.

By this time, his father-in-law had been round, removed the contents of the freezer, taken the busted unit into the front garden, arranged for its safe collection and ordered a new one to arrive within twenty-four hours.

Sometimes he failed to plan. It was his only downfall. That and the plan he had hatched with his new ally, Jude Watson.

Perhaps his wife would see a way out onto the other side.

The issue was never going to be as simple as the council coming to take away the problem. If it was that simple, he would have made the call himself. That was how desperate he was; he was even prepared to clear up his own mess on this occasion.

'Do you remember that night I came back from the East Rise Players' emergency meeting?' he said, chancing a look up into the eyes of a furious woman.

'The one that you and Jude walked out on?'

'Yes,' he said with a sigh. 'That's the one.'

'If I remember rightly,' Elaine said, 'you both walked out and went straight into the pub.'

'OK, OK. Are you going to let me tell you what happened?'

She reached down to her handbag which she'd dropped to the floor, pulled out a packet of cigarettes and put one in her mouth.

'What?' she said, the lighter held to her face. 'You can bring the police to my door asking questions about a murdered paedophile that you pranced about on stage with, have your fingerprints taken, but I can't have a smoke? Don't make me out to be the bad guy here.'

He recognized that it probably wasn't the best time to mention that he thought they'd given up smoking together six years ago, so Jonathan continued.

'Jude and me sat at the meeting, thinking it was going to be about raising extra funds or selling tickets or something. We had no idea that Eric Samuels, prick of the parish, was going to drop a bombshell about one of the members being a sex pest.' He glanced up at the smoke as it curled towards the white ceiling. He thought about reaching out and taking a cigarette himself. Instead he carried on.

'You know that I only went along because Jude's wife made him go and he didn't want to go by himself. At first, when Jude got so angry at what Samuels said, I wondered if it was because he only wanted a reason to storm out, something to tell his wife that she couldn't argue with. Well, once we left the Cressy Arms, we walked to the Hake and Billet. Jude didn't say a word the whole way.

'Once we sat down, he started ranting about Woodville and what he'd like to do to him. We drew a few looks in the pub, I can tell you. I had to shut him up cos we were on the verge of getting barred.'

He watched his wife tap her cigarette ash into an

empty coffee mug on the table, something he had never seen her do in all the years of knowing her. Even when they were students and couldn't afford an ashtray, it wasn't a level he'd ever seen her sink to. That action more than anything struck a chord in him – he was reducing his wife to pitiful.

He knew he couldn't tell her the truth. Even if their marriage survived, he wasn't sure she was up to it.

'Elaine,' he said, putting his hands on top of her left hand, idle on the table. He felt the gold wedding band touch his palm. 'We didn't kill Woodville. Could I look you in the eye and tell you such a bare-faced lie? Could I? After all the years we've been married, known each other, loved each other? You do believe me, don't you?'

'Then why were the police here?'

It was said without feeling, without accusation, with a cold detachment.

He put his hands up to his temples and leaned on his elbows.

'Because we were the only two blokes at the amateur dramatic society who weren't over sixty and actually had a backbone. Everyone sat and tutted at that meeting; a few people, including Samuels, said that the police had it wrong and hadn't given us all of the facts.

'I don't have much time for the filth but they don't tell you someone's a nonce when they really mean that he forgot to pay his bloody television licence. They don't work like that. Me and Jude were horrified that someone like that was walking amongst us.

We reacted; the rest of them didn't. I can't help that. What's done is done.'

He waited for his wife to say something, even if it was another accusation.

More worrying than that was that now she said nothing.

Elaine ground out her cigarette on the side of the *I love Cyprus* mug, picked up her handbag and walked out of the front door.

Jonathan sat at the kitchen table and heard the sound of his wife's car start as she drove away from him.

His stomach lurched. He was certain she'd be back soon. Certain that she would be back this time.

He tried to think in terms of the momentary reprieve he had before Elaine came back and started asking him more questions. She'd driven away from him when he'd lied to her. He didn't want to think what she would do to him when she learnt the truth.

Chapter 43

It was taking a little longer than expected for DC Hazel Hamilton and DC Pierre Rainer to reach their final destination. It was only a couple of hours' drive from East Rise to the small Sussex town where Dean Stillbrook had lived, but Hazel suggested that they make another stop.

'Are you sure you're all right to carry on driving?' she asked for the third time. 'I thought we were going to swap over when we stopped for a coffee.'

She couldn't continually ask him as it sounded to her own ears as if she was nagging him.

'I know you've only just flown back from your holiday and that's the fourth time you've stifled a yawn. And I know it's not because I'm anything other than fascinating company.'

Pierre laughed and said, 'OK. Let's have breakfast. I am pretty hungry and that'll give us a chance to plan how we tackle this enquiry.'

A few minutes later, they were sitting opposite one

another, steaming mugs of coffee and a silver serviette container partially filling the gap between them.

While they waited for their food to arrive, Pierre said, 'I'm not entirely sure that we need to stay overnight. I got the impression that Harry wanted it sorted out in one go, less chance of us going back to the incident room and being bombarded with questions from the others until we've got as much from the young girl as possible.'

He stopped stirring sugar into his drink and glanced up, catching the look on Hazel's face.

'Perhaps it's because I'm new,' she said as she picked up her coffee mug, 'but looking at it impartially, I think it's because if it's a planned overnight enquiry, they don't have to pay us an overnight allowance for being away from home. If the DI plans ahead and we don't need to stay over, he can cancel the hotel, the department gets its money back and the cost is nil.'

For a few seconds, Hazel wasn't sure if she had spoken out of turn. She didn't want her new team to dislike her, although she wasn't about to hide her forthright attitude. She bit her tongue, not wanting to say anything unpleasant about her new detective inspector before she got the lie of the land and had sounded out Pierre's thoughts.

'Harry's one of the good guys,' he said.

She felt herself raise her eyebrows at him. 'I know he is. He's the sort of bloke that everyone likes, even those who don't agree with him. I did my homework before I came here. It's just that's what I'd do if it was down to me – I'd plan ahead and save money. It makes good business sense.'

She glanced in the direction of the kitchen, wanting their food to appear. Right at that moment, she felt she needed the distraction. She wanted to make a good impression on her new work colleague and desperately churned her mind over to find something neutral to talk about.

She was grateful when Pierre came to her rescue.

'So when you're not at work, leaving disastrous relationships out of the equation, what else do you get up to?'

Hazel smiled and felt her shoulders relax. 'I foster dogs,' she said. 'Usually only for a day or two because of work but I love helping out.'

Pierre picked up his coffee mug and studied her face. He didn't take a sip, simply continued to look at her. She took it as her cue to continue and for the first time that morning she was happy to talk, to tell him about the many dogs over the years she had cuddled up to, walked, fed, sat on the sofa with at night, their heads in her lap.

'It started when I was on the domestic violence unit.' She turned her gaze to the window, not really seeing what was the other side of the glass and not really caring.

'Vanessa Meaden went back to her violent husband three times in as many years. He used to beat her for a period of weeks and eventually, when he'd put her in the hospital, we'd get involved, he'd get arrested and go to court. He always got a ridiculously short sentence, if he got one at all.

'Anyway, she always went back to him, whatever he did to her. I'd ask her over and over again why she didn't leave him.'

Hazel sat at the Formica table retelling the tale she had told herself so often, knowing that she couldn't have prevented what happened, but accepting that it was possible for such situations to have a different outcome. Of all the things she stressed about, this was one she never gave herself a difficult time over. There'd been a problem she hadn't been aware of, and all she could do now was play her tiny part in making things easier in the future for victims of domestic abuse, such as Vanessa Meaden.

'She used to tell me that she couldn't leave because she had nowhere to go.' Hazel looked at Pierre, saw him open his mouth to say something, pause and sit back in his plastic seat. 'I'd guess that you were about to say a refuge. The thing is, refuges take women and children, but they don't take pets, especially not Great Danes. She wouldn't leave because she had nowhere to go where she could keep the dog.

'Her lowlife, piece-of-crap husband gave the dog a kicking too on a couple of occasions. I put people who are cruel to children, animals, the elderly, the disabled, wife-beaters and paedophiles in the same category – worthless human beings. They pick on the weak and those who won't or can't tell.'

She swirled the remains of her coffee around the bottom of the mug.

'What happened?' said Pierre. 'Although I have a pretty good idea.'

'He beat her again, pushed her down the stairs and she lay behind the front door until the postman called the next day, looked through the letterbox and saw the dog sitting beside her dead body. According to the neighbours, who had stopped calling the police because of the abuse they got from him when he inevitably got released from custody, the row started about midnight so the dog probably sat there for something like eight or nine hours.'

'So you foster dogs so that women like Vanessa can make a fresh start?'

'That's the idea. I'm happy to help out usually only for a day or two because of work, on my days off, something like that.'

Pierre was still holding his mug. She saw him look at it, place it on the table and lean towards her. He looked a little uncomfortable at what he was about to say next. Hazel told herself that whatever it was she wouldn't be offended.

'It seems as though everything you do is for someone else,' he said in what she gauged to be the least judgemental tone he could muster.

'Not really. I get a lot out of looking after the dogs. I fostered one for a fortnight a while ago and he was a nervous and timid dog when he came to me. By the time he left, he was a lot livelier and cowered less. I really got a kick out of that.'

The waiter appeared with their plates of food, giving

Hazel a few more seconds to think before she spoke again, or Pierre asked her anything else. She was keen to come across as level-headed and show herself in a good light, especially so early on in a department she had walked away from once. She couldn't afford to mess this up.

'So,' he said as he sawed into his breakfast, 'getting back to what we've got to do today, do you have a plan any better than knock on the door and say to the parents, "Can we speak to your daughter about the allegation she made against Dean Stillbrook?"'

Hazel ripped a corner from a piece of brown toast and forced it into the top of her fried egg, watching the yolk run towards the bacon before she said, 'I do, but it'll have to wait until I've finished. No one likes a cold fry-up.'

Eventually, Hazel pushed her plate to one side and said, 'With any luck, when we get there, at least one of Monica Lewis's parents will be home. She should be at school but I think that if we start by speaking to her mum or dad ... then once she's home from school we can go back and chat with her. I'm not ...'

Pierre looked up from his plate, last mouthful on his fork. 'Go on,' he said before he chewed on the piece of fried bread and mushroom.

Once again, Hazel was torn between saying what she was thinking and testing the waters. She tapped her fingernails on the edge of the table top.

'I appreciate what you said about Harry, and I don't

disagree with you. My only comment would be that perhaps we should have called the Lewis family and arranged to see Monica at a different time. The reactions of victims of any crime are difficult to predict, none more so than those of an eleven-year-old girl who's gone through such an ordeal. The element of surprise is all very good in the right circumstances. I'm very worried about freaking this poor kid out.'

He nodded his head at her but something about his expression told her that he wasn't about to agree.

'It's a judgement call, isn't it?' he said. 'If we call and make an appointment and the parents tell Monica, then she may fret for days. If we turn up, we possibly uncover something that we would have otherwise missed.'

'The classic police damned if you do, damned if you don't,' she said. 'I know what you mean, but I'm all about the bigger picture here. A successful murder investigation is one thing, a traumatized kid messed up for life is quite another.'

'What was the real reason you left Major Crime?' asked Pierre.

Hazel didn't want to answer. She couldn't avoid the truth forever, though she thought she had done a very good job of dodging the question by talking about Gordon Letchford and their disastrous relationship. It was her safest option, the option that didn't let on how every day she tortured herself that she hadn't seen the warning signs and had been too busy to do anything to help before it was too late. Pierre seemed too astute and it would be hard for her to fob him off without appearing rude.

She liked Pierre and wanted to tell him. The enquiry they were about to carry out probably meant he deserved her honesty. Besides, he could always ask around. Someone was bound to tell him eventually. It might as well be her.

She took a deep breath.

'I worked on the department for about four years. It was the usual mix of euphoria when we sent a murderer down for twenty, twenty-five years and total despair when we didn't have enough evidence to get the suspect to court or the jury acquitted them. You do your best and ride the highs and try to survive the lows.'

Hazel began to inspect her immaculate fingernails.

'Sometimes the lows overtake you. I walked into the incident room one morning and was told that there had been a rape overnight. An eighteen-year-old girl – well, I suppose she was a woman although I never saw her as that. She'd had a couple of drinks in town with her friends, had wandered off and been raped at the back of a supermarket, next to some industrial waste-bins.'

By now Hazel felt she should at least look him in the eye as she told the rest of the tale.

'She was a nice young girl but she wasn't showing any signs of shock and she didn't even cry. The police are a cynical bunch and I wasn't convinced that she was telling the entire truth. I wondered if she'd met some fella during the evening and gone willingly with him to have sex somewhere, and then when her friends found her they'd got the wrong end of the stick and reported it as rape.

'The investigation started and it was soon obvious from the CCTV that this wasn't a consensual act. She was staggering along the High Street, tripping up and bumping into the wall. She went to a cash point – her friends later confirmed that's why she wandered off – but then she walked into an alley which led to the back of the supermarket. I watched the footage of the arsehole as he followed her along the street and then down the alley.'

'I understand that you felt bad for not believing her at first,' said Pierre, 'but you're right. We are cynical because people lie to us and she wouldn't be the first person to claim she was raped when she wasn't.'

He paused when he saw the dark look Hazel gave him from under her fringe before he added, 'I'll guess that there's more to it than that.'

Her reply came in the form of a nod.

'You don't have to tell me,' he said after a few more seconds of silence.

'I know that I don't,' she said. 'We found him, we arrested him and we took him to court. It turned out that the jury didn't believe her either. He'd picked a victim who didn't present very well in court, and unfortunately, he came across very well. He had no previous convictions, a job, a girlfriend, he said it had been consensual sex despite her injuries, and twelve men and women chosen at random believed him.'

'That's still not your fault,' said Pierre.

'I don't think that any of it was, up until the point my broken victim left court, insisted that she was all right, despite being completely humiliated by an obnoxious defence barrister, went home and took an overdose. She was dead before the ambulance got her to hospital.'

It was probably the first time that Hazel had unburdened herself of the sorrowful story and not cried. She knew that it wasn't because she was hardening to it, merely that this was a public place and not the sanctuary of a counsellor's office.

'That a young girl killed herself is something I'll have to live with. I know that I'm not directly responsible for her death. I did everything that I could to help her. I even told her that court wasn't like the kind of carry-on you see on the television with pompous barristers shouting and hollering and judges failing to intervene. That's exactly what happened when we got there. I couldn't believe it. Isn't this all supposed to be about the victim? It's a fucking disgrace.'

'I've seen similar happen myself,' said Pierre quietly. 'If it was a friend or relative of yours, what would you tell them?'

Hazel sat for a moment, staring into space past Pierre. 'I don't really know. I suppose that I'd say speak to the police, they'll believe you, they'll help you. I'd definitely leave out the bit where I tell them that, once they get to court, the defence are likely to degrade them all over again. After all, the only other option is that they never tell a soul. And who can live with that?'

Chapter 44

As DC Gabrielle Royston stood at the combined photocopier and printer in the stationery cupboard, she concentrated on putting her pin number onto the screen to get her documents to print. She let out a sigh at the futility of yet another task she had to perform time and time again to save the force money. She knew it wouldn't bother her so much if over a million pounds hadn't been spent on PR during the last year. She wasn't exactly sure that the police required PR, and certainly not over a million pounds' worth of it. It wasn't as though the public had an alternative, but it was another of life's mysteries that she knew she shouldn't dwell on. She had more pressing matters to worry about.

A noise behind her over the whirring of the printer as it came to life made her glance round, scowl still attached to her face.

'Soph,' she said as she turned to her colleague. 'I won't be long if you need to copy something. I'm waiting on a PNC print but it's about twenty pages in total.'

'It's OK,' said Sophia as she leaned against the door frame. 'I wondered if you needed any help. Tom and I are waiting for a couple of people to call us back and for some stuff from intel, so if you've got anything urgent, I can come out with you for an hour or so.'

Gabrielle recognized the gesture for what it was but hesitated to take up the offer. She didn't think for one minute that Sophia really could spare anywhere in the region of sixty minutes from the work she had stacking up. Whilst she stood contemplating whether she should accept, she watched Sophia's eyes narrow so minutely that it was unlikely that she was aware of it. The way she seemed to force her mouth to relax gave her an unhappy face. If that hadn't been enough in itself, the tensing of her shoulders as she pushed herself away from the frame was confirmation that Gabrielle's hesitation had snapped the olive branch in two.

The last thing she needed at that moment was anyone trying to get to know her a little better, asking about her personal life, wanting to be her friend. This raced through her mind as she cobbled together a brush-off that wouldn't be offensive.

She gained a little time by reaching for the papers churning out of the printer, redirecting her attention to Sophia and arranging what she hoped resembled a smile.

'Thanks so much, but I'm on top of my work at the moment. I was about to make a round of teas though. Can I get you one?'

'That would be great,' said Sophia. 'I'll meet you in the kitchen with my mug.'

Papers in hand, Gabrielle made her way back to the incident room, Sophia in front of her almost at a gallop.

One of the things she had learned during her career was that police officers rarely turned down a cup of tea, and if all else failed, doughnuts usually did the trick.

She tucked her paperwork under her arm, got her phone out of her pocket and set a reminder to call in at the baker's later that day.

Chapter 45

No sooner were Ian Hocking's eyes open than he started to regret the amount he had drunk the previous night. His alcohol consumption was something he thought about every morning as he awoke, plus on many occasions throughout the day. Lately though, he would be the first to admit, to himself at least, that the all-consuming thought was his sister and her children. He himself had never met the right woman and doubted he ever would, so all his efforts, energy and love when it came to having a family of his own were diverted in their direction.

As he turned over in bed, pushing his face against the pillowcase that should have been changed and washed two weeks ago along with the rest of the bedding, he felt the familiar anger that not only had his niece and nephew been denied a father as they grew up, but their mother had chosen a sex offender as her boyfriend.

Ian loved his sister and had tried to look out for her without smothering her with his affection, so it was almost a relief when his friend Dave Lyle first clamped eyes on her and told him that he was besotted with her and would one day marry her.

He smiled to himself when he thought back to the image of Dave's chubby spotty teenage face, a couple of lonely hairs sprouting out of his chin, as his friend looked over at him on their walk home from school and said, 'Your sister's easy on the eye. What do you reckon of me marrying her and being your brother-in-law?'

'I think you're a tosser,' had been his reply. 'She's only thirteen. Just because we've got to read *Romeo and Juliet* for English, it doesn't mean that you have to get married when you're still at school. Besides, the football season starts soon and you'll be too busy to plan a wedding.'

Right at that particular moment, Ian wasn't sure where the years between walking home from school with the occasional trip to the sweet shop for a can of Coke or to McDonald's for a milkshake and the present-day adult mess of his life had gone.

None of it was supposed to be this way. He had planned to get a great job, meet a beautiful woman – though after six years without having sex he had stopped pretending she'd be a lingerie model – and his life would have been complete. He hadn't wanted fame, fortune and his own yacht but a home and family. Most importantly of all, he had wanted to be happy.

If he couldn't have a home and family, he was at

least pleased when his sister Millie got them. He had been genuinely fond of her husband Clive and they had shared many a pint and a laugh together. He had even told him of Dave's adoration of Millie.

The power of the memory was too much for Ian and he turned himself over suddenly in bed, wrapped within his stale duvet cover. Head thrown back against the pillow and arm across his face, he couldn't stop his mind playing back to him the conversation they had shared. He wanted to block it out as he had wanted to on so many previous occasions, but it was still no good.

'I know Dave's crazy about her,' said Clive as he downed his lager. 'What bloke wouldn't be? She's beautiful, kind and sweet. Almost an innocence about her.'

Ian was able to picture the ten-pound note Clive pulled out of his wallet and waved at the barmaid, a tall, slim brunette, who clearly had a queue of customers vying for her attention. Like most people, she couldn't help being drawn to Clive, ignoring the other waiting punters and smiling as she took his empty glass and refilled it.

With a shake of his head, Ian had turned his back to the bar and taken a pull on his drink. Clive really seemed to have everything to make his life complete and if he hadn't have been such a thoroughly decent person, it would have been annoying. All Ian had ever wanted was a shot at a life like his brother-in-law's. That was of course before it all went tragically wrong.

One morning, Clive left for work and didn't come home. That was the hideous part of life that no one could ever avoid. The hand of fate had decided one particular morning that Clive would get into his car and drive his usual route to work, except on this day a lorry would jackknife, career across the central reservation and hit Clive's car head on, killing him instantly.

The thought of such a waste of human life, sweeping everything in its wake, was enough to cause tears to form in the corners of Ian's eyes. He rubbed them away, not wanting to begin another day wallowing in self-pity. It was, after all, a much bigger loss to his sister and her children, but Ian couldn't help but feel devastated at the thought of what Millie and the children went through every day. If they suffered, he suffered.

It was something he always kept bottled up, as he realized that people might misinterpret his feelings and think that it was only for his own sake that he mourned the loss of his friend and brother-in-law. He had once or twice been out drinking with Clive and attracted the attention of beautiful and interesting women. He was no fool: he understood that it was Clive who radiated charm and warmth; he merely happened to be in his company. The conversations always began the same way with Clive introducing his very single brother-in-law and telling everyone that he was happily married to Ian's sister.

Ian missed his drinking partner and confidant, and

whilst there was nothing he could do to bring him back from the dead, what he could do was look after Millie and her children.

It was something he had always done, although he had got out of the habit of concerning himself with her quite so much once she met Clive.

That was the fundamental flaw in Ian's personality – he didn't know where to draw the line and back off. That was usually the problem of those with an obsessive personality.

He knew that he couldn't lie in bed all day, especially as the smell of the sheets had started to make his hangover worse. He uncurled himself from the duvet, gathered the bedclothes and made his way with them to the washing machine.

Whilst he got himself ready for the walk to his sister's house, he allowed himself the luxury of a whole new torment by wondering how Millie was coping after her world had been turned upside down once again by the monster that went by the name of Albert Woodville.

Chapter 46

'Here goes then,' said Pierre as Hazel brought the car to a stop outside a semi-detached house in a busy road, cars passing by every few seconds. 'It doesn't look like the worst part of Sussex.'

'It looks OK,' said Hazel as she ran an eye over the street.

Pierre thought about asking her if she was feeling all right, but stopped himself when he glanced over and recognized the look of a hardened detective who wasn't about to go to pieces, was just going to get the job done.

They walked to the front door, Pierre stepping to the side to allow Hazel to knock. He watched her from the corner of his eye as she straightened her blouse, smoothed her jacket down and shook her hair back from her eyes. Then she gave a short, sharp knock, let out a sigh that Pierre assumed he wasn't supposed to hear, and waited.

A short, petite, middle-aged woman opened the door to them, surprise registering on her face at the sight of two people on her property on a Monday morning who were either door-to-door salespeople or police officers.

'Morning, Mrs Lewis,' began Hazel. 'Nothing to worry about. I'm DC Hamilton and this is DC Rainer. We'd like to speak to you about Monica, please.'

She allowed her words to hang in the air as Pierre scrutinized Mrs Lewis's face for one of the fundamentals of police work – the initial reaction. There was nothing that came close to observing the involuntary realigning of facial muscles and flash of emotion across the eyes. It replaced a hundred questions and answers and even the most poised witnesses and suspects rarely masked what they were really thinking.

A little wave of fright swept across her face, followed swiftly by a glance towards the staircase behind her.

As he stood impassive on the doorstep, Pierre took all this in and concluded that Monica was at home upstairs, probably in her bedroom. It explained why the initial signs of trepidation displayed by Mrs Lewis were now being replaced by interest and annoyance.

She folded her arms across her chest and said, 'I'd rather you didn't bother her, she's off sick from school.'

'I'm sorry to hear that,' said Hazel. 'We're not from Sussex police and we've come a fair distance to speak to her. Can we at least come in and talk to you?'

Perhaps her curiosity got the better of her or maybe Mrs Lewis had more time for the police than Pierre had expected. Whatever it was, she dropped her hands to her sides and let them into her home.

She led them to the dining room at the back of the house. Most of the area was taken up with a large table and eight chairs, along with a glass-fronted display cabinet.

After closing the door, Mrs Lewis pulled out a chair for herself and said, 'Please take a seat. It's not the most comfortable of rooms but Monica's bedroom is at the front of the house and there's less chance of her overhearing us if we're in here.'

'What's the matter with her, Mrs Lewis?' said Hazel. 'I don't want to intrude if it's serious.'

'Call me Louise. I wouldn't say serious.' Her eyes fluttered up to the ceiling, in the direction of the front of the house. She seemed to sag as she thought about her answer.

'What happened to Monica was horrendous and we have to live with it every day. I'm probably far too lenient with her. Bruce tells me that I let her get away with too much. He's probably right but I can't help but think I've got to try to make it up to her. I let her down. My own daughter and I failed to protect her. She was in the street one minute and gone the next.'

It was simply stated as if she wasn't expecting an answer. Something no doubt that had become her mantra over the last six months.

'She's twelve now, it was her birthday last week, and she seems so grown-up compared to how she was before all this nightmare began. Ever wish you could turn back the clock and do one thing differently?'

Again, Louise Lewis didn't seem to expect an

answer; she seemed to be talking to herself if anything. The two detectives at her dining table let her speak.

'There are days, if I'm honest, when I think she loves the attention. I know what a terrible thing that is to say about your own daughter, especially one so young who's been through so much. Monica has always known how to manipulate me, never more so than the day Dean Stillbrook took her into his house and ...'

Her voice cracked and she began to clasp and unclasp her hands in her lap.

'We don't want to upset you, Louise,' said Pierre, who intended to let Hazel do most of the talking but felt he should contribute something. 'We know what happened to Monica. Hazel and I are here to ask some questions about Dean.'

His years as a police officer, particularly those spent investigating murders, had taught him that sometimes the less said the better.

'I hope you don't think that we had something to do with why he committed suicide?' she said, a harsher edge to her words. 'He moved away from here as soon as he was arrested and bailed from the police station. He shouldn't even have been let out. For an offence as serious as that, he should have stayed in prison.'

It was something that hadn't passed Pierre by. He wondered, not for the first time, why Dean Stillbrook hadn't been remanded for a sexual offence against a child. He kept his thoughts to himself, not wanting to interrupt Louise. He found himself automatically nodding at her, trying to coax more out of her.

'I'm not entirely sure that Dean was all there,' she continued. 'For a start, what sort of a monster wants to make an eleven-year-old girl do stuff like that with them? God. Would you listen to me? After all that's happened, I still can't bring myself to say what he did to her. You'd have thought I'd have toughened up a bit, wouldn't you?'

This time, Pierre thought that he needed to speak, to keep her on track, if nothing else.

'Why did you think Dean Stillbrook had difficulties?' he asked, not wanting to use her exact words.

'He seemed a bit of a simpleton, he always had. That was before he messed about with Monica. His family had little to do with him and I think that he struggled with some day-to-day things. It doesn't excuse for one minute what he did, although perhaps if he'd had the right guidance, he would have kept his nose clean and led a better life. At least, that's what I like to think. The alternative is that he was born a monster. The fact that he took his own life too. I appreciate that committing suicide doesn't mean someone is of limited intelligence, far from it. I had a cousin who killed himself and he was so smart. As far as Dean's suicide goes, his family have my deepest sympathies. I know what it feels like to wonder if you could have spotted the signs, could have made the call you'd been putting off because you were so busy. That leaves you thinking if only you'd made a bit more of an effort, the whole outcome could have been—'

She broke off and stared first at Pierre, then at Hazel.

'I think that Dean Stillbrook expected to go to prison for what he'd done and when he didn't, he took the only option he thought was available to him.'

'You're right. Suicide is a terrible thing,' said Hazel, inching forward in her seat towards Louise. 'The thing is, we're not entirely convinced it was suicide.'

Once more, Pierre studied their witness's face. He watched her blanch.

'You, you ... You think someone killed him?' Louise said. 'We didn't have anything to do with it, if that's why you're here. I don't have the strength, my son's only seven and Bruce has a heart condition. We hate that bloody man, but none of us would kill him or even hurt him. The police sort out the criminals. That's what you do, isn't it? If the police don't deal with it, then the mob take over. What if they get the wrong man?'

Her voice had got louder and louder, so much so that none of them heard Monica walk downstairs and open the dining-room door.

A round-faced young girl, grey nightshirt, messy brown hair, stood watching them from the doorway. Her eyes were wide open, her mouth gaping slightly.

'Mum, I—' she started to say.

'It's OK, sweetheart,' said Louise. 'I didn't hear you get up. Go back to bed and I'll bring you up a drink. These officers are about to leave.'

The girl's face filled with panic. She stepped forward, one bare foot in front of the other.

'Please don't go yet,' she whispered. 'I've got

something I need to tell you. Mum, don't hate me. I've done a terrible thing.'

No one spoke. There was a chance that the three adults in the room were holding their breath.

'I heard you say that Dean didn't kill himself.' She looked at Pierre, her blue eyes full of tears.

He nodded at her.

'If someone killed him, then it might have been because of me.'

'That's not something—' Louise said but Monica put out a shaky hand to stop her, eyes still locked on Pierre.

'He didn't do it, you see,' said Monica, cheeks now awash with tears. 'It got out of hand when everyone was asking me where I'd been. He didn't lay a finger on me. Please don't hate me, Mum. I didn't know how to make it stop.'

Chapter 47

Pleased by the effort he had made to shower and put on clean clothes, never mind the petrol-station flowers he had stopped to buy his sister, Ian paused at the front door, finger poised at the doorbell.

If he wasn't mistaken, he heard the sound of laughter tinkle along the hallway as he stood stock-still at the stained-glass window to the side of the heavy wooden door. He thought he could make out the shape of two people sitting at the kitchen table. Through the uneven glass, which distorted everything in his eager eye line, it was difficult to distinguish his sister from the other person sounding as though they were lifting her mood. Something he had been intent on doing.

It certainly wasn't how he'd seen his morning with his little sister heading.

As tempted as Ian was to stand outside and listen, his desire to get inside the house and find out who she was talking to was greater.

He pressed the bell.

The sound of Millie tripping down the hallway was loud and clear as he imagined her racing towards the front door and flinging it wide, welcoming him in.

She at least hastened in his direction.

The gap between the door and the frame didn't grow as fast or as large as Ian had expected. Even then, if he wasn't very much mistaken, no sooner had she opened the door than Millie stepped street-side of it and pulled it behind her.

This was definitely a first.

'Mills,' he said, moving to his right to try to see through to the kitchen. 'Everything OK?'

A three-second pause told him that it wasn't.

'Ian,' she said as she forced her face into a smile. 'Lovely to see you. Are those for me?'

He had forgotten that he was holding a bunch of £4.99 carnations from a petrol- station bucket. He held them out and leaned in for a kiss.

'Come on in,' she said. 'Dave's here too. We were just talking about you.'

He hesitated before he stepped over the threshold. 'I heard laughter.'

If Millie thought he was implying something, she didn't show it.

'We were also talking about Clive,' she said as she made her way back to Dave, leaving Ian to shut the door after himself, flowers still in his hand.

He followed her into the kitchen.

'Hi Dave,' said Ian. 'Thought you'd be at work this morning.'

'All right?' said Dave. 'I had some leave to take so thought I'd use it wisely. How are you?'

'Not too bad. I wanted to see my sister and bring her some flowers.'

'Thank you, Ian,' she said, 'they're lovely.'

He handed them over, and the briefest of genuine smiles appeared on her face. His pleasure at her reaction was equally as fleeting as his eyes were drawn towards the enormous floral display next to the sink.

She looked at him over her shoulder as she ran water into the washing-up bowl and said, 'Dave brought me some too. I don't get flowers for ages and then you both bring them on the same day. What's brought this on?'

Ian glanced over at his friend who sat watching him, half-drunk mug of coffee on the table in front of him.

'Well, I know that I can't speak for your brother,' began Dave, raising his voice to be heard over the sound of the running water, 'but I wanted to make sure that you're OK after all that's happened. I'd guess that he wants to do the same.'

For a few seconds they locked eyes, Ian risking Millie turning round and seeing the grim expression on his face as he stared at the one person who could be the undoing of him.

The abrupt silence as soon as Millie turned the tap off forced Ian to say something.

'Yeah, that's right. I wanted to check how you were bearing up and apologize for ringing you the other night when I'd been drinking. I know you hate it when I do that.'

He stood with his hands in his pockets in the centre of the kitchen, Dave to his right at the table, his back to the wall, and his sister to his left, still at the sink, now removing cellophane from the pink carnations. He hadn't expected the morning to begin like this. He had envisaged a long chat with Millie, a catch-up about the children and then gently coaxing out of her how she was feeling and exactly how her weekend had gone.

He hadn't factored Dave into the equation, although going by the look on Dave's face, he hadn't expected company either.

'Sorry if this is a bad time,' Ian said. 'I can come back later.'

'Don't be daft,' said Millie. 'I put another pot of coffee on minutes before you arrived. I'm glad you're both here.'

She walked over to the table with a fresh mug of coffee and took the chair furthest away from Dave. Ian was convinced it wasn't the one she had been sitting on before he rang the doorbell, and he couldn't fathom out why he should be so bothered about that. This whole scenario was making him feel uneasy and the reason for it was escaping him. There was a time when he would have welcomed Dave into his family, and been only too pleased for his best friend and his sister to get together. That, of course, was before Clive.

It was also before Albert Woodville.

'The coffee's for you,' she said, staring straight at her brother. 'Why don't you sit down? You look as though there's something on your mind.'

Her eyes smiled at him as he stood feet away from the two of them, unable to say what he had been so intent on sharing that morning when he set out from his own home.

'I meant to call you over the weekend,' Ian said as he pulled out a chair.

'Which one of us are you talking to?' asked Dave.

'Both of you, I suppose. Mills, I'm sorry that I called you so late on Friday night. I was drunk and I shouldn't have risked waking the kids.'

The more awkward part of Ian's apology was still to come, so to avoid having to turn in his friend's direction, he leaned across to pick up his coffee. At the same time as he navigated his trembling hand through the milk jug and sugar bowl, he said, 'And Dave, ta for, you know, making sure that I got home all right from the pub and putting me to bed.'

'Not the first time, mate,' came the reply. 'I tried to wake you up to say bye, but you were dead to the world.'

A small gasp came from Millie at the word 'dead' and her hand went up to her forehead.

Ian's shaking hand shot in the direction of her arm, narrowly missing the coffee.

'Hey, sis. What's wrong?'

As she rested her head in her hands, Millie said, 'Tell me that you didn't do anything daft?'

'Me?' said Ian. 'Why would I do something daft? What are you on about?'

'Please don't lie to me.'

He took his hand away from her arm, gave a sigh and said, 'I shouldn't have called you and said that Woodville wouldn't bother you again. I hope you don't think I went round to his place and beat him up. I'm not stupid.'

She closed her eyes and spoke in a whisper. 'Then when you telephoned me on Friday night, how did you know he was dead?'

'Dead? Woodville's dead?' said Ian.

'Bloody hell, Millie,' said Dave. 'Isn't Woodville the bloke that you were seeing?'

'As drunk as I was,' said Ian, 'I know that I told you not to worry about him any more. I certainly didn't tell you that I'd killed him. I warned him, that was all. I bumped into him in town coming out of one of the coffee shops, and I told him to stay away from you and the kids. That was it.'

Several seconds of silence followed before Dave said, 'We were out together that evening, so anywhere Ian went, I went. We didn't see him and we certainly didn't kill him.'

'Aren't you going to ask how I know this?' she said through her tears. 'I find it a little odd that you haven't asked how I know he's dead.'

'Was it on the news?' asked Ian before he took a sip of his drink. He saw Millie fix her reddened eyes on him. He hated that she was so sad. At least the pervert couldn't hurt her any more, whatever she was going through.

'No, the police came round to see me.'

Ian knew that his reaction was a little slower than it should have been.

'The police came here?' he said, almost dropping his mug to the table. 'You should have called me.'

'I watch television, you know.' Millie looked from her brother to Dave and back again. 'The police do stuff like check telephone records. You'd already rung me once on Friday night. The last thing I wanted was a whole load of calls going backwards and forwards.'

Now it was her turn to lean over and place her hand on his sleeve. 'I'll only ask you this once: did you go to Albie's and do anything to him?'

He stroked the back of her hand with his fingers. 'I didn't touch him. Me and Dave went out for a couple of jars, went back to mine and I all but passed out. Ain't that right, Dave?'

'That's exactly what happened,' said Dave. 'What did you tell the police?'

'I didn't tell them that Ian called me on Friday and told me not to worry about Albie any more. I think they'd have come straight round to see you otherwise. They asked me who else knew that I was seeing him and about his, well, you know ... past.'

'And what did you tell them?' said Ian, unintentionally applying a little more pressure to the back of his sister's hand with his fingertips.

'I couldn't lie,' she said. 'I told them that you both knew. I left out the part about how angry and upset you were, Ian.'

Unable to resist, she found herself casting an eye over the cracked glass oven door, a vivid reminder of when, only ten days ago, her brother had shouted at her, 'How can you be so bloody stupid?' immediately before he picked up a stoneware casserole dish from the worktop and threw it across the kitchen.

Chapter 48

Once again, murder was very much on DCI Barbara
Venice's mind. She had thought about little else for
most of the morning and even earned herself a very
worrying pep talk from Assistant Chief Constable
Barrett.

Barbara liked Sally Barrett and despite the fact that
the woman was half her age and had got to a rank
higher than Barbara had even set her sights on, she
was a decent woman.

At the end of the meeting, Sally followed her along
the corridor and asked her if everything was OK.

It had led to much reassurance on Barbara's
part that everything was excellent and apologies if
she hadn't contributed all that she should have to
the weekly meeting, but her daughter was getting
married and only minutes before the start of the
wedding-planning get-together, she had called her
with a crisis.

Nothing of the sort had happened; it was all she
could think of after receiving a text from her daughter

asking if she was still free to run into town at lunchtime to check out the price of bouquets. Barbara Venice was a thoroughly professional woman who wouldn't normally have dreamt of such base behaviour. Never in all of her years of police work had she ever used her family as an excuse for not committing herself to the task in hand when on duty.

She held back from kicking herself in the shins before hurrying towards the sanctury of Harry Powell's office.

'All right, Babs,' he said as he looked up and saw her in the doorway.

'I've been better. Any update?'

Harry pushed himself back from the desk, blue striped shirt beginning to strain at the middle-aged spread. He sighed and put his hands behind his head.

'Have a seat and I'll tell you a very sorry tale,' he began, eyes on the overhead fluorescent lights. 'Pierre called me about twenty minutes ago. He and Hazel got to Sussex, went to see the Lewis family and as they were speaking to Mum, Monica walked into the room and said that she'd made up the entire rape allegation against Dean Stillbrook.'

'Oh good grief.'

'That's putting it much milder than I did. If there was a swear box in here, I'd need to set up a direct debit. They're taking Monica to the nearest nick for a voluntary interview. Her mum's going too, but for crying out loud, if he never touched her and he was murdered because of what he did – or didn't do in this case – we've not only got a vigilante, but a vigilante who's been led up the garden path and so far, has got away with murder.'

Even though he had an idea of the impact of his words on her, Harry couldn't begin to know how worried and fragile the entire situation was making her feel.

She shut her eyes, only for a moment. When she opened them again, Detective Inspector Harry Powell had pitched forward in his seat, heavily lined forehead wrinkled to such an extent it made Barbara laugh.

'What?' he said.

'You look like a man with the weight of the world on his shoulders. I understand that you're the senior investigating officer but I've come to you and told you of my concerns about all this. You know my feelings on the original investigation. Do you have any good news?'

'Woodville seems to have complied with the terms of his Sex Offender Prevention Orders as far as not having a computer goes.'

'Thanks, Harry. Any update regarding not buggering children?'

She saw him grimace. Harry Powell had actually pulled an uncomfortable face in front of her. This was the point where she knew it was time for her to take a break and step back.

Everyone had that one job, that murder, that investigation that should have been when they drew the line.

Perhaps this was her swansong.

It happened.

Barbara wasn't the first and wouldn't be the last. She had known CSIs who had attended one mutilated body too many, officers who had taken dead babies to the nearest hospital because of an ambulance strike, off-duty colleagues who had been attacked by disgruntled criminals whilst they were out with their families. So many of those people had reached the point where giving up their own lives no longer held an allure, and they had decided to take back a life for themselves.

It was probably time to make crime someone else's problem again.

'I've had enough,' she said. 'I don't only mean about this, but generally with this job. I'm thinking of putting my ticket in. You know what I mean. I could do something else while I've got the chance.'

She stared at a blank-faced Harry.

'I've never seen you so quiet,' she said. 'Please say something.'

'We've all had the dream of giving this up,' he said. 'Everyone thinks that the life of a detective is a calling and why would anyone with such a job do anything different. I can bloody well tell you why. It's fucking hard work to hang on to your sanity. Don't do it, Barbara. Don't leave.'

She smiled and said, 'Just for calling me Barbara and not Babs, I'll see this one out before I make any decision.'

Barbara got up to go.

'One more thing before I leave you to it,' she said. 'At some point, can you let me have an update on the death threats Albert Woodville got? And don't look at me like that. All the time I'm still here, I'll do the best job I possibly can.'

She walked out, leaving Harry with the thought that any chance of Barbara letting the fight go out of her was inconceivable.

Chapter 49

The weather always had a huge impact on Leon and Toby's working day. Rain meant that they lost money, and often overspent in cafés and pubs if it was set in for the day. Toby would happily have gone home on those occasions but never let on that he stayed with Leon to keep his friend company.

Today, as they made their way back to the van from their breakfast, Toby knew that, if the heavens were to open, he would rather be indoors on his own than trying to drag out a conversation with Leon. He had never known his friend to be so quiet. A dry day meant that he would at least have to make the effort with him.

'You know where we're off to first?' said Toby as Leon started the engine.

He watched Leon's profile as his enormous head gave a tiny nod and possibly heard 'Mmm' come from his pursed lips.

'It's that young woman with the two kids. She always offers us a cup of tea. She gave us cake last month. This'll be a good start to the week.'

'I can't do it.'

Leon sat with his hands on the steering wheel, breaths long and slow, chest rising and falling beneath his fleece jacket.

'Can't do what? I get the impression you're not talking about eating chocolate cake?'

'I'm thinking of going to the police—'

'The police?' said Toby. 'What the fuck for? Are you crazy?'

'Isn't it better that I go and tell them what I've done, what we've done, than they find out and nick us? It'll look better for us.'

Toby slumped back against the van door, partly to distance himself from his friend and his ludicrous suggestion, and partly to observe him. He felt his heart racing and he suddenly felt hot and cold at the same time. If he hadn't known better, Toby would have said it was the start of a panic attack.

The two of them remained where they were for some time before Leon turned his head so slowly to the passenger seat it was as if he was scared of what he might see there.

'You know that I'm not very good at coping with serious stuff,' Leon said at last. 'I don't know what to do.'

'Mate, you've got to leave it behind you, like we left what happened to us at the children's home behind us. We left it years before we felt strong enough to do anything about it, and now, we do the same. We walk away and carry on as before. We talked about this.'

'How do you cope? I don't mean about Woodville's death. I mean how do you deal with what he did to you?'

The words hung in the air between them, suspended in the stifling hot blasts spilling from the dashboard's heaters.

It was the first time that Leon had ever asked Toby outright; it was an unwritten rule they had that they never spoke of their sexual abuse. Toby loved that their invisible bond was there, even though it came from something so hideous. It was the worst kind of burning shame that they never discussed, merely lived with it every day.

When seven-year-old Toby had walked into the bedroom he shared with Leon in the home, and seen the expression on his roommate's face, he knew what had happened to him. There was no mistaking that look of hurt and humiliation.

The same bedraggled, lost look was once again back. It had taken hold of every part of his features and Toby knew that he was watching someone who was within touching distance of despair. Everything torturous up to that point, they had gone through together, and he wasn't about to change it now.

Toby spoke before he could change his mind.

'If you really want to go to the police, I'll come with you.'

Even as he said the words, he wasn't entirely sure that he would see it through. The police would never believe their story and time in prison wasn't something he was cut out for. Leon even less so. No one knew better than Toby that his friend was a huge, gentle man who under any other circumstances wouldn't have hurt anyone. He had only become embroiled in the planning of Albert Woodville's murder because he was a loyal individual who couldn't bring himself to walk away from someone in their hour of need, even if that meant going to prison.

All Toby could do was guess at what Leon might actually say if he went to the police, but what he did know was that he regretted drawing him into the whole sorry escapade. If he hadn't shared with Leon that, whilst out shopping with his wife and kids, he had seen Albie Woodville as he strolled along East Rise High Street, head held high, as if he didn't have a care in the world, and the old familiar feelings of humiliation and degradation had returned in an instant, Leon would not be reacting this way now. Those feelings were back so fast, it was as if the last twenty years of building a life, family, home and business had never happened. He was instantly in his bedroom in the children's home, hiding under the bed covers and praying to a God he didn't believe in that tonight would be someone else's turn.

No, he should never have told Leon about that chance sighting of their tormentor. He should have done it alone.

Except he knew that he needed Leon to be by his side.

That was the most selfish act he had ever carried out and, ever since, throughout every minute of their plotting, not a day went past when he didn't regret that he had involved Leon.

The contempt he had for himself was overwhelming: all those years ago, he had had the chance to take a pair of scissors or knife from the kitchen and ram the blade into Woodville's jugular on any of the nights when he had sat beside his bed, hands creeping under the covers, gasping as his fingers stroked Toby's flesh. Why hadn't he killed him then? Surely the other children in the home would have backed him up. None of this would now be happening.

He despised himself for failing to act all those years ago and save himself, Leon and the others he knew were being harmed; and he despised himself for not being strong enough to face this alone.

If Leon felt that he should go to the police and tell them what they had done, he would go with him. Needless to say, they still needed a plan.

'Do you really mean it?' said Leon. 'We'll go together?'

'I really mean it. The only thing is, what we tell them. We have to decide and then stick to it. They've already been to see me, so I don't think it'll be long before they pay you a visit.'

'Bloody hell. What have you told them about me?'

'Don't panic, Dilly. They asked me where I was on Friday night. I was with you. We already worked that bit out a long time ago.'

'Yeah, yeah. I'm sorry. It's the nerves setting in. So what do we do?'

Leon released his grip on the steering wheel and ran his hands across his head before dropping them down to his sides.

'You know that I need your help,' said Leon. 'You've always been the brains of this outfit.' He waved away the beginning of a protest from the person he trusted most in the world before he continued with what he wanted to say. 'I've not been completely honest with you. Remember that day you came back to our room at the children's home? Woodville had walked out as you were coming up the stairs?'

He looked across and saw his friend nod.

'Christ. I've practised telling you this for what seems like a thousand years. I knew I'd struggle. I didn't realize how much until now.'

Leon took a deep breath and let out the secret he had kept for as long as Toby had felt the need to take to his skin with a wire brush to scour away the imagined dirt.

'The thing is that Woodville didn't touch me. Not in the way he touched you anyway.'

The silence was louder than the noise of the air rushing towards them through the vents.

'I wanted to tell you, Toby, really I did. You watched out for me in the home and I idolized you. You'd got it wrong about him sexually abusing me but he still made my life a misery. He made me eat food from the floor, stand naked in the freezing corridor if I didn't clean the floor properly afterwards, he kidney-punched me more times than I can remember. You know why he didn't interfere with me, do the stuff to me that he did to the rest of you?'

A miserable shake of the head from Toby.

'Because he told me that I was too fat. He didn't fancy fat kids. It was such a relief to know that he wasn't going to mess about with me, but do you know the fucking ridiculous thing? It made me feel left out. What the sodding hell is wrong with me?'

'We were children,' said Toby quietly. 'We were only kids. I think that we'd better go to work now, and let me think about what we do next.'

'I didn't want to tell you this. I'm so sorry.'

'Sorry for what? Sorry that you weren't sexually abused? Let me think. We'll talk about it later.'

'I can't leave things like this all day between us,' said Leon. He rubbed at his eyes, possibly so that he didn't have to look at Toby as he spoke. Toby couldn't tell. In fact, he felt that he couldn't tell the truth of any situation any more.

Toby had got everything so wrong: he felt as though he had perhaps failed to grasp any aspect of his life properly. He had misinterpreted an expression so many years ago, and now it was shaping his whole life. He needed time to think. Time away from Leon.

'I need to tell you, Tobe, of the total humiliation that man put me through. It wasn't only what he said to me about being fat, it was worse than that.'

At this point Leon stopped rubbing his eyes and turned in the driver's seat to look at Toby face to face.

He saw now why Leon had spent the last several seconds with his fingers over his eyes. It was an attempt to stop the tears, and it hadn't worked.

'Woodville came up to the bedroom after he sent you to the shops. He obviously knew you'd be a while and I was on my own. He kicked the door shut and I remember as clear as if it was yesterday, I thought to myself: This is it. Today it's my turn. The most stupid thing was I didn't want to let him see me cry. Reducing me to a sobbing eight-year-old seemed like the most terrible thing that could happen.

'He, he . . . pushed me up against the wall, grabbed my privates. I was a fucking kid, for God's sake. What could a grown man get from touching an eight-year-old's dick? I told him to leave me alone, that I'd tell. I was petrified but like with all bullies, I thought if I stood up to him, he'd back down.'

Leon paused to wipe the tears from his cheeks. His enormous hands merely pushed the wetness down to his chin.

'Little chance of him backing down,' continued Leon. 'He put one hand around my throat and squeezed it. With the other hand, he undid my trousers and pulled them down. I thought he was going to touch me again. Instead, he let go, stood back, looked me up and down and said, 'What would I ever see in a fat little bastard like you? You're disgusting.' It was probably the most mentally cruel thing he could have done to me.'

Both men sat still. Neither spoke. Eventually Leon was aware that Toby was trying to say something. He put his hand out and turned the heater off to stop the noise of the blower from carrying away his friend's words.

Leon leaned forward until his ear was almost level with Toby's mouth.

'You might have put off telling me for years, Leon. It's important that you understand that, even if he didn't rape you, touching you is still sexual abuse.'

For the first time in their lives, the two men sat and cried together.

Chapter 50

'Hi, everyone,' said Harry to a crowded incident room. There was an immediate drop in the noise level, although one or two people were making phone calls so the detective inspector raised his voice to be heard over the sound of a murder team's buzz. 'I've got an update from Hazel and Pierre although I'd rather keep it for the briefing. Let's make it at midday. I realize that's a lot later than normal but I want to speak to them again and catch up on a couple of things. In the meantime, can someone work out if any of the former witnesses in the 1990s investigation are currently living in Sussex so Hazel and Pierre can double up their enquiries, and then can someone tell me where Gabrielle is?'

Several heads made as though they were scanning the room, most were going through the motions. The detective inspector was asking the question so his staff seemed to make the effort to care but they all had their own tasks to get on with. Looking for a wayward member of staff wasn't a murder-investigation line of enquiry, so it didn't feature on most of their radars. Besides, he had little doubt that judging by the general apathy towards Gabrielle, most of them didn't have much time for her.

He hadn't failed to notice that things in his briefing room were a little strained. He paid attention and was a man who cared about both the investigation and his staff. One wasn't possible without the other, and the pressure was on, especially as it wasn't long ago he was a detective sergeant and was keener than ever to show his capability as a DI.

As he was about to return to his office, the main door opened and Gabrielle walked towards him, take-away coffee in hand.

'Just the person,' he said to her. If he wasn't very much mistaken, her cheeks instantly dotted pink. To Harry's mind, she was giving the appearance of having been caught doing something she shouldn't.

'Have you got a minute?' he said. 'Bring your drink, although it won't take long.'

He stood by his office door, Gabrielle seconds behind him, and waited for her to go inside.

With the door shut, he sat behind his desk and watched her place her cardboard cup on the table and take a seat.

'After our chat, I wanted to make sure that now you've had time to think about things you're still OK on this murder investigation,' he said. 'It is a difficult one, I'll be the first to admit. No one likes paedophiles, but most people aren't overly fond of murderers either.

I want to make sure that you're comfortable dealing with this because it hasn't escaped my notice that you may not be. I'd be a pretty crap boss if I didn't pay attention to my team.'

Harry saw her eyes widen as he spoke, her lips parted as if she was going to say something, and then she looked down at her hands in her lap. From the corner of his eye, he saw her clasp them together.

'Has someone said that I'm not pulling my weight?' she said, eyes still down.

'No, no. It's nothing like that. I know that you'll get on with anything you're given but with your background in child investigations, it's natural that you'll have more of an insight into these things. I'm the same; I don't sympathize with people who get their sexual gratification from hurting and abusing children although I don't want to see them murdered either. Especially in our county.'

He found himself looking at the top of her head as she seemed to be folding into her own lap. She really was a strange young woman. Harry was on the verge of asking her if she was all right, when she sat up straight and said, 'I loathe them all. I know now that I probably stayed on child protection for too long. It got to me, got under my skin. I saw so many children whose lives and futures were ruined by lowlifes not fit to walk the earth, let alone be amongst babies and kids, it made me sick. Properly, physically ill. I couldn't stand it any longer, though I should have seen the signs and moved on. You know what it's like. You've been there. Trouble is, walking away seems like giving in and letting them win. I know that my attitude should always have been that I had the best job in the world. I got to arrest and lock up people who rape children, but when you do it constantly, week after week, disgusting pervert after disgusting pervert, you know that however hard you work, whatever you do, you'll never stem the tide. It won't stop, will it? More and more cases are coming to light, especially involving those who hold positions of authority, and should support the children in their care. Kids who have no one else to turn to. Who are isolated and vulnerable. It's the tip of an enormous iceberg, except instead of ice, it's made of the torment of children.

'Some days, it was difficult to get out of bed and go in to work. I thought about resigning constantly and making it all someone else's problem. Why should I go through so many innocents' horror with them, reliving it all, feeling the way they do and damage my own sanity? I could simply walk away. But then, I couldn't, could I?'

She stopped talking, eyes glistening, her face immo bilized by a mask of misery.

The room was still. Harry gave her a moment before he said, 'I know, Gab, I've been there. You leave, who takes on your caseload? The problem is, it won't ever disappear completely, no matter how hard you work at it. You aren't responsible for the entire planet's ills. I think, for your sake as much as anything, you should be on another investigation. You see this?' He pointed towards the wall, adorned with a whiteboard with a list of twelve other operation names written on it.

She nodded.

'Pick one of them, any one of them, and there'll be plenty to do. I'll speak to one of the detective sergeants, Sandra probably, and she can give you some work on something else, something that's not going to cause you sleepless nights and internal conflict. In the meantime, I think that a trip to welfare is probably in order.'

Gabrielle opened her mouth, then nodded at him again.

'And you know,' he said, 'if you need some time off, I can give you a day or two at home, but only if you'd rather not be around people. Sometimes it helps, sometimes it doesn't. I'll let Sandra know if you want to disappear off for the rest of the day.'

He was unsure whether he had overdone it as she looked like she was going to burst into tears. Harry definitely didn't want it getting out that he was losing his touch and had gone soft, but he could tell when someone was in distress. He felt guilty that it came as a relief to him that this went some way to explaining her odd behaviour. There was nothing more sinister involved.

Right now, he was probably looking at a woman on the edge and in need of help. He knew how difficult it was sometimes to ask for it, and Gabrielle was showing all the signs of heading for depression, if she didn't have it already.

'Promise me one thing,' said Harry as she stood up

to go, dabbing the corner of her eyes with a tissue. 'If you feel like this, talk to someone about it.'

He thought he heard her mumble 'OK'. There was possibly the beginning of 'Thank you', and then as she turned to go back into the incident room, she said, 'I need to nip into town. OK if I go before the briefing?'

'Course.'

She shut the door behind her and he watched her through the small glass panel reinforced with chicken wire as she made her way back across the bustling incident room.

Harry leaned back in his chair and put his hands behind his head.

'Never underestimate people's emotions and what makes them tick,' he said to the ceiling.

He was about to throw himself back into work, tired already so early in the day, when a Tannoy announcement from the police station's front counter assistant caught his attention.

'Visitor for DI Powell at the front counter, visitor for DI Powell at the front counter.'

He sat for a moment as he decided whether to call and find out who it was or face the music. His hand hovered above the phone, then he sprang from the chair, took his suit jacket from the hook on the wall and walked out through his incident room.

Once again, he ran an appreciative eye over his staff as they typed reports, made phone calls and rushed to each other's assistance over queries, and listened to the good-natured banter between them all.

He let himself out of the department's security door and walked down the stairs towards his visitor.

Through the security glass, Harry saw the familiar figure of Martha Lipton poised on one of the plastic seats inside the public entrance.

She sat with her legs crossed, black stiletto dangling down from her foot as she absently waved it backwards and forwards. She glanced down at her watch with a frown but, as she looked up, she caught Harry watching her and gave him a wink.

He pushed the door open with enough force to take the front-counter assistant off guard.

'Thanks, Julie,' he said to her. 'I'll take Miss Lipton here into one of the side rooms.'

Martha picked her bag up from the floor and followed him across the foyer to a small windowless room furnished only with a desk, three odd chairs and a mess of blank statement forms and leaflets offering all manner of advice from how to spot extremists to security-marking personal property.

'Morning,' said Harry when they'd sat down opposite each other.

'Good morning. I expected you to send one of your underlings.'

'I think you mean my team. And they're very busy. They've not only got a murder to investigate, but now an arson with intent to endanger life.'

She bristled.

'I've come here about both matters.'

If Harry wasn't very much mistaken, Martha did

have the good grace to seem as if she'd been knocked off her pedestal.

'Please, Harry,' she said, hand outstretched across the table towards him, 'I knew nothing about the fire. It could have been anyone. What I can help you with is the name of a new member of the Volunteer Army who might have been involved with the murder of Woodville.'

'Go on.'

She drummed her fingertips on the smooth surface of the table, deftly avoiding a tea stain from a previous member of the public.

'You didn't get this from me and I'll deny I ever told you this. You know that I can't be seen to betray my members.'

Harry held in a laugh.

'Give me a name,' he said, 'and leave the rest to me.'

'I was in the High Street handing out leaflets. I gave one to a fella called Jonathan Tey. He came along to one of our meetings and afterwards we got chatting. He knew Albert Woodville and had a real problem with him, said he was in an amateur dramatic society with him and Woodville was using it to gain access to kids. Tey seemed quite, well, volatile. Possibly dangerous.'

Harry pinched the pleats in his trouser legs, leaned forward and said, 'Let me get this right here, you run a group of vigilantes who want to alert the public to the whereabouts of sex offenders in their neighbourhood, and you're acting all surprised that someone's

251

come along to one of your shindigs and may have a propensity for violence.'

'If you don't need my help, there's no point in my being here.'

She stood up to go.

'Martha, thank you for your time and for coming to see me.'

He felt the words sticking in his throat but he knew a useful source when he saw one.

'One last thing,' he said as she turned towards the door, 'the fire . . .'

He watched her take a large breath and her shoulders inch a little higher. He had no idea why he wanted her to feel better about herself when he said, 'We've got someone in custody for it. He said he acted alone, thought he'd teach a few people a lesson. He's got no idea who or what the Volunteer Army are. He's well known to the police, carried out a spate of crimes, including low-scale arson.'

She turned back round to face him. 'Thanks, Harry.'

'What I need from you now,' he said, benevolent feelings all but forgotten, 'is a statement that you didn't have anything to do with the fire and don't know anyone by the name of Chris Enfield.'

She raised a plucked eyebrow at him. 'The fire-starter, I presume?'

'Think about it,' he said as he pulled the pile of statement sheets towards him. 'You've come down the nick and given me a name in a murder investigation. What better way to justify your actions than making a statement about a completely different crime that possibly would implicate you if you didn't cooperate?'

Martha Lipton, convicted sex offender, sat back down and smiled at Harry.

'Under different circumstances,' she said, 'we might have got along together. It would only take the small matter of you forgetting my past.'

Glad that he could turn his attention to the task of finding a pen and flattening out the edges of the paper, Harry looked away from her.

One of the biggest personal torments of being a police officer was cajoling those you loathed when you needed their assistance. Some days, Harry just knew he had to break bread with a monster to get what he wanted.

The sacrifice to his own self-respect at least meant that he now had Jonathan Tey very much in his sights.

Chapter 51

'If I'd realized you were going to have coffee,' said Jonathan Tey when he came back from the bar, 'I wouldn't have suggested meeting in a boozer.'

He shoved the cup and saucer down in front of Jude whose face was now demonstrating equal displeasure at the latte as it spilled into the saucer.

'It's only a quarter past eleven,' said Jude. 'We're not even having lunch. I can't go out and get drunk at lunchtime. I've got a council planning meeting this afternoon at the Town Hall.'

'It's hardly Cobra, is it?'

'If you're going to take the mickey, I'm going.'

Jonathan rested his arm on the back of the chair next to him, untouched pint on the table. He kept his voice as low as possible and said, 'We've got things to discuss.'

He had got to the pub first and chosen a table near the window with the bright November sun on his back. When he leaned forward to pick up his drink, he cast a shadow across Jude's face. Fully aware of what he was doing, Jonathan added, 'So it's a really good idea if you stay put.'

'Well, I'm getting a serviette first,' said Jude.

He walked over to the end of the bar to the condiments and cutlery and made a great show of taking three paper napkins, one at a time, before he took his seat again.

Jonathan waited whilst his unlikely partner in crime mopped up the spilt drink from the saucer, wiped the bottom of the cup twice, stirred the latte, added sugar and then stirred it again.

He was showing no signs of the angry outburst he had displayed at the East Rise Players' emergency meeting when Eric Samuels had dropped his sexual-offender bombshell. It was the only reason that Jonathan had considered Jude for sorting out Albie Woodville. He was now beginning to think that he might have made a very grave mistake. There appeared to be extremes to Jude's character but right at this moment, all he was experiencing were the prissy and lame parts.

'Finished?' asked Jonathan when the white serviettes were brown and sodden.

'Yes, thank you. Now what are we going to do? We've both had the police round and I certainly don't want them coming back.'

'We do nothing,' said Jonathan. He picked up his pint and gulped half of it down, smacked his lips and leaned forward again. 'We stick to what we've already decided. Nothing can go wrong if we do that.

Remember that, if we start to panic, we'll draw attention to ourselves and that's the worst thing that can happen. Agreed?'

Jude shot him a dark look, drained the rest of his coffee and said, 'That was about the worst latte I've ever had.'

'Why are you being such a dick? We've got much more important things to worry about.'

'You told me to behave normally. I'm drinking coffee and commenting on it. That's normal. Meeting you in a pub before noon and us whispering across the table to each other isn't normal. We're not gangsters. You're an accountant and I work for East Rise council's planning department.'

This was proving to be more difficult that Jonathan had envisaged. He cast his mind back to the moment he left the Cressy Arms with Jude when they had vented their anger about Albert Woodville and all that he represented. Neither of them at the time had seriously considered their intentions to be more than simply words spat from their lips in a rage as they'd goaded each other on with their fantasy of what they would do to the man if they were left alone with him.

Then of course, they were alone with him. And it was no longer only words.

The thought of what they had imagined doing to him forced Jonathan to fidget in his hard wooden pub chair, bothered by the memory of his own channelled hatred.

If he was being honest with himself, he had enjoyed

discussing the pain they'd wanted to cause Woodville. Few people knew the real Jonathan because he understood it was better that some things stayed hidden. One stupid mistake many years ago had almost been the undoing of him, but his wife Elaine, his girlfriend then, had come to his rescue. Only the two of them knew the truth, and he certainly wasn't about to share it with Jude. Jonathan wasn't entirely sure he could trust him to keep quiet about his own crime: he most certainly couldn't risk a twenty-year-old secret getting out on top of an attack on a sex offender.

'You're staring at me,' said Jude. 'If I'm honest, it's alarming me. What's wrong?'

'Nothing's wrong, so long as you've sorted your clothes from that night, like we agreed, and you don't tell anyone about Woodville, and us going to his flat. If you've done that, we're home and dry.'

'It's done,' said Jude. 'If we're to act normal, that means going back to the East Risc Players. Do you think we'll be welcome there?'

Jonathan shrugged and said, 'I don't see why not. Samuels can't afford to keep losing members. He's already down one costume assistant. Don't pull that face.'

'It's a bit distasteful, Jonathan.'

'I'm distasteful? If you'd had your way, we'd have strung him up from the nearest lamp-post. At least I wanted to be discreet.'

Jude drummed his fingers on the table and said, 'It doesn't really matter now. It's done. He's dead.'

'I'm glad that you understand that there's no point in overthinking this. What's done is done and nothing can change it now.'

'I know, I know,' said Jude. The thing is, I'm racked with guilt over what we did, so someone somewhere is sitting with the weight of the world on their shoulders. I'm not really sure how they're coping.'

'My thoughts exactly,' said Jonathan. 'There's one thing I'm clear about and that's if we ever find out who it was, I'd like to shake them by the hand.'

Chapter 52

DCI Barbara Venice checked her phone for messages as she crossed the police station's back yard. A number of marked and unmarked cars were parked in the bays, a number next to the custody entrance. She nodded and said hello to some of the officers, a few addressing her as 'ma'am', a few clearly not having a clue who she was though her security badge allowed her unhindered access.

She let herself out with the same badge, unlocked the ten-foot-high metal gate and surprised herself at how different she felt on the civilian side of the fence.

Within minutes, she was outside the florist's shop where she had arranged to meet her daughter. It was the largest one in East Rise and gave over half its floor space to unusual Christmas gifts at this time of the year. Feeling a touch chilly and arriving a little ahead of the arranged time, Barbara ducked inside the shop, keen to start her shopping early this year and not leave it all to the last minute and allow the internet to take care of it.

Lost in thought and browsing Christmas pomanders and wicker reindeer at the back of the shop, she heard a familiar voice from the direction of the till.

Stuck for a moment as to who the voice belonged to, she stayed where she was behind the rows of baubles, vases and garlands. She popped her head out from behind a rack of dried fruit and coloured moss and saw Gabrielle Royston at the counter engrossed in conversation with the florist.

Unsure whether to approach them or not, Barbara elected to stay where she was. Flowers were a very personal thing and she didn't want to encroach on something that was none of her business.

Her hesitation turned to a mild panic when she realized that the young detective constable from her department was ordering funeral flowers. Now she found herself trapped at the back of the shop, unable to leave but aware that her daughter was about to arrive at any moment and would be sure to seek her out and want to talk her through all the floral stock available.

Barbara made her mind up that she was going to step out from the rows of bric-a-brac acting as her cover when Gabrielle said, 'My nephew was only six. He had leukaemia. I'm not sure what would be best, a teddy-bear wreath or his favourite football-club colours.'

Barbara took a cautious step backwards.

She took her mobile phone from her coat pocket, turned it to silent and tapped out her daughter a message that she would be another hour, had been called back to work and would explain shortly.

No sooner had she pressed send on her phone than she heard the florist offer a compromise.

'We can make you a teddy-bear wreath in his team's colours if you'd prefer that.'

DCI Barbara Venice looked around the shop for the staff-only area and wondered if she could get away with hiding there until Gabrielle had finished her heart-breaking order.

Chapter 53

With Toby's words of warning still ringing in his ears, Leon walked up the steps of East Rise Police Station. The automatic doors parted and he stepped inside.

Two women of about forty years of age sat behind a high counter. One was occupied with a telephone call but the other looked up at him and smiled.

'Hello,' she said. 'Can I help you?'

He glanced around the sparse foyer, eyes lingering on a row of plastic seats bolted to the floor. Only one was occupied by a sulky-looking teenager, who was paying no attention to Leon.

He lingered in front of the counter, unsure what to say. He'd expected to be able to speak to someone in private, not like this in public.

For a moment, he considered walking back down the steps, forgetting about the entire thing. Toby had tried to warn him that what he was about to do was an incredibly bad idea. He had even resorted to pleading with him, but Leon's mind was made up.

He took a deep breath and said, 'Can I speak to a police officer, please?'

The woman behind the counter had a pleasant face. If Leon were forced to describe her demeanour, he would call it open and welcoming. That look disappeared and was replaced by concern as soon as he added, 'It's about Albert Woodville.'

'Take a seat, please,' she said. 'I'll get someone.'

He chose the seat furthest from the angry boy who was now tutting and scuffing the floor with his brand-new, £120 trainers.

Leon watched as the woman at the counter picked up the phone and put it to her ear. She spoke softly although he could still hear her ask for an officer to come and speak to him.

'What's your name, sir?' she said, having to stand up to see him over the raised wooden ledge now he'd moved to the far side of the foyer.

'Leon Edwards.'

He heard the name whispered into the phone and he sat and awaited his fate.

After a remarkably short time, the door opened and a young man in a suit walked towards Leon to where he sat on one of the cheapest chairs in East Rise.

'Hello,' said the man. 'I'm Tom Delayhoyde. I'm a detective constable. Do you want to step into this side room and we can speak in private?'

He gestured towards a wooden door to the left of where Leon was sitting. It crossed Leon's mind that he could still get up and walk out. As far as the very fresh-faced officer knew, he hadn't done anything wrong. He didn't feel discouraged that DC Delayhoyde was so young, although he could see little difference in age between the officer and the angry teenager who was now frantically pressing buttons on his phone and talking to himself under his breath. It crossed his mind to help out the police officer and the nice woman behind the counter by punching the teenager as he left, but figured he was in enough trouble as it was. The phrase 'You might as well be hung for a sheep as for a lamb' popped into his head although even in his crowded mind, he recognized that this wasn't going to be the smartest thing he had ever done.

Tom Delayhoyde opened the door with his security pass and the two of them went inside and sat across from one another at the large table which was taking up most of the room.

'You mentioned Albert Woodville,' said Tom in an even tone.

Leon felt his mouth go dry and convinced himself that he could feel his pulse racing and heart speeding up. He didn't need to let his imagination work overtime when it came to sweating profusely: the perspiration was running down his face to the end of his nose.

He wiped his face on the sleeve of his fleece.

'I know something about Albert Woodville,' he said. His voice was much smaller than he would have liked. He was out of his depth.

'Go on.'

He unzipped his fleece jacket, pulled his T-shirt away from his clammy body.

'I did something stupid. Something criminal.'

The sound of the truculent young man who was still waiting at the front counter filled the room as he demanded to know how long he was going to be kept waiting.

'Go on,' said Tom again.

'I knew Albie Woodville from years ago. I was at the children's home he ran. He was a right horrible bastard – sorry about the language.'

Tom held up a hand and waved Leon on with his tale.

'I hated him. We all hated him. He was nasty and spiteful. It doesn't excuse what I did. I have to live with that now and it's very important you know that I did this on my own.'

He tried to imagine what the detective was now seeing but it was laborious enough for Leon to form in-depth views from his own perspective without trying to envisage what others might have on their minds. He got as far as interpreting the officer's raised eyebrows as interest and thought that he should continue.

'No one else was to blame or involved. That's important. When I saw Mr Woodville after all these years, I couldn't believe my eyes. It had been so long and I thought that I was over what he did. I suppose that you never put aside what's happened to you as a kid, especially when it's something so bad. He was a nasty piece of work, you see. I knew that I had to do something, so I did.'

He paused, at first expecting and indeed then hoping that the officer would stop him talking.

When he saw the detective was about to speak, though, he knew that he had to get the words out so he said in a rush, 'I did it. I told Albert Woodville I was going to kill him. I suppose you're going to nick me now?'

'You told him that you were going to kill him?' asked Tom. 'When was this?'

'Right before he died.'

Even as Leon gave his answer, he knew he had said the wrong thing to the officer but it was too late now. His fate was sealed.

Chapter 54

Even as Tom said the words, 'I'm arresting you for the murder of Albert Woodville,' and began to caution his prisoner, he wondered if perhaps he was being a little hasty. The man in front of him didn't strike him as a murderer, just a bit of a sad individual who had come into the police station to claim that he had threatened to kill Woodville. Nevertheless, Tom knew Edwards's name as Toby Carvell's alibi for Woodville's murder, and the chances of him not being responsible or involved in some way were extremely unlikely. Especially after he voluntarily came into the station and told him that he threatened to kill their murder victim.

What had really tipped the balance was the nervous, sweaty way the man, now his prisoner, conducted himself. Tom knew he had to get him into custody without the very large individual stumbling upon the notion that he wasn't going to allow himself to have his liberty taken away after all, especially by someone half his size.

What Tom realized was that, if he had the murderer standing in front of him, it was most certainly his lucky day. His suspicion of the man's guilt was almost confirmed when following the caution Leon said, 'I never actually told you that I killed him.'

Regardless, he followed Tom towards custody where the officer began the tedious process of booking him in and explaining to the custody sergeant exactly why he had made an arrest for murder, before Leon was searched and led to a cell to await interview. His only comment was once again, 'I never actually told you that I killed him.'

Tom and the uniform sergeant exchanged a look at these words before Tom went off to explain to his detective inspector what had unfolded within the confines of the police station. It had, all in all, been an unremarkable arrest although the officer was already planning in his head how he could talk this one up to his colleagues. Detectives, after all, went in for a lot of swinging the old blue lamp. It passed the time between investigations.

It would have been difficult for Tom to deny that he was relishing having been the one who happened to answer the phone to the front-counter staff at that moment. The request for an officer to speak to the member of the public who had decided to drop into the police station about a murder was the best bit of luck he'd had for a while. He knew it was no more than luck that he'd been in the right place at the right time, but he felt the spread of excitement at the thought of going to tell the senior investigating officer that there was a man in the cells who might be responsible for taking another's life.

As ever, talking to someone suspected of killing brought out mixed feelings: on the one hand it was thrilling, on the other it was disturbing because of the sheer horror of the act of finality involved.

He made his way back to the Major Crime offices and through the incident room to the conference room. He hesitated for only a moment before opening the door and stepping inside to tell the entire team, SIO and all, what had happened only metres away from them. He didn't want to show off, but it wasn't every day he got to announce to everyone that he had made an arrest for murder. He decided against calling Harry Powell outside so that he could tell him in private. After all, it was a briefing. Surely his next step would have been to tell everyone else anyway. It was impossible to brief an investigation team without filling in the details.

All eyes turned to him as he pushed the door open, stood at the front of the room and said, 'Sorry to bother you, sir. The man we've been looking for, Leon Edwards, has come to the front counter and said that he threatened to kill Albert Woodville shortly before he died. I've arrested him for murder and he's waiting in the cells now.'

If Tom had been expecting a fanfare, he was disappointed. He wasn't even sure that he saw surprise flash across the DI's face.

'Come on in and take a seat,' he said. 'Oh, and well done. Want to tell us any more about it?'

Tom took a seat and ran through his mind everything that he so far knew about Leon Edwards. The realization that he knew very little hit him full on. He stumbled on his words and struggled to have anything further to add to what he had already said. Then it dawned on him that, in fact, he did.

'His reply after caution and again after he was booked into custody was . . .'

Tom read the words from his notebook, although he knew full well what they were. 'Leon Edwards said, "I never actually told you that I killed him."'

The young, keen detective was now beginning to think he hadn't minutes ago arrested the man who murdered Albert Woodville, but someone who perhaps made a habit of attending police stations and confessing to crimes he hadn't committed. It happened, although so far it hadn't happened to him.

As he was about to squirm in his seat, Harry Powell's voice carried across the conference room. 'Nice one, Tom. You made the right decision. As you all know, if Tom had allowed him to leave the nick, you'd all now be scouring the streets of East Rise trying to find him. Not asking too many questions was the right way to go.'

Harry rubbed his hands together and said, 'So what else do we know about Leon Edwards?'

'I recognize the name, of course, from the initial investigation.' DCI Barbara Venice had once again taken a seat at the back of the room behind Gabrielle, unknown to Tom, as she had remained silent up until that moment.

He glanced back at Harry, who had an air of surprise. Tom wasn't exactly sure why the DI should be so mystified by his superior's comments, and then it hit him. Barbara Venice wasn't really anything to do with this investigation, yet she appeared to be on the periphery of all that the team did. The only way she could have much knowledge of Leon Edwards was if she had been reading up on the case.

That in itself wouldn't have been significant, as a DCI in charge of an incident room should have an insight into all investigations, although perhaps not knowledge of all the details; it was the look that Harry was giving her that piqued Tom's interest.

'Leon Edwards never claimed to have been a victim of Woodville's sexual offending,' said Barbara, 'although he was at the children's home with Toby Carvell and was subject to physical abuse and bullying. It's where he and Carvell met and as we already know they now have a window-cleaning business together.'

'I've just been reminded of something I need to check on,' said Harry. 'Who was finding out if they were the firm who cleaned Woodville's windows? It would explain how they knew where he lived, not to mention being aware from looking in through his windows of his failure to manage his sexual interest in children.'

Everyone in the room had spent more time than they'd wanted to examining the scene photographs and the CSI's virtual tour of every room in Woodville's flat. They didn't need reminding of the depths of depravity the man had sunk to.

'No, sir,' said DS Sandra Beckinsale who was sitting to his side. She nodded in the direction of Sophia and added, 'We checked that out after Sophia and Tom came back from their enquiries with Carvell. The contract for cleaning all the flat windows in both blocks is with a London-based firm won under a tender. Carvell and Edwards are local with a smaller round.'

'OK, so no prizes for guessing who'll be interviewing today then, Tom,' said Harry. 'Possibly tomorrow too, depending on what Edwards has got to say for himself. Soph, you able to do that with him straight after the briefing? We shouldn't be much longer here.'

He got a thumbs-up in answer to his question and continued speaking to his team.

Tom tried his best to pay attention but he was preoccupied with his imminent interview and the task of establishing exactly what Leon Edwards knew about Woodville's murder.

His thoughts were interrupted by the DI saying his name again.

'What you missed, Tom, when you were making the arrest, was that DC Hazel Hamilton, our newest member of staff, and Pierre, went to Sussex early this morning to investigate what appeared to be a suicide from six months ago. Dean Stillbrook was found hanging from a tree after being acquitted of the rape of an eleven-year-old girl, Monica Lewis.

'It seems that it wasn't suicide, what with the illiterate Stillbrook writing a suicide note and stuffing it in his pocket before he hanged himself on the way to work. When Hazel and Pierre got to her house this morning, Monica was there and told them that she'd made the whole thing up. They're with her now. The problem we have, other than dead bodies popping up, is that if someone killed Dean in an act of what they considered to be justice for raping a child, they were very much misguided.'

He stopped and scanned the room.

'I don't need to remind you that taking the law into your own hands is a very dangerous way to mete out justice. People en masse will panic and mob rule always ends badly. If Leon Edwards is part of that mob rule, he's going to prison. No pressure though, Tom. Let me know how you get on.'

Chapter 55

Getting drunk was always Ian's default setting. He left his sister's house in something of a mood and started to walk home. He turned down a lift from Dave, preferring to be by himself. He recognized the warning signs that he was about to get himself into a state and would find it difficult to lift himself out of it.

He couldn't help it. He had spent many years of his life looking out for his sister, and when during the Clive years he didn't have to, he'd allowed himself the luxury of relaxing. The best way for him to do that was through alcohol.

His route home took him past six pubs, seven if he went twenty metres out of his way. He pushed open the door of the first one he came to.

The bar was empty except for two men sitting at a table by the window. Ian noticed that one was much larger than the other, who seemed nervous and was clutching a cup and saucer. Their heads were bent together and they seemed to be going to some lengths to keep their conversation secret. It wasn't difficult in the deserted public bar and Ian wasn't interested in anything they had to say.

He propped himself against the sticky bar top and ordered a pint of lager and a large Scotch. Neither lasted very long.

By the time he was on his third pint, Ian thought it was probably time he sat down. He hadn't eaten all morning and the effects of the alcohol had taken hold. He scanned the bar for a seat where he could still make it to the counter for service without anything blocking his way. Lately, he had been refused further service in several pubs after falling over the furniture and he felt the need to drink in this particular one until he was so intoxicated he wouldn't remember being thrown out onto the pavement.

He chose a seat at the table in the window recently vacated by the two men he hadn't noticed leave. He pushed the discarded empty pint glass and cup and saucer to one side and left his mobile phone on the table.

The lagers and Scotch had taken the edge off his mood and he was now at the point where he wanted to talk to Millie but wasn't quite prepared to return any of her three missed calls. He hadn't even summoned the energy to listen to her voicemail.

Now he felt ready.

Ian, please call me back. I'm worried about you. You looked upset when you were here earlier. Dave's gone now but he's also concerned. I know that the whole mess with ... with Albie is horrible. You seem to have taken it harder than me and I took it badly ...

There was a hesitation in her voice and he sat with the phone pressed to his ear, eyes focused on the bubbles rushing to the surface of his dwindling pint, as he waited to hear what she had to say next.

Ian, I need you to tell me that you had nothing to do with Albie's death. I'll believe you if I hear it from you. Please, don't have done anything stupid, especially on my behalf. I love you ...

The last three words brought the tears that he had been trying for so long to hold back.

Memory was his worst enemy so that made alcohol his friend. It helped to block out what he'd had to endure for so many years. Millie couldn't know, she could never know. She knew that he watched out for her, especially since Clive's death, but the one thing he wanted to keep from her was his own childhood sexual abuse.

It was beneath the surface of everything he did, and although he fought so hard to stop it defining who he was, it most certainly had shaped him, angered him and urged him to watch out for his sister.

It had started when he was ten and his sister was six. He still remembered the uneasy feeling he had the first time the family friend had babysat for him and Millie. He couldn't understand why he felt so odd in the man's presence. Ian had nothing to base it on and no idea he could be in danger in his own cosy home, so he put it down to one of those things and went off to bed when he was told to, after brushing his teeth and getting changed into his pyjamas.

Late that night, Ian had heard his bedroom door open.

He sat up in bed and rubbed his eyes, hoping that his mum and dad had come home early and it was his mummy coming to kiss him goodnight and tuck him in.

The silhouette of a man, clearly not his father, appeared in the doorway. Ian didn't suspect anything was wrong at first, then the uneasy feeling returned. But here was an adult and they took care of children. At least they always had in Ian's world up until that point. It was the day his life changed.

'This will be our secret,' he said to Ian, who was petrified at what was happening. 'It's part of growing up. Everyone does it.'

He wanted to stop it, he tried so hard to resist but what could a ten-year-old boy do to stop a fully grown man?

'You have to keep this our secret,' was the threat. 'If you tell, your parents won't believe you. They'll send you away and it'll leave your sister all alone. She's only six. You wouldn't want that, would you?'

The thought of leaving Millie to this man's mercy was even more horrifying than what he was going through. Surely if he could do only one good thing with his life, it was to look after his little sister.

She was always a ray of sunshine, and at the tender age of ten, he already felt that he had the weight of the world on his shoulders.

Twenty-five years later and that feeling had never gone away.

Chapter 56

'At least this address is on our way back,' said Hazel as she concentrated on the satnav on the windscreen. 'Do we know any more about Charles Culverton than the checks Sandra Beckinsale ran through with us a moment ago?'

'Don't think so,' said Pierre as he ran an eye over his own paperwork. 'I wasn't really expecting to do this today. Before we got here, I thought that we'd spend a lot longer with Monica and her parents once she got home from school at four o'clock or so.'

'I know what you mean. I thought that Harry was wasting our time a bit, making us leave so early. I realize that he didn't want the rest of the department, other than the enquiry team, knowing what we were off to do, but I expected to sit around most of the day, and then finish very late.'

'Can't believe that someone used some common sense though,' said Pierre, still thumbing through his own notes. 'They actually applied some thought to having us see two people in the same county. Bet it was Harry himself.'

'Remind me again,' said Hazel. 'Charles Culverton was at the home when?'

'He was at Cuxington Children's Home from 1975 until 1985. He was five when he went there and left when he was fifteen. The notes were incomplete so we're not sure where he went after that. He's got no previous convictions and his address shows nothing of note, except he was burgled about seven years ago. Quite a lot stolen.'

As Hazel drove on she asked Pierre a few more questions about the running of the department and he made her laugh on more than one occasion. By the time Hazel pulled up outside the address, and they both got out of the car, she felt as though her working day so far had been one of the more interesting and varied.

'Nice drum,' said Pierre as he gazed up at the cream façade of a beautiful home nestled in the woods. The gently sloping road they had followed meandered through the trees in such a leisurely fashion that neither of them realized they were climbing so high or that they'd be met with such magnificent views.

Hazel breathed in the fresh air and ran an appreciative eye over the green, lush landscape. Gentle hills were visible the other side of the canopy of trees and several of the fields were dotted with grazing sheep.

'Charles Culverton certainly did OK for himself,' she muttered. They had parked some metres away from the house on the wide sweeping driveway so she didn't think anyone would hear her, though she thought to herself that if she lived in such an isolated spot one of the first things she would do would be to install CCTV cameras. This was no doubt the police prudence in her.

Paperwork in their hands, the two detective constables crunched their way over the driveway to the door, knocked and waited.

Just as Pierre raised his hand to knock again, they both heard the sound of the door being unlocked.

A man of about forty-five, tall and slim with greying hair, dressed in trousers and a golfing jumper, opened the door, glanced from one to the other and said with a smile, 'Hello.'

'Mr Charles Culverton?' asked Pierre. 'I'm Detective Constable Pierre Rainer and this is Detective Constable Hazel Hamilton. Sorry to bother you. We're here on an enquiry about Cuxington Children's Home.'

The transformation of his face was instant. Their words had lifted a veil.

He went white and lost his composure for just a fleeting moment.

'You had better come in then, officers,' he said after taking their identification from their hands and studying it for some time.

'I wanted to make sure that you actually are police,' he said, 'and not reporters. That happened once. It upset the wife. Not the reporters, but my reaction to them.'

He led them along a vast, open hallway that reached back several metres with a number of doors and a staircase leading to other parts of the house.

'Nice place,' said Pierre as they walked along the carpeted area, more corridor than hallway. 'What do you do for a living?'

'I worked in finance in the City for more than twenty years,' Charles Culverton said over his shoulder as he pushed open a large wooden door at the end of the hall. 'I was very lucky and made enough money to semi-retire and work from home when I need to.'

All three of them stood inside the entrance to a beautiful room, almost the entire far side of it made of glass with stunning views of the countryside. The sun streamed in, throwing light on the furniture and décor.

'That's some scenery,' said Hazel as she took in the view.

'I've done well for myself,' said their host. 'Please take a seat and tell me why you're here. I must admit that I'm curious to know why, after all this time, two officers who have travelled some distance from the look of your warrant cards have knocked on my door with regard to Cuxington Children's Home.'

He sat back in an armchair, which probably cost more than every item of Hazel's furniture collectively, and listened.

'Well,' she began. 'We know that you were at the home as a child and that you gave evidence in the trial against Albert Woodville.'

She saw Charles shift forward and cross his legs.

Probably an involuntary movement, perhaps a nervous reaction, she couldn't tell.

'When did you last see Albert Woodville?' she asked.

He rested his elbows on the arms of the chair, placed his fingertips together and said, 'It would have been the trial. I went along and did my bit. I had no idea how I came across, and no idea how the others had done. The police didn't tell me and I didn't want to be there for the entire thing. I was told that I could go along for the verdicts, but I have to admit that I . . .'

He looked out of the window, an expression of concentration playing on his face.

'I don't know really,' he continued. 'I did my bit and I wanted no more to do with it. There were many children at the home, boys and girls, who came from terrible backgrounds. My own story was simply that my mum couldn't cope with so many of us after my dad died. It's ridiculous to think that I ended up in a home because of that, but I did.'

Charles looked back towards Hazel and smiled. 'I don't have much to complain about though. I got a good education, qualifications, left school and went to work in a bank. I know that I was one of the lucky ones and I have Cuxington Children's Home to thank for that, in a way.'

He paused again and turned his attention to Pierre. 'I was sexually abused in the home by Albert Woodville. It was the worst time of my life, obviously. All the time it was going on, I kept thinking to myself that I was going to get out of there as soon as possible and make something of my life.'

Once again, he gave a smile, but one without happiness. 'I loved school and learning. The teachers at school were fantastic and a couple showed me how to study for exams, helped me with job applications, one even came with me when I had my interview at the bank. I felt so sorry for a lot of the kids at the home, and I knew that some would be fortunate like me and some wouldn't. That's a sad part of life. I don't feel smug about it, although I'm glad I wasn't one of the unfortunate. Makes me a bad person, doesn't it?'

Both Hazel and Pierre shook their heads. 'No,' said Hazel, 'I think it makes you lucky, as you've said. However, above all, I think that it makes you remarkable.'

He tried to bat the comment away but Hazel felt compelled to say something else. 'There are some who would have given up. You chose not to. That takes determination. Everyone's different and I don't want to imagine how I would have fared in your position. I like to think that I would have gone on to make something of my life. I can't say.'

'Life's not fair,' said Charles. 'I know that I might have come across better to the jury at Woodville's trial because I'd been working at the bank for a couple of years, I had a good suit on, I hadn't been in trouble with the police. I can't talk for the rest of them who gave evidence, but I know that some of them were younger than me, some by a few years. How well they came across, I don't know. It's who the jury believe at the end of the day. They chose to believe what I said happened to me, and they chose not to believe a couple of the others.'

'Did you know the others?' said Pierre.

'I knew Rochelle Harbour,' he said. 'She died of cancer some years ago. I also knew Andrea Wellington, although I haven't seen her since I left the home. She attempted suicide at some point. I'm not sure what happened to her. The other two, I didn't know.'

The sun went behind a cloud and the room suddenly took on a gloomy feel.

'I'm not sure there's much more I can help you with,' he said. 'It's not that I want to be rude, but my wife and son will be home soon. She doesn't know about any of this, you see. We've been married for twenty-two years, together for twenty-four years, and I've never told her that I was sexually abused in a children's home and gave evidence at a child molester's trial. It's not something I ever talk about. It's why I slung the reporters off my property.

'If she should come back and you're still here, would you humour me and tell her that you're here to give some crime-prevention advice? She's always on at me to get some more security installed.'

'Of course we will,' said Hazel. 'All we need to know now is your whereabouts on Friday night.'

'I left the house with my wife at six o'clock. We drove to Arundel, met some friends for dinner at seven o'clock in the Winchester Arms and left there at about nine-thirty. We're in there fairly often, so they know me and should be able to confirm it. Can I ask why?'

'Albert Woodville was murdered on Friday the fifth of November,' said Hazel.

'Oh,' said Charles Culverton. 'I'm not a particularly religious man, but I hope that he's burning in hell.'

Chapter 57

Sophia and Tom sat side by side in the farthest corner of the incident room, she at the computer typing furiously, he leafing through sheet after sheet of paper and occasionally reading something out. Now and again she put her hand up to stop him so she could check she had recorded everything accurately.

'Are we almost done?' she asked. 'I think we've got most of what we need.'

'I think so,' Tom replied. 'I'd rather get down and interview him as soon as—'

Sophia looked away from the screen to find out what had distracted him. Her eyes were drawn to Gabrielle who had walked across the room and was unpacking two plastic carrier bags of cakes and doughnuts. She was placing the unopened packets on the communal table reserved mostly for the office diary and the collection of unwashed, germ-riddled mugs that lived there until someone was desperate enough for a drink and carted them off to the kitchen.

The only other things Sophia had ever known to find

their way to the table were items of food purchased for the incident-room staff's general consumption.

This had the hallmark of Gabrielle making an effort.

'Is it your birthday, Gabs?' called out Tom.

She looked across, a packet of greasy, sugar-coated goodies in her hand. She held them in his direction and said, 'No, but I thought it's Monday, so why not? Jam or custard?'

'Who buys custard doughnuts?' muttered Sophia, earning herself a warning look from Tom.

'I'll have a custard one, ta,' he said as he stood up.

'Stay there,' said Gabrielle, 'you've got enough to do.'

She strode across, a selection of wrapped cakes in her arms. She put them down on the desk in front of the two DCs and, concentrating on arranging the packets in a perfect line, said, 'I bought them before you arrested Leon Edwards. They won't keep you going all day but I can go out and get you both something else if you haven't had lunch if you like.'

'Well, we, er, thanks,' said Sophia. 'I'm not sure, that, er—'

'That's really kind of you,' said Tom. 'We'll see how we get on and perhaps give you a shout later, if that's OK?'

He ripped apart the wrapping and made a grab for a custard doughnut.

Gabrielle watched him as he took a bite and gave her a satisfied smile, or as much as he could manage with his mouth full of one of the unhealthiest but most loved snacks to be found in East Rise Police Station's incident room.

She hesitated before she took herself away from Tom and Sophia, compelling Sophia to call out, 'Thanks, Gabs. Really kind of you.'

Sophia watched her give a little wave over her shoulder and disappear down the corridor.

'Go on then,' said Tom, turning to Sophia. 'I know that you can't wait to say something unpleasant about her. I'm sure you'll find something.'

'I like her skirt,' said Sophia, but couldn't resist adding, 'even though there's not much of it.'

Tom mumbled, 'Give me strength,' and returned to his paperwork.

Chapter 58

Evening of Monday 8 November

'Take a look at us couple of hell-raisers,' said Josh Walker when Harry came back from the bar with a pint of lager shandy and an orange juice.

'I've already had a pint and I've got a feeling that I'm going to have to go back to work this evening,' said Harry. 'Even so, I fully expect a flurry of phone calls. I've told the interview team to give me a ring too.'

'Can I ask how it's going?' said Josh. 'I saw that you'd nicked someone.'

Harry took a sip of his orange juice, pulled a face and said, 'Really? What's the point of orange juice in a pub unless it's got vodka in it?'

'Want me to get you one?'

There was a slight hesitation before Harry answered, 'No ta. Best stick to this. The murder? It's an odd one all right. Young lad on the team, Tom Delayhoyde, made an arrest of a bloke this morning who came into the police station and said that he'd threatened to kill

Woodville just before he died. Got to be fair to Tom, when I first met him, I wasn't sure that he could detect his own arse with two hands, but he's done well on this one.'

'Technically, if you threatened to kill someone and then killed them, you've committed a threat to kill but the bigger picture is clearly that they're now dead.'

'That, Josh, is why you reached the lofty heights of inspector years before I did.' Harry rested the base of his glass in his palm and turned the glass around. 'It's times like these I wished I smoked. At least I could get some enjoyment from this vitamin C. I could have done with a straightforward murder. Those lucky bastards at Riverstone have just picked one up where the whole thing's on CCTV. Not me. I have to get the nonce with a cable-tie around his throat, possibly linked to a bloke who apparently committed suicide who obviously didn't. Throw in an arson for good measure and then this bloke today coming in and telling us that he threatened to kill Woodville.'

'What's he said up to now in interview?'

'Tom and Soph hadn't got all that far when I left,' said Harry. 'By the time they took his DNA, samples and clothing, they'd had one interview where he said that his only involvement was sending death threats through the post to Woodville.'

'Any reason?'

The look Josh received in answer made him smile. He knew that Harry was about to rip into him for what was clearly a stupid question.

'Because the man thought it was OK to rape children. That's usually enough. What's wrong with you?'

'I get that, Harry, but it's not like sex offenders are a dying breed. If anything, they seem to be flourishing. What I meant was, why Leon Edwards and Woodville? What's the link between them?'

'Years ago, Edwards was at a children's home which was run by Woodville. Also at the home was Toby Carvell. He's someone we've already been out to see and something doesn't seem quite right there either. Carvell was part of the original enquiry into Woodville when he was sent down in the nineties. The only problem was, Woodville was acquitted of offences against Carvell.'

'How about Leon Edwards? Was he part of the original investigation too?' said Josh.

Harry shook his head. 'Reading through the notes, he claimed that Woodville beat him a lot but nothing sexual. He didn't even make a statement. It doesn't seem right that nothing happened to him as a child, yet much later he decides to send death threats to a man he hadn't seen for over twenty years.'

'So what's the next step?'

'The usual forensic run with stuff going off to the lab, left, right and centre. Woodville took the letters he got in the post into the nick and gave them to Laura Ward. She was the ViSOR officer keeping an eye on him. We've had a conversation about what a high risk he was but she did all she could to find out who sent the letters.'

'Fingerprints?' asked Josh.

'Nothing on the envelopes' contents so someone was being careful. The outside isn't helpful as it gets handled by God only knows how many people until it gets to its destination. We are, however, talking about a bit of a fuckwit who decided to lick the seal on the envelope. All we need to do now is determine whoever's DNA it is by finding a match. The envelope went off ages ago to the lab but matched nothing already on the database. Might turn out to be Leon Edwards's now we've got a sample from him.'

He pushed himself back in his chair and smiled. 'What would that actually prove? We've got someone who's now dead being threatened weeks before their murder. If the person sending the threats is the same person as the murderer, the threat to kill is too minor to worry about. If the offender isn't one and the same, how are we going to prosecute? Woodville won't be coming to court to give evidence to say how scared he was.

'We have enough of a problem getting jobs home at court when the victim's alive, let alone a fucking corpse. Can you see us even getting a charge authorized for this?'

'Leon Edwards may accept a caution,' said Josh.

When they both stopped laughing at this, Harry asked, 'One for the road?'

'You're willing to suffer another orange juice?' said Josh.

'It's either that, go back to work – and I'm probably

going to out of sheer nosiness – or go home to the wife. I'd rather sit here and talk about detecting this murder. It's more cheerful than being at home right now.'

'Sorry to hear that things are still so bad indoors. Have you made any decisions?'

Harry pondered his answer. He knew that he avoided thinking about his domestic set-up but on the rare occasions he was asked a direct question about it it at least started him off on a train of thought, even if he didn't always feel comfortable with it.

He rubbed at his stubble with both hands, recognizing it as a sign of thinking too deeply for his own good. One hand was habit, two were a bad omen. He preferred not to cogitate, especially when it came to his wife. He didn't like the idea that his marriage was struggling because of his work. Better to blame the fact that his domestic arrangement was far from blissful, so he was forced to spend so much time in the office.

It wasn't his fault then.

He opened his mouth to ask Josh how things were with him: he had meant to ask him, when his phone rang.

Harry saw Tom Delayhoyde's name appear on the screen and answered. He could hear the excitement in the DC's voice.

'Boss, great news. Leon Edwards is talking, as you know. He admitted to sending the death threats through the post simply to put the frighteners on Woodville. He's still insisting that he did it alone but when we pushed him on whether he'd ever been to Woodville's flat or knew where it was, he went very quiet to begin with. Then came the good part.'

There was a pause whilst Tom got his breath back.

'He said that he was in the area near to Woodville's flat on the evening he was murdered. He saw Woodville come out of the Co-op and walk home. It looked like a car was driving slowly up and down past the victim. It only did it twice, something we probably hadn't picked up on yet. Edwards thought it looked odd.

'I'll grant you, boss, it could be because he's clutching at straws but right at the moment, we're reviewing that bit of CCTV footage.'

'It's a start,' said Harry, 'but have we got any chance of identifying the car or the occupants?'

'We've got the CCTV from the Co-op,' said Tom. 'The really brilliant news is that a bus goes past Woodville as he's about to turn the corner to his road. We've got the CCTV from the bus and it shows someone in the car, though it's a bit grainy. I've got to get it enhanced, but I think we should be able to get the registration at least.'

'Fucking hell,' said Harry, 'you bloody genius. I'm on my way.'

Chapter 59

The day had been an interesting albeit difficult one for Hazel. Pierre had seemed out of sorts too, although he spoke on the journey back about Charles Culverton, and also about Monica Lewis's big revelation with an openness that Hazel couldn't seem to muster. She admired him for the common-sense stance he took when it came to children telling lies and not knowing how much trouble they could get someone into, but every time she pushed the girl's admission from her mind up sprang the image of Dean Stillbrook hanging from a tree.

By the time they got back to East Rise Police Station, she didn't know which she wanted to do first: vomit or take a long hot shower. At least she had come across someone who proved there could be survivors of childhood sexual abuse. With that thought she managed to salvage something good from her day.

The two detectives trudged up the stairs to the incident room and dropped their paperwork off on their desks.

'You get off home,' Hazel said to Pierre. 'It's only your first day back from your holiday. I wanted to have a chat to the DI if he's still about.'

'Are you sure you don't mind?' he said. 'It was an early start, though at least we didn't end up staying overnight. I was happy to book into a hotel, but I'm even happier to be going home.'

'Yeah, goodnight and thanks for your company today,' she said. 'I'll catch up with you in the morning.'

She waited until Pierre had signed out in the diary and made sure that there was no one else around before she took the short walk along the corridor to Harry Powell's office.

Even as Hazel stealthily made her way along the worn blue carpet-tiles, she wasn't entirely sure why she felt the need to ensure she was alone. It wasn't as if she was doing anything wrong by wanting to speak to Harry on his own. She tried to rationalize it and paused outside the disabled toilet when a thought hit her. She wanted to talk to him because she had him down as someone she could confide in and trust.

Such a perception about someone she had only met fourteen hours ago was an extremely odd one. Few people gained her trust, even after years.

Either he was remarkable or she wasn't herself.

Disappointment hit her when she got to his door and realized that his office was empty.

A lamp was lit on the far side of his desk, illuminating the back corner of the small room where there was a small circular table with two chairs. One of the chairs had a broken arm and there was a hole in the carpet. The only thing in the room that gave the impression of being relatively new was the enormous whiteboard hanging on the wall.

Hazel stood for a moment, absorbed in the list of operation names written in black marker pen, some going back two years. Nothing from Operation Rotation 2015 to Operation Hydrant 2014 rang any bells with her, merely made her feel that the country was awash with crimes that most people either knew nothing of, or chose to remain ignorant of.

She heard a noise behind her and for a second she thought that Harry had found her in his office, lost in thought, staring at the wall.

'Hello,' said a voice. 'Are you after Harry?'

Hazel turned to see an older woman, attractive, kind face, smiling at her. Something about her said senior officer, although Hazel couldn't put her finger on what it was.

'I'm sorry,' she said. 'I'm DC Hazel Hamilton. I started here this morning. I can come back later.'

'I'm Barbara Venice. Have you got time for a coffee? I know that you and Pierre had an early start today.'

Her name rang an immediate bell, loud and clear. Hazel knew that she was talking to the DCI and if truth be told she was desperate to get away now that she knew Harry wasn't there. Even so, she didn't think it would do any harm to pass half an hour warming herself with a drink and chatting to her new boss.

'Thanks,' she heard herself say before she could change her mind. 'I'll make it.'

'No, I'll do it. Take a seat in my office and I'll be with you in a minute.'

'OK, ma'am. Milk, no sugar, please.'

Hazel followed the direction Barbara waved towards, having also guessed that the DCI's office would be where it had always been.

A photograph of what was clearly the Venice family took pride of place on the desk, confirming that Hazel was in the correct room. Hazel didn't have to wait long before she heard a woman's footsteps coming towards her.

'How was your first day?' said Barbara once she'd handed her a mug and they'd both sat down.

'Odd, if I'm honest.' Hazel blew on the coffee to cool it, although the benefit of instant water from a tap on the wall was that it was rarely too hot. Still, it gave her time to collect her thoughts. She decided to keep her forthright attitude under wraps until her feet were firmly under the table.

When it was clear that Barbara expected her to expand on her comment, she continued. 'It was hard going today speaking to Monica Lewis. I've mixed emotions about the whole thing: on one hand, she's a petrified little girl who didn't know what to do when the balloon went up and everyone started to believe what she was saying; on the other hand, she did something so stupid, eventually she cost an innocent man his life by saying he'd touched her when he'd done nothing of the sort.

'It's the problem with one person's word against another's, isn't it? Monica was accusing Dean Stillbrook of something that wouldn't necessarily lead to DNA evidence, and certainly not in this case. Especially as it didn't happen anyway.'

Barbara sat and listened. She allowed Hazel to unburden herself of the day's events and after some time, said, 'Well, according to what's been happening in the cells whilst you've been in Sussex, it seems that we may have some progress on who murdered Albert Woodville. I've a sneaking suspicion that it may well be the same people who put a rope around Dean's neck and hoisted him into the trees.'

Hazel's eyes opened wide.

'Really? That's great news. We hadn't been told this. What's happened?'

'There was a vehicle seen near to Woodville as he came out of the shop minutes before he was murdered. Two figures got out and followed him. We've got a partial registration and we're narrowing down the owner. I think we'll have made some arrests by morning.'

'That's us set for another long day tomorrow,' said Hazel, memories of working through the night flooding back.

'Have you missed all this?' said Barbara. 'I doubt much has changed in the time you've been gone.'

Hazel hesitated to say any more but the long day with its mental strain and being new in the job meant she found herself letting her guard down.

She took a breath and said, 'The work's unique, I'll

say that much. I left Major Crime once because of a mistake I made. I failed to recognize the signs that one of my rape victims showed and she took her own life.'

Both of them sat and absorbed the weight and sadness of Hazel's words.

'I know it wasn't my fault. At least that's what I tell myself. It didn't stop me feeling bad and I can't help thinking that the eighteen-year-old girl would now be twenty-two. She might have got married, had a baby, I don't know, become a scientist and made inroads into the cure for cancer. Instead, a random man with no thought further than his own sexual gratification and the need to pretend that his own bloody miserable existence on this planet meant something, raped her and made her feel like shit.

'The physical act is bad enough, isn't it? A disgusting stranger with who knows what diseases forcing himself on you, but the constant, never-ending feeling that must stay with you morning, noon and night that something bad has happened . . .'

Hazel paused for breath. The feeling didn't escape her that she had probably said too much. And Barbara was the second person she had told in one day. The expression on Barbara's face was of mild concern, but largely interest.

'We all make mistakes,' she said. 'If someone goes through their entire life without making a mistake, they're either extremely lucky or a dictator. It can't happen that in thirty or so years of police work none of us will ever go wrong. It's impossible.'

'Can I ask,' said Hazel, 'what thought fills your mind and keeps you awake at night?'

A shadow passed across Barbara's face. It might have been the lighting but Hazel thought she recognized the flicker of a personal torment. The glance away, sideways to the left, confirmed to her that she wasn't about to get the truth.

'There have been a few, you know,' she said with a liar's smile. 'There's no single specific thing but now and again I remember something I hesitated to pass on, or recall that I left an enquiry for a day longer than I should have. As SIO, I have to make bigger decisions, follow my instinct and lead the team in a particular direction. I suppose that I wouldn't always know if I'd got it wrong. Take one pathway and you're never going to know where the other one would have led.'

They sat in silence for a second or two: Barbara knowing she had said something that was completely untrue and Hazel suspecting it.

'You're right about not blaming yourself,' said the DCI, 'though I doubt that my words help. Every victim of crime reacts differently, especially to something as serious as rape or child abuse.'

'I know and I expect that's why I found today so tricky. It would have been bad enough if Dean Stillbrook had committed suicide, but the fact that he was murdered for something he didn't even do ... that young girl is going to have some serious issues in her later life. Something that huge will always come back to haunt us.'

Chapter 60

'Tell me a bit more about who you saw following Albert,' said Tom to Leon that evening.

He sat on one side of the interview-room table, Leon opposite him and Sophia to the side. It was the third interview, and the fourth time Leon had turned down the opportunity of having a solicitor present.

If truth be known, Tom would have felt more comfortable with a brief there. He couldn't insist but he had never known a prisoner suspected of such a serious crime as murder to go it alone.

Leon's bulk took up most of his side of the table and his backside was hanging over both sides of the wooden chair. He was dressed in police-custody-issue grey tracksuit bottoms and top, the largest size they had. Both were stretched to capacity and almost required a trip to the shops when nothing they had in the store seemed to fit. The jailer managed to rummage in the recently laundered returns and save them a dash into East Rise High Street's many discount clothes shops.

Only once had Tom known a prisoner to decide that he wasn't going to be interviewed and walk out. His money was on Leon seeing it through to the end, although he didn't fancy his chances of stopping him if he chose otherwise. The man was massive.

Fortunately, he also seemed to be passive with it.

'Look,' said Leon, picking up one of the three paper cups of water he had been supplied with, 'I came in here to tell you that I'd sent Mr Woodville death threats through the post. It's not something I'm proud of. It was poxy stupid of me. I know it now and knew it at the time. He was a total git to me when I was a kid but I wouldn't kill the man.

'The size of me, it wouldn't take much to hurt him but I know that two wrongs don't make a right. I wasn't going to tell you about the bloke in the car I saw that night. I may not be the fizziest cola in the fridge but I do know that I've just put myself near his flat on the night he was killed. I couldn't help myself. I knew where he lived and I wanted to see what he was up to. He lived near to a school and there's always kids hanging around those shops. I suppose if I saw him talking to kids or doing something he shouldn't be doing, it would've made me feel less shitty about sending him death threats.

'I feel bad that someone's killed him, though I can't say I feel any sadness that he's dead.'

'The bloke?' asked Tom.

Leon's forehead creased and his eyebrows became reacquainted.

'Now you mention it, fella, it must have been a bloke in the car.'

Out of the corner of his eye, Tom saw Sophia smirk at the suspect calling him fella. Tom had bigger issues than what the prisoner was calling him. He needed details. They helped detect murders and put those responsible inside.

'Tell me about him,' said Tom.

He watched Leon as he put the paper cup down and screwed his eyes shut.

'He was driving slowly, it's why I remember the car now, though it's the first time I've thought about it.' He paused and opened his eyes. 'I probably shouldn't be telling you any of this. I followed Mr Woodville and I know that it's not right what I did, but driving past a bloke's flat one time, that's not a crime, is it?'

Leon put the question to no one in particular and the only response he got from Tom was a shrug. He didn't want to interrupt his prisoner.

'I can't help you any more than that. I felt uneasy being there, watching him, like I was doing something wrong. I didn't take a lot of notice of anyone else because I needed to get away to meet Toby.'

He threw himself back in his seat, tiredness showing in the dark rings under his eyes, now with a gentle crease around them as a smile played over his mouth.

He didn't strike Tom as being particularly intelligent, although he had to admit he was getting to like him. He hadn't given them any cause for trouble and had walked into the police station of his own accord.

And now he was here, wearing himself out trying to help them find the identity of Woodville's killer.

Perhaps it was too good to be true. Tom had seen *The Usual Suspects*.

He couldn't argue with the CCTV from the number 72 bus, something they might not have got round to looking at for some time if it hadn't been for Leon. Eventually, someone would have viewed it along with about two hundred hours of other footage, and that might have taken weeks depending on what other murders, kidnaps and stabbings had come their way, constantly pulling staff in a myriad of directions. Leon's arrest had saved them days: something he would never know.

'Is there anything else you can tell me about the car or driver?' said Tom. He was aware that Sophia had sat forward in her seat, a sign that she was ready with her mop-up questions when Tom had asked his last.

'No, no, fella,' he said with a shake of his head, jowl wobbling. 'I'm sorry. That's it from me. If I could think of anything else, I promise I'd tell you. I wouldn't have come in here and fed you half a story about Mr Woodville and the threats I made. I wasn't going to mention the night he died, but now I have, I've let you have the lot. I'm certainly not someone who'd jump straight on the nines and call you lot if there's a problem but now I'm here, why would I hold back?'

He shrugged, his ears disappearing under his enormous shoulders, neck nestled in his chest.

Sophia moved into Leon's eyeline and tilted her head to one side.

'Leon,' she said, 'other than when you saw Albert Woodville on Friday the fifth of November, the day he died, when was the last time you saw him?'

It was a flash of his eyes to the empty paper cup in front of him and a rapid licking of his lips that Tom took in.

'Saw Mr Woodville?' Leon said, voice dropping a level. 'Blimey, I'm not too sure of the date. Toby saw him in town before I did, and be clear on this, he had nothing to do with what I'm telling you I did. I, I suppose I saw him in town a week or so after Toby warned me that he was about and that was what started the whole thing off. As I said before, it was seeing him wandering around, seeming not to have a care in the world.'

'What was he doing that last time?'

Another ear-swallowing shrug.

'Nothing really, love. He was walking around the shops. Hang on ...'

A frown so deep engulfed Leon's forehead it was more trench than lines.

'Of course, of bloody course. That was the start of it.'

He pointed his index finger at her.

'He was carrying a Toys 'R' Us bag. I can't believe I'd forgotten that either. The dirty, dirty fucker. Oh sorry, sweetheart.'

Sophia waved away his apology.

'That's why I followed him. He went to a café and ordered a drink. I went inside and asked for a sandwich, not really knowing if I'd get it and finish it before he left. Obviously, judging from the size of me, eating it in one mouthful wasn't too much of a challenge but I didn't know how long I'd have to wait for it to arrive. Anyway, I thought I'd leave it to chance and besides, that's not important. I got the grub, and he was still sitting there.

'That was when I started to wonder what I was doing. I suppose I wanted him to see me and recognize me. Perhaps if he'd have come over and chatted, explained, apologized for the crappy way he treated me, I might even have felt differently. I would never have forgiven him but it might have made things a bit better. Oh, I don't know.'

He leaned forward and put his head in his hands, elbows resting on the table.

'I thought of moving away to another part of the country. I didn't do anything wrong though, did I? I didn't suffer as badly as some of the kids at the home, and there have been other places he was messing around with children, so I read in the paper. That particular time I saw him in town and he went to the café, I remember it was a cold day. For October, the weather was really on the turn. In my line of work, you're always on the lookout for rain and when it freezes it cracks the skin on your hands.'

He held out his massive hands to demonstrate what that looked like. Both detectives stared pointlessly at his palms.

'Anyway,' he said, 'what I'm saying is that it was cold that day. Two men came into the café. I was sitting at the back and there wasn't much room. People taking a break from the cold. They'd warned there'd be a frost and I keep an eye on the weather. Have to, you see. It's important for our job.

'The two who came in couldn't sit at the back. I'd taken the last table. There seemed to be a bit of a problem between them and one wanted to go out again, but the other insisted they stay. I couldn't hear, only see. They were standing between me and Mr Woodville. It's the only reason, I think, that I noticed them.'

He paused, his face strained.

'Maybe it's because I've not let myself think about it,' he said. 'I waited until Mr Woodville was ready to leave, made sure I'd paid my bill so I didn't draw attention to myself and the fact I was about to follow him, when the two blokes made towards the door as if they were leaving too.'

From the expression that Leon was sporting, he thought that a revelation. Tom wasn't so sure.

Just as Tom was about to break the bad news to him that two men walking out of a café weeks before Woodville's murder wasn't necessarily relevant, Leon gave the best bit of information to date.

'The thing was, a woman walked past the café with two young kids, a boy and a girl, I think, and Mr Woodville rushed out. The two men in the café looked so worried. One of them went to the toilet downstairs and it was only a couple of seconds before the other one joined him. It made me think that they knew the woman but didn't want her to recognize them. I'm not sure if it's important but I thought I should tell you.'

Both Sophia and Tom maintained the Home Office-approved po-faced expression on being given the best bit of news so far.

'It's possibly important, Leon,' said Tom. 'Leave it with us and we'll look into it.'

Inside his heart was singing.

Chapter 61

One thing was for sure, Hazel was glad that her first shift back in Major Crime was over. She was tired and it had been a long day. For the first time since leaving the house that morning, she was able to relax.

She was pleased to be home and to have the time to appreciate simpler everyday things, such as opening her front door and a seeing a pile of letters lying on the doormat. They were real, tangible things that had been posted through the letterbox by a real person.

And there was something in there that she had been hoping for.

Kicking off her shoes and picking up the post in almost one motion, she forced the front door closed with one of her stockinged feet and sat on the bottom stair, mail on her lap. She ripped open the envelope in question and scanned the letter.

Hazel had waited for some time now for a building quote for an outside kennel. She had enough money saved for a modest run in the garden, but had held out for the right person, and the right price, so that she'd get exactly what she needed for overnight emergencies.

Despite the preoccupations of the day, there had been a small part of her brain set aside to fret about what it was going to cost her to give dogs a temporary home when their owners were fleeing from domestic violence.

She didn't want to dwell on the real reason why it was such a relief to see that she could afford the kennel, which was that dog fostering was a way of putting her mind at ease over the death of Vanessa Meaden.

She crumpled the letter in her hands, held it to her chest, head bent.

The ferocity of her sobbing surprised her. By the time she'd sat listening to her own heart breaking for what seemed to be an eternity, she felt worn out, but a little less angry at herself or the world.

There was nothing she could do about Vanessa's death; and she couldn't prevent Vanessa's husband – who by now must have served his time for killing his wife – from finding another victim of domestic abuse. But what she could do was play her tiny part in helping other women, other families escape from a dangerous and volatile home life.

And if she took pleasure from that, and from canine company, surely everyone benefited.

Chapter 62

The day had been a strange one for Dave Lyle.

Now he sat in his lounge, lights off, television on mute, third can of lager in his hand. He popped the top and guzzled almost half of the drink in one chug.

All his motives for visiting Millie were valid, he felt. He cared for her and she had been through a horrible ordeal, but he would be kidding himself if he didn't admit that part of the reason he had gone to see her was to establish exactly how vulnerable she was. Finding out about her boyfriend's sexual offending, and then his murder, had indeed weakened her resolve. The last thing he wanted was any more harm to come to her, although he couldn't deny the feelings he still had for her.

It made him feel as though he too was a sexual predator but he had always admired her from afar, a little afraid of her rejecting him. He had hung back for far too long and when Clive came along, he knew that he had missed his chance. Begrudgingly, Dave had really taken to Clive. He had been that sort of person. Even if Dave had been seeking out reasons not to like him, he would have been hard pushed to find one.

Then there was the Ian factor.

Ever since they had met and become friends at school decades ago, they had looked out for each other. There had been something a little reckless about Ian, not that Dave was able to define it at the age of eleven when they were thrown together in the first year of their secondary school. It was a place that had seemed very daunting at the time, although they would never have admitted it then, not even to each other.

They had kept an eye out for one another, but as the years went by it was usually Dave who was reining in Ian, and the favour wasn't often returned.

The pattern of his friend's behaviour had become as familiar to him as the taste of the lager that was hitting the back of his throat now, although it was doing nothing to take away the memory of the day's events. The look on Ian's face that he had seen today in Millie's kitchen, he had seen countless times before. No one single act or comment appeared to spark the reaction, and Ian had explained that even he couldn't put his finger on what it was that made him feel so exposed and raw, and then angry and resentful.

That look was Dave's cue to help out his oldest and best friend who had always been there for him.

He shook the lager can from side to side, found it was empty and contemplated the walk to the fridge to get another. On the short distance to the kitchen, he smiled as he remembered the open-ended flight he had booked a few years back for Ian so that he could get away to Crete and try a new way of life, even if for only a few months. It had cost Dave his own holiday money, but that was what friends did for each other. It wasn't in his nature to turn his back on a friend in his hour of need.

Chapter 63

Tuesday 9 November

A very bleary-eyed Harry Powell opened that morning's briefing with a rapid check around the room of who had turned up. He knew that Sophia and Tom had finished late and probably got no more than three hours' sleep each, but both looked very good on it, and Pierre and Hazel had returned from Sussex much earlier than expected, via Charles Culverton. He was pleased to see that Gabrielle had taken his advice and was nowhere to be seen.

He still made a mental note to get someone to call her as he didn't want her to forget she was part of the team and think she was out of their thoughts as soon as she was absent.

'Morning,' he said at the same moment he realized he didn't have enough staff. One was on maternity leave and the flexible working arrangements meant that two of his DCs didn't work on Tuesdays. He would have to ask DS Sandra Beckinsale to rustle up more officers, although heaven knew from where.

'A fair bit happened yesterday after our midday get-together. Some of you know what Leon Edwards told us about the car and two men acting oddly in the café. It may be relevant, it may not be. Someone get the CCTV from the town centre. Often they keep it for a month or so, so we may still be in luck.

'The car from outside the Co-op is a silver Renault Clio from the looks of it and we've got a partial registration of EA52. Intel have run some checks overnight and whittled it down to a list of several thousand, merely hundreds in and around East Rise. We'll start local and widen it as we go. There are obvious links to Sussex on this investigation so we're getting some assistance from them too. Any Clios with the same partial registration as our vehicle are a priority and the analyst has been tasked with putting together a chart, updating it as we get the results.'

He paused to scan his investigation team. Some were writing, most were looking at him, awaiting his orders. He had been in their position many years ago, sitting in the briefing room, wondering what the day would bring, guessing what role they would be given, and some keener to stay on well beyond their eight-hour shift than others.

'Any questions so far?'

Silence. A few shakes of the head.

'OK, good,' he said. 'There are several lines of enquiry that Sandra will be allocating today. Any links between the Clio and the mystery café men will be, in police speak, a right fucking touch.

'In the meantime, I've listened to all that Tom and Sophia have told me about Leon Edwards. The upshot being the absence of a feel for him as Woodville's murderer. However, he hasn't given a plausible account for why he was following him and why he was outside his flat on the night he died. His mate in all this, despite Edwards's insistence he was alone on Friday evening, is Toby Carvell. We know that later on Friday evening the two of them were together. This plus Carvell being one of Woodville's original victims – who the jury chose not to believe – leaves only one option.'

Harry took a breath, and said, 'I've raised Toby Carvell to suspect status. He needs to be arrested on suspicion of Albert Woodville's murder and then we go back and visit the other remaining victims of sexual abuse from the 1990s.'

He looked at Hazel. 'I know that you and Pierre started this yesterday. I'll have to leave the rest to you as I've got no other staff. I'm ruling nothing out, including the possibility that even those who saw Woodville convicted for what he did to them might still have some sort of grudge as regards his further offending and what they perceive as leniency by the courts.'

'Actually,' Hazel said, 'apart from Carvell, who's getting arrested, we've seen one. One's dead and so that only leaves two. One of them was a not guilty against Woodville, the other a guilty.'

Harry thought about it for a couple of seconds and then said, 'There's a chance that one of the five of them, including Toby Carvell, had something to do with our victim's death. We still need to make sure that Rochelle Harbour is dead. That'll make us look bloody stupid if she's alive and killed him. Let's see what they've all got to say unless you get any strong feelings otherwise. Anyone got anything else they want to bring up?'

Harry went around the room asking each member of his staff, including police officers, civilian investigators and the HOLMES staff and typists. He listened to suggestions, complaints about not having enough resources and pleas from those in charge of the tea fund for everyone to pay their subs, and then the room was suddenly empty except for him and Barbara Venice.

'How's tricks, Babs?' he said.

'I remember all five of them, you know. It was my one and only brush with sexual abuse of children at ground level. It wasn't something I ever wanted to deal with but I did my best, despite it not ending in a conviction for everyone involved.'

'Think through our legal system,' said Harry. 'There's a murder, the police are called. Trained crime scene investigators turn up, gather the evidence, send it to a lab where scientists in sterile conditions work away and return their findings to the police. The investigators, in the meantime, gather the evidence with their years of experience and detective training, liaise with the Crown Prosecution Service and fully qualified barristers who've cut their teeth on thefts, assaults and robberies, and then what happens? We take twelve random people off the street, say "have a look at this" and they say guilty or not guilty.'

'Do you have a better system, Harry?'

'Not one that the civil liberties people would let me get away with. Listen, my point is that you can't predict or legislate for what untrained, random strangers are going to do. We'll never know why the jury didn't return a guilty verdict for Toby Carvell or—' Harry hesitated. 'Shit, I'm embarrassed. I can't remember who the other person was the jury didn't convict against.'

'His name was Russell Wilson,' said Barbara, no pretence at having to trawl her memory for him. 'The other three, as you know, were Charles Culverton, Rochelle Harbour and Andrea Wellington.'

'We'll find out a bit more when Hazel and P ring back in,' said Harry. 'The possibility that they all got together and did it hasn't escaped me completely. The only thing so far to disprove that is the DNA returns aren't showing very much at all and the only fingerprints the senior CSI found were Woodville's. Common sense says that, if four or five of them had done it, it would look like a DNA bomb had gone off in there.'

'Or more likely, someone wouldn't be able to keep their mouth shut.'

'Once again, it seems that we're at the mercy of the

public telling us what's gone on. I only hope that Hazel and Pierre come up with something whilst they're out.'

'Are they starting with Russell today?' said Barbara.

Harry made no comment on the fact she'd referred to a crime victim from twenty-five years ago by his first name.

'Yeah. I thought it was the best place to start as he'd be the one with the most to feel aggrieved about, and he's only about half an hour away.'

'He'll be a good place to start. He was always very accepting of what happened to him at the time, although how he's coped over the years is anyone's guess.'

Chapter 64

'What the fuck do you want?' were the first words from Russell Wilson's mouth when Hazel and Pierre knocked on his door and introduced themselves as police officers.

'We'd like to come in and talk to you about Cuxington Children's Home,' said Hazel, standing her ground.

The transformation of his face was completed in an instant: it went from a mask of anger and hatred to one of torment. Hazel put him at the same height as her, five feet nine inches, and with the physique of someone who spent a lot of time weightlifting.

His biceps were straining at the sleeves of his T-shirt, and made to appear a little more menacing by his hands clenched into fists.

They were by his side but very visible from the corner of her eye.

His mouth hung open slightly and he dropped his shoulders, stretched his fingers out and considered his options.

At the point where it was looking as if the door was

about to be slammed in their faces, he said, 'Suppose you'd better come in then.'

They followed him to a sparse lounge with a tiny wooden table and single chair pushed into the corner. The window was covered by a blue bed sheet nailed up below the empty curtain rail and an old television set sat on a bowed coffee table opposite the two-seater sofa.

Russell Wilson stood in the kitchen doorway staring at them both, arms crossed. He took up most of the doorway although Hazel noticed that the washing up was draining behind him and she had certainly been in worst-kept flats.

'What do you want?' he said and then immediately began to grind his teeth, chest visibly rising and falling beneath the taut cotton top.

'We know that you were a part of the investigation into Albert Woodville in the 1990s,' Hazel said. 'When was the last time you saw him?'

'That worthless piece of shit? Let me think. Oh yeah, it was the day he was found not guilty of what he did to me.'

This didn't seem to be the same man who had opened the door to them and cursed in their faces: he was beginning to crumble in front of their eyes.

'Is it all right to sit down?' said Pierre, as he headed in the direction of the dining chair, leaving the other two to take the sofa.

'You haven't seen him or heard from him since the trial?' Hazel said.

'I heard from him all right,' said Russell. 'He fucking well wrote to me from prison. He had the neck to tell me that he forgave me for telling lies.'

He choked up at this point, voice catching on a bad memory, the beginnings of a sob forced into a shout, probably to cover his embarrassment at being caught leaking emotion.

'Do you know what got me the most?' he asked, although neither officer attempted to answer. 'He wasn't even very nice to me when I was at that bloody home. Some of the boys he played about with at night, they got toys and games, taken out for meals after he'd done what he wanted with them. You could tell who his next victim was, even if the shock all over their face wasn't a total giveaway. They'd be the ones with the new football or a train set or something to keep them quiet.

'So what's the nasty bastard done now? You wouldn't be here otherwise.'

Hazel said, 'He's dead. He was murdered.'

There was a momentary appearance of surprise, followed swiftly by Russell throwing his head back and laughing.

'Please tell me it was slow and painful. That would make my day. You have no idea what that bastard did to me. I'm not only talking about physical stuff, but how he messed about up here too.'

He put his hand up to his head and tapped his temple with his finger.

'He was a horrible, manipulative man. I bet he

begged for his miserable life, saying it wasn't his fault and he didn't do anything wrong. I had to hear all that bollocks at the trial, despite being told it wasn't a good idea I sat in and listened.'

After an uncomfortable silence, he asked, 'So why exactly are you here?'

'Did you have anything to do with his murder?' asked Pierre.

Russell sneered. 'No, of course I didn't. I have to be honest, I wish I did. For years I didn't know what to do. I went from Cuxington Children's Home to another one that was much better, but I couldn't settle. The staff there tried their best but I didn't want to know, didn't want to talk to adults again. One had already abused me and hurt me, lied about what he'd done and now I was back in the system that had let me down in the first place. I was lost and I have been for years, but it never for one moment made me want to go and kill the evil son of a bitch.'

He stopped talking and sighed. 'He really messed me up. It's not only the thought of him touching me and making me do stuff to him that got inside my head, it was other stuff. For years I thought I was gay, I even had a relationship with another man. It didn't work out, probably because I'm not gay. At least I don't think I am. I've struggled with relationships with women too.'

He picked at his thumbnail. 'I doubt that I'll ever lead what people call a normal life. I've been in trouble with the police, although you probably know that. Done a bit of drugs too. I thought it would make it better. It didn't of course. The problem was still there when I came round and remembered how fucked up I was. How am I supposed to get over what happened all those years ago if I'm still reliving it on a daily basis?'

Hazel knew that whatever she said next would sound crass, but she went ahead anyway.

'Have you tried talking to anyone about what happened to you?' She kept a close eye on his reaction. 'I mean someone professional who might have been through the very same thing?'

'No, love.' He gave a long slow breath out and said, 'Perhaps I should. The last few weeks have been OK. I got a new job and thought I'd make a clean slate of things. I couldn't face going in today. I was all right until last night when the newspaper headlines caught my eye on the way home. They were about children's homes shutting down, though not because of perverts caught with their hands in kids' pyjamas, but it still freaked me out. I called in sick, so here's hoping they still want me in tomorrow.'

His face formed a smile. Hazel couldn't bring herself to mirror it.

'I can leave you some leaflets if you like,' she said as she opened her file. When no objection was forthcoming, she took out pamphlets from three different charities and handed them to him.

'Thanks,' he said. 'If I'm upfront with you, I wasn't even going to let you in. I fucking hate the police. You let me down.'

'We're glad you decided to talk to us,' said Pierre. 'Any chance we can really push our luck and get a statement from you?'

For the first time, Russell gave them a genuine smile. 'You're a couple of cheeky sods, aren't you? This is what happens when you cooperate.'

It took Hazel some time to get the information she wanted from him, but the longer she spoke to him, the more she warmed to him. It was always impossible to establish exactly what someone was thinking, but up until her rapid exit from Major Crime she had prided herself on being a good judge of what was going on inside someone's head. It was something she rarely trusted herself with these days.

In spite of that, he seemed to be giving them a cast-iron alibi for where he was on the evening of Friday the 5th of November.

'So there were seven of you in the Smugglers' Inn on Friday?' said Hazel.

'Yep, straight from work at four p.m. and I left with two of the others at about half ten. I was pissed as a handcart but walked home as I didn't think a cab would take me. Besides, it's only about a twenty-minute walk back to here.'

Hazel knew that it was at least twenty-five minutes' walk to Albert Woodville's flat from the Smugglers' Inn. It still needed checking out, although it appeared highly unlikely Russell Wilson could have sneaked out after a couple of hours of drinking, strangled Woodville, and then rushed back. And they suspected that two people had carried out the murder.

Even so, trust no one, believe nothing.

When they had all they wanted, including Wilson's fingerprints and DNA, Pierre and Hazel stood up to leave.

'Is it OK if we come back, Russell?' said Hazel. 'In case there's anything we've forgotten.'

'Course you can, although I hope to be back at work tomorrow.'

'And good luck if you decide to make a call.'

She turned her gaze to the leaflets left on the arm of the sofa, encouraging him to look at the same thing. Above all, Hazel wanted to leave him with the thought of asking for help.

Back in their car, Hazel sat in the passenger seat, running her hands down her face.

'That's a big sigh,' said Pierre. 'Never mind Russell Wilson, are you doing OK?'

'The more I hear about Albert Woodville, the more I'm glad he's dead.'

'I don't think you're alone in that, his killers aside.'

She turned in her seat to watch Pierre's reaction when she said, 'If I'm truthful, I don't want to find who murdered Woodville. One less sex offender on the books.'

She was disappointed to see that her colleague exhibited no sign of outrage, just gave a smile and said, 'We don't get to choose whose murders are worthy of our dedication: they all are. Besides, what if whoever killed Woodville also killed Dean Stillbrook, the innocent man?'

This was something that sent a chill down her spine. Hazel shivered, despite the suit jacket she was wearing and the heating turned up to the highest setting.

'You're absolutely right,' she said. 'Mob rule gone wrong. We've already seen where that can lead. It's that all this is getting to me more than I want people to know. Not you. You strike me as trustworthy.'

He smiled at her and said, 'I'm not one to argue. Where to next?'

Hazel opened her file to check the next closest address and automatically got her phone out of her bag.

'Missed call,' she said. 'It was on silent. It's from Harry.'

She sat listening to his message, hung up and said, 'We can definitely cross Rochelle Harbour off the list. He's had it confirmed that she died of cancer four years ago.'

'Was she the one in Yorkshire?'

'Yes, that's her. Married with three children, owned her own restaurant according to Harry's message.'

'Let's head for Andrea Wellington next. She's only about ten miles past Riverstone.'

Hazel didn't say very much on the journey to their next port of call. She didn't fail to notice that as Pierre drove them past Russell Wilson's flat, he was standing at the living-room window, watching them until their car was out of sight.

Chapter 65

Afternoon of Tuesday 9 November

Things were troubling Toby Carvell. His life revolved around his family, business and Leon. His oldest and best friend. With no family of his own to count on for as long as he could remember before Shirley had come along, he had relied on Leon.

As soon as social services took him from his abusive father, his older brother and younger sister were also removed from his life. It wasn't part of the deal; they merely disappeared into the ether. Leon filled the hole they left in every respect.

Toby was putting one foot in front of the other with little thought as to what he was doing. The streets he walked along took him from his home, blurring into one as he made his way towards the heart of East Rise, through the newer, modernized part with its department stores and restaurants and out onto the other more rundown side. He was moving automatically, in a daze.

Leon was his hero. He always had been since the first conversation they had shared. His admiration for him had ballooned the more he got to know him.

The path that Toby now walked was one he was familiar with. East Rise had been his home town ever since he first met Shirley and she insisted they move there to be near to her family. It was essential to her that her mum was near by for when their children came along.

The smile on Toby's lips didn't register with him as he made his way to Gallery Street. The thought of Shirley's announcement all those years ago that they were going to start planning for a family together hadn't fazed him in the slightest. They had only been dating for three weeks.

He went out and bought the ring the very next morning.

He felt a pain when he thought of how Leon had let him believe for all these years that he had suffered the same horrendous sexual abuse at the hands of Woodville. Toby had tried to cast his mind back to what Leon had told him Woodville had done to him.

That was the thing with sexual abuse: it made the victim, the perfectly innocent victim, feel like the one who had done wrong. Like they were the one with something to hide. Who wanted to shout from the rooftops about what had happened to them? Or about what they perceived they had allowed to happen to them.

It was so perfect for the perpetrators of these crimes that they went undiscussed, repelling even their very victims. If no one dared speak its name, it didn't exist.

Except it did.

Toby couldn't allow himself to contemplate what else might be happening up and down the country.

His own children were safe. That was a start.

He stopped, ran his tongue around his teeth, a nervous habit, and stepped towards the automatic glass doors of East Rise Police Station.

If the woman on duty felt any surprise at the words of the man standing feet away from her, albeit on the other side of her safety net in the guise of a raised counter, she certainly didn't show it.

'My name's Toby Carvell. I need to speak to someone about the murder of Albert Woodville,' he said in a rush, with no discernible breath.

'Take a seat please, sir. I'll call someone for you.'

Toby had no idea that he now occupied the same seat that Leon had picked only the day before.

He sat and waited, sure that it wouldn't be long before he was in the cells.

He leaned back, head resting against the wall, and closed his eyes, replaying last night's local news in his mind. *Police have confirmed that they've been granted further time to question a thirty-seven-year old man in connection with the murder of Albert Woodville. Their enquiries continue and they aren't ruling out anything at this stage ...*

He knew that it was standard television-speak but

this time it related to someone he knew. That someone was a lifelong friend.

'Toby Carvell?' said a voice. He wanted to play the part so he counted to four, opened his eyes, uncrossed his ankles and said, 'That's me, darling.'

'I'm Detective Sergeant Beckinsale,' said the owner of the stern voice. 'Would you come through?'

He got to his feet, followed her to a side room and was about to speak when the door behind her opened and a man Toby guessed to be in his late thirties walked in.

'Hello,' he said. 'I'm Pierre Rainer, a detective constable here at East Rise Police Station. Please take a seat.'

Detective Sergeant Beckinsale walked out of the room and Toby couldn't help but notice that the look on the detective constable's face was a picture.

Toby was about to make a comment when the door opened again and a blonde woman walked in.

'Sorry about that messing around,' she said. 'I'm Detective Constable Hazel Hamilton. The sergeant was waiting until I was free.'

As far as Toby was concerned, he couldn't care less if he spoke to a sergeant, inspector or the chief constable. All he wanted was to tell someone what happened.

'I need to tell you that whatever my mate Leon Edwards has told you, I was there too.'

He half expected the two detectives to exchange some sort of glance. Instead, the man moved towards the door. It hadn't escaped Toby's notice that it was the one behind him that led onto the street and his freedom.

'Take a seat,' were the woman's only words.

Now he was here, he wasn't entirely sure how things were going to go, but he wasn't leaving until he had told them what he came to say.

'My friend, Leon Edwards, is here,' he said, switching his stare from one impassive face to another. 'Whatever he's told you he's done, I've done it too.'

This was the moment that they actually did exchange glances.

'What do you mean by "whatever he's told you he's done, I've done"?' asked the male detective.

'Well, it's obvious, isn't it? About Albie Woodville. Me and Leon, we did it together.'

It took a few seconds for the matter to sink in with the two police officers in the room with him, but the woman was the first to her feet.

'I'm arresting you on suspicion of the murder of Albert Woodville.'

She only got a few words into the caution when Toby said, 'Hang on. Murder? Oh no, no. It wasn't murder. He wasn't dead. He was still alive.'

Unfortunately for Toby, the door he tried to let himself out of needed a pass card, something that he didn't have. He thought about struggling, making a run for it. He was the one who had walked in voluntarily. All he had wanted to do was support his friend, not get arrested for murder. The shock had hit him as soon as the officer told him what the reason was for his liberty being taken away. Fighting wouldn't look good. Toby understood that. He surrendered to his circumstances after a brief pretence of trying to get back out again to the public area at the front of the police station.

It took only seconds for the two detectives to escort him to custody where he allowed himself to be searched and put into a cell. His momentary panic left him and was replaced by despair.

Things were not going according to plan now. Toby didn't imagine for one minute that Leon had confessed to murdering Woodville. He knew that his friend wasn't blessed with intelligence but he wasn't entirely stupid.

At the first opportunity, Toby got himself a solicitor who told him to wait until she got there before saying anything else to the police.

As he waited for her arrival, he sat himself on the bench in his cell, read the graffiti, used the toilet and then ran out of things to do. He tried listening out for sounds of Leon but then wondered what on earth he was listening for. They would hardly be torturing him or beating him up. So far the police officers he had seen were no match for Leon and as for the jailers, they had the word *Civilian* embossed on their uniform. Surely they wouldn't punch a prisoner.

He glanced at his watch, one of the few things they had allowed him to keep. Only half an hour had passed. He was going to have to keep an eye on himself as he was aware he was already beginning to think total nonsense.

Eventually the door opened and he was led to a room and introduced to his solicitor. Some hours later, they had finished discussing what Toby had done. Now it was time to tell the police about it.

The two detectives from earlier took them to a police-interview room and Toby watched them unwrap the DVDs and put them in the recording equipment with a kind of detached fascination. On more than one occasion, he had to remind himself that this was indeed happening to him, a married man with his own business, and in spite of not having had the best start in life someone who'd always been on the right side of the law and had never been stopped by the police or caught speeding. Now he was under arrest for murder.

After what seemed like a long time, the woman detective spoke. She went through question after question about his legal rights and his welfare and then at last, they got down to business.

'OK. 'You're under arrest for the murder of Albert Woodville, Toby. It may sound like an odd question, but what's your understanding of murder?'

He held his hands up in the air. 'Yes, it is a·stupid question. It's when someone kills someone but I didn't kill him. Neither did Leon—'

His solicitor intervened. 'Toby, don't concern yourself with Leon.'

'Yes, yes,' he said. 'I know. When I got nicked I said me and Leon did it together. I think I need to explain—'

Once again, his solicitor cut across him. 'You know my advice, Toby.'

'Yes, thanks, I do, but where Leon's concerned, I'm not going to sit here and say no comment to everything Hazel asks me.'

The somewhat dowdy-looking legal representative raised an eyebrow at the familiar use of the very attractive interviewing officer's name. It was something that Pierre noticed, only Hazel herself seemed oblivious to it.

'Go on,' was all she said.

'We didn't kill him, we didn't even hurt Woodville, the horrible fat bastard. Sorry about the language, love.'

His solicitor put her pen down.

'Oh, you and all,' Toby said. 'I'll tell you a bit about me and Leon. We met years ago at Cuxington Children's Home. He looked out for me and kept Woodville away from me. There were a couple of occasions when he physically stood in between me and Woodville and took slaps and punches that were coming my way. Up until very recently, I thought that Leon took a lot more for me too.'

Toby's eyes had begun to mist over. He continued with a catch in his voice.

'For years I've been under the impression that all those horrible things he did to me, he did to Leon too.' He started to rub his hands up and down his arms, shoulders hunched up to his ears, no eye contact now.

'I still owe him though. He went through as tough

a time as me, only in a different way. We used to talk about Woodville from time to time, how much we both hated him. Sometimes there were happier memories. It wasn't all bad. There were some other really good kids in the home. A lot of them were little sods but we used to play practical jokes on the staff, not Woodville, never Woodville, but a few of them were great. I always thought that they knew what was going on, only no one spoke about it. Things are a bit different now, but it's still the last taboo.'

Toby looked up into Hazel's eyes. 'We spoke about what we'd do to Woodville if we ever saw him again, and then one day, I did see him in town. I couldn't believe what I was seeing. He'd aged, of course, but it was him, as large as life.

'I'd gone into Pets at Home to look for something for my daughter's birthday, so I know it was about June time. She wanted a guinea pig, not that that's important but I wandered around the corner and he was picking out a dog lead. He's petrified of dogs. I remember that because I used to lie awake at night at the home, praying it wasn't my turn, and it would be some other poor little bastard's, and I used to fantasize that I'd buy a pack of dogs when I grew up and train them to chew his fucking face off. I never did though.'

Hazel gave a small smile.

Toby gave a big sigh, ran his hand across his brow and said, 'Couldn't help it, could I? I got straight on the phone to Leon. We met at the pub about half an hour later. I was a right mess. A fully grown man sitting in his local boozer on the verge of crying. I could barely put a sentence together. Have you ever heard anything more pitiful? Thing was, it took me right back there, see? I was seven years old again, a little petrified kid, being ... being interfered with all over again.'

For the first time in the interview, Toby looked across at Pierre who sat making notes, but glancing up from time to time.

'Leon was great,' said Toby. 'I wanted to go round and give Woodville a kicking right away. Leon pointed out that not only did we have no idea where Woodville lived, but also that we'd both end up in prison for it. We decided that we'd find out a bit more about him and bide our time.'

Toby glanced across at his solicitor. She repeated her advice to answer 'No comment' to the questions. Toby ignored her.

'We weren't ever going to kill him or physically hurt him, we were looking to put the frighteners up him. Send him some threats, so he didn't know where they were coming from. We wanted to cause him pain up here.' He tapped the side of his head. 'Just like he did to us all those years ago. The physical stuff was bad enough, but it was the lingering effects of what it did to my mind. That doesn't go away.

'We followed him a few times, tried to—'

'Toby,' said his solicitor, 'we've spoken about this. My advice to you is to answer "No comment" from now on.'

He sat and mulled it over.

'OK,' he said, 'but I don't want you to think I'm not cooperating. We followed him home and knew he had a routine on a Friday night when he went to the Co-op on the corner and bought some grub.

'I'm going to tell them this bit,' he said to his brief, 'and then no more. We talked about getting into his flat one night when he'd gone out, and then jumping out from behind the sofa or cupboard or whatever. I've never been in there so I don't know what furniture he's got. It was only to scare him, not beat him up and definitely not kill him.'

'When were you going to do this?' said Hazel.

'That break you mentioned at the beginning,' said Toby, 'the one you told me I could take any time I like, I'd like it now, please.'

Hazel set about turning off the DVDs and glanced over at Pierre. She had an idea that from here on Toby would choose to say nothing or very little in answer to her questions.

Her train of thought was interrupted by Toby asking his solicitor if they could speak in private and Pierre leading them to a consultation room.

When he returned, he pushed the door behind him and said, 'What do you think?'

'Mmm,' she murmured. 'I think that's all he'll say, but for a minute I thought that his brief was going to let him confess to a conspiracy to murder along with Leon.'

'I've dealt with his solicitor before. She's a pretty

switched-on cookie. I'm still surprised she let him say anything at all.'

'I don't think she had much choice. It was difficult to shut him up. Besides, it's usually the ones who have, shall we say, "limited intelligence" who struggle with the concept of talking to a point and then declining to answer. I thought he did OK, not that it takes us much further.'

'You're right,' said Pierre. 'He still hasn't said where he was on Friday night when Woodville was murdered. We know from the CCTV he was still alive at 6.20 at night and by the time the patrols got there shortly after eight o'clock he was dead.'

Toby and his solicitor's arrival at the interview-room door put an end to the officers' conversation.

As Hazel had predicted, for the rest of Toby's interview she and Pierre did most of the talking, with 'No comment' coming from the interviewee each time he was asked anything.

That was more than could be said for Leon, although at that very moment an unexpected alibi was coming his way. His luck was about to change for the better.

Chapter 66

The automatic front doors of East Rise Police Station opened once again on the fading afternoon sunlight, attracting the attention of the front-counter assistant. She looked up and smiled at the young woman walking across the brightly lit foyer towards her.

'Hello,' she said. 'How can I help you?'

'I need to speak to someone about Dilly, well, Leon Edwards. Everyone calls him Dilly, but his real name's Leon. He's here, isn't he?'

'I don't know. Who is it you want to speak to?'

'It said on the news that a bloke had been arrested for the murder of the old bloke in Pleasure Lane but I know it wasn't Dilly. Let me speak to someone about it.'

The incident-room phone rang and was answered by Harry. He didn't usually make a habit of answering other people's phones, but it was ringing on the desk he stopped at to talk to Sophia and Tom, who were taking a break from interviewing Leon.

'Really?' he said into the receiver. 'I'll get someone to come and speak to her. Thanks.'

'It seems,' he said to the pair sitting opposite him, 'that a woman has given your prisoner, Edwards, an alibi for Friday night. Go and see her, will you? She's at the front counter.'

'What's her name, boss?' said Sophia.

'Lorraine Butterfield. She works in some diner and said that Leon was there most of Friday evening.'

'Oh good,' said Tom. 'Shall we just let our prisoner go now?'

'Less cheek and less sarcasm, Thomas,' said Harry. 'She may be lying, or mistaken. Come and let me know, would you?'

Harry wondered whether his team would ever find out who had murdered Albert Woodville. He was certain that Leon Edwards and Toby Carvell had been doing more than passing by his flat to see how he was doing since his release from prison, but neither of them were daft enough to admit to planning to or trying to kill him.

At the moment, all he had was two men in custody, one admitting to sending death threats to a man who was now dead, and the other claiming some of the responsibility for it, possibly through misguided loyalty.

He made himself a cup of coffee and took the steaming drink to his office, glad of the chance to close the door and shut out the incident room. Only minutes before, he had heard that there was something else going on in East Rise and Harry knew that he wouldn't be able to hold on to his staff for very much longer. It was one of the curses of dealing with major incidents – they all demanded immediate attention.

The last thing he needed was to find Sandra Beckinsale waiting for him at his desk.

'Sandra,' he said. 'What can I do for you?'

'You can get me more staff.'

'No, I can't. Anything else?'

She handed him a printed piece of paper. 'Not sure if this is relevant to us or not. A woman living near the seafront was on her way to the shops on Monday morning when she saw a man throw what looked like a black holdall or rucksack into the water.'

She placed the sheet on the desk and they both stared at it.

'Want me to get someone to go and see her?' she asked.

'Yeah,' sighed Harry. 'I'm sure we've got another box of coppers somewhere. Haven't we got anyone?'

'Gabrielle's back.'

For a moment, Harry wondered if he should speak to Gabrielle himself before sending her out on enquiries but then reasoned that she wouldn't have come back to work after only taking a couple of hours off if she wasn't fully up to being there.

'OK,' he said. 'Send Gabrielle but brief her fully. I don't want her only knowing half the details.'

*

Having been brought up to speed by DS Beckinsale, DC Gabrielle Royston sat in Joyce Slattery's kitchen. Gabrielle hadn't really wanted to come in to work this afternoon but her mood was lifted by the view across the harbour from the woman's breakfast bar. She was aware that the witness was still talking to her, although she had to admit she hadn't been paying her all that much attention.

She wanted to get this right and put to one side her personal life and at the same time her outburst to Harry. Sex offenders would not be her downfall: she was going to do all she could to work as hard as possible to find the murderers, even if she really wanted to shake them by the hand. Gabrielle pushed the thought from her mind and smiled.

'Beautiful view to start your day, Mrs Slattery,' she said.

'It is, dear. I couldn't believe my luck when this flat became available. Hilda downstairs waited twelve years to get one of these at the top but then she had to get her hip done, and missed out. Anyway, that's not why you've come here. Biscuit to go with that tea?'

Gabrielle turned down the biscuit and concentrated on the task in hand.

'Where was I?' said the seventy-five-year-old widow. 'Oh, that's right. Most mornings, I'm up early at about 6.30. It doesn't get light until later now, so I put the light on, but I always turn it off when the sun comes up, to save a bit, you see.

'Anyway, I've got my set routine and I don't go to

the shops until just after nine. I wait until the school-children are out of the way and those going to work are wherever they're supposed to be, and then I leave. If I time it right, I'm out of the flat and on my way to the shops by five past. From habit, I lock the balcony doors when I go out. Daft, I know.'

She pointed her index finger at the glass balcony doors, five floors from the ground.

'Not daft,' said Gabrielle. 'It's sensible.'

'Anyhow, I locked the balcony doors as normal and, as I did so, I glanced down and saw a man throw a bag into the sea. He was the other side of that bus stop down there so I didn't get a good look at his face, and he was dressed in dark clothing. I could see, even from this distanceand with the rain coming down, he was quite a well-built man and if I had to say, I'd guess that he was a youngish fella. When I say young, I mean in his thirties or forties. That is young to me.'

She laughed and Gabrielle smiled.

'I don't know if it's of any help to you, but as they've sent someone out, and a detective too, I suppose it must be. Did you say you were from Major Crime? Is it important? Sorry, I shouldn't ask, should I?'

Gabrielle thought through her answer to the kind lady in front of her and stalled by taking a sip of tea.

'You never know,' she said in a non-committal fashion. 'I'm very grateful that you called. It's a good starting point – I can look into it further.'

Gabrielle left the flat with mixed emotions: she was

making inroads into an enquiry that she felt more passionate about not investigating than investigating. She understood that she had a job to do though, despite her doubts about the career choice she had made. She seemed to be fighting a losing battle when it came to separating her personal feelings from any ethics the police had tried to teach her.

At least it made her human. At least it meant she cared.

The rest of the afternoon she easily filled by making calls, attending locations and gathering exactly what she needed until she was ready to return to the incident room. She recognized it for what it was: she was keeping busy enough to stop her own grief from taking hold.

It was early evening when Gabrielle made her entrance at the incident room, and was at least cheered to see the DI and DCI Barbara Venice talking to the interview teams who were on a break.

'Gabs,' said Harry. 'How was the witness?'

She took a seat and smiled. She waved her paperwork at him. 'She was lovely, made me tea, has a great view of the harbour and so had a great view of a man chucking a bag into the water. I've got the CCTV, tracked most of the route he took to the seafront and back, and I'm pretty sure that I know who he is. The only thing I don't know is what he was throwing in the drink and why, although I could have a good guess at that one.'

The young detective surveyed the stunned faces of her colleagues. She couldn't help but feel a little superior and extremely glad that she had been sent out to work by herself that afternoon. This glory was all hers.

'Nice one,' said Harry, as he pitched forward on his chair. 'Don't stop there.'

'OK,' she said, as she unfolded a map of East Rise with the CCTV cameras marked on it. 'I picked this up today when I got the footage downloads. Wasn't sure if we already had one, but thought I'd get one to be on the safe side.'

As she smoothed down the edges of the paper, Gabrielle cast an eye in Harry's direction. He gave her a nod of approval.

'What I've been thinking about,' she said, 'is who's come into this enquiry so far whose movements we haven't accounted for on Monday morning. Toby and Leon were on their window-cleaning round, which started early, and we're bottoming that out. There are the two men in the café with Woodville, seen by Leon on a previous occasion, and then there are Jude Watson and Jonathan Tey. Watson's not a particularly big bloke, but Jonathan Tey is. And he lives here.' Gabrielle pointed to his street with the tip of her pen. 'He's already told us that he works from home some days, and Monday's one of them.'

'Fucking hell,' said Tom across the table top to Sophia. 'When me and Soph got to his house on Monday morning, he wasn't in. His wife said how strange it was that he'd gone out without his phone.'

'Bastard was trying to outsmart us,' said Sophia, cheeks tinged with pink. 'Hindsight's a wonderful thing, but when I think back on it now, he did seem to be acting a little defensively. I put it down to nerves at being spoken to by the police for a murder. I won't make that mistake again.'

'Listen, you two,' said Barbara, 'this is new information. We didn't know about a man lobbing stuff into the sea until Joyce Slattery called in last night. Don't fret over it, but I have to say, good work, Gabrielle.'

'Gabs,' said Harry as he put his hands behind his head and eased himself back in the chair, 'you've just made my day. All we need to do is get Jonathan Tey and Jude Watson arrested, find some sort of evidence and we're laughing.'

What Harry wasn't about to share with his team was that Martha Lipton had flagged the name Jonathan Tey up to him over twenty-four hours ago.

He trusted them not to leak the information but he wasn't about to risk anything going wrong. He knew how much rested on him getting this right, so what did it matter if he kept his team temporarily in the dark? A successful outcome was far more important than the danger of offending the ones who thought they had the right to know everything that was going on, whether it directly affected them or not.

The wheels were in motion: first thing in the morning, before the sun came up, two very experienced, no-nonsense teams of rapid-entry uniform officers would descend on the home addresses of Jude Watson and Jonathan Tey.

Harry couldn't help it. He indulged himself with a self-satisfied smirk.

Chapter 67

Wednesday 10 November

Harry's office overlooked the rear yard of the police station and he had a good view of the vans arriving as they brought the prisoners in to custody. Partly because Tey was of larger build than Watson, and partly because of the way he swaggered out of the back of the van, Harry could easily make out which of the two of them he was looking at. It was no mean feat for a man in handcuffs whose head was almost level with the roof of the transit once he was standing beside it. Harry saw him try to shrug off the hands of the uniform officer who led him to the custody security door. He couldn't help a smile to himself when he saw that the PC escorting him was Karl Roundtree, six foot seven and a very good match for Tey's size.

There was a conversation, short on Tey's part, and Harry saw the prisoner toss his head back and refuse to answer. He thought he heard Karl say something along the lines of, 'Get that looked at by the nurse.'

That was all it needed to get Harry's interest. He took his jacket from the back of his chair and left his office, heading in the direction of custody.

He knew that he had no actual reason for being in the cell block: he wasn't interviewing, he wasn't needed for any custody matters as they were being dealt with by Sandra Beckinsale, but he was nosy.

He let himself in with his security pass, stood in the time lock and waited for the external solid metal door to slam shut behind him before he attempted to release the inner cage door. All the while he was listening out for sounds of the prisoners being brought in from the holding area.

'Harry,' said a voice from behind the raised custody counter, 'what are you doing down here? You do know that you're a detective inspector? Are you lost?'

'Colin,' said Harry as he held out his hand for the custody sergeant to shake. 'Still keeping you in the dungeons, I see?'

'These two yours?' said Colin as he jerked his head in the direction of the holding cell.

'Yeah. They're not both in there together, are they? Don't want them talking.'

'No, Karl's keeping one in there but the other's been booked in already. You were too slow, old man.'

'You've put on a bit of weight,' said Harry. 'That gut of yours is probably spreading so fast because it thinks you're in perpetual hibernation.'

'I'm trying not to swear at you,' said Colin with a laugh, 'only because of the cameras. We can go out the back and I'll tell you what a tosser I think you are.'

Harry held up his hand as he heard the sound of an officer's rubber soles squeaking on the polished floor, in step with the inflexible tread of his prisoner's shoes.

The two approached the custody bench, arrogance running amok over Tey's face. Nevertheless, he stood awkwardly in front of the high counter, designed to stop prisoners, and no doubt police officers, from leaning on the ledge. The counter reached Tey's chest level, so he stood with his arms at his sides, glancing around from time to time. His gaze met Harry's.

Something about him wasn't giving Harry the impression he was Albie Woodville's murderer. Thug and half-wit, yes, but not paedophile murderer.

Harry moved behind the counter and stood beside the custody sergeant where he had no choice but to look down on the prisoner because of the raised platform. He took full advantage. Karl Roundtree caught his eye as he stood just out of Tey's line of vision. He glanced across at the officer who was tapping the back of his right hand with his left index finger.

Harry picked up on the cue immediately and took a step forward to glance down at Tey's right hand. He saw a large welt, not completely healed, on the back of it. In reply to the discreet signal, Harry gave a small nod to the officer and then stood back and watched the remainder of the booking-in procedure.

'Yes, I want a solicitor,' Tey said when asked, but said little else.

When Harry had seen enough, he made his way back to the incident room and did his best to muster his tired team.

He stood in the centre of the room, rubbed his hands together and said, 'As you know, both Jonathan Tey and Jude Watson are in custody. I watched Tey being booked in and he's got what looks like a cut to his hand. It doesn't appear to be that recent but it looks like a very deep and nasty wound, so you never know if it's going to be relevant.'

'Er, sorry, sir,' said Gabrielle, going her standard shade of pink when all eyes, especially the DI's, were on her. 'I took the statement from Eric Samuels, the chairman of the East Rise Players. He told me about a row that Jude and Jonathan had when they were cutting something out for the scenery and Jonathan cut his hand. He ended up blaming Jude for moving the piece of cardboard. His hand bled quite a lot at the time.'

The DI stared at her.

'It's all in the statement I submitted,' she said.

'All is not lost,' said Harry, determined to bolster the morale of his troops if it was the last thing he did. 'If he had that nasty cut and went round to Woodville's flat and murdered him, his blood may turn up there somewhere.'

'I don't want to piss on your parade, boss,' said Hazel from her desk in the corner, 'but if we don't find his blood, and the cut was bleeding badly, that points away from his involvement. Anyway, you said the cut doesn't look recent and Woodville's murder was only five days ago.'

He mulled this over for a second or two and said, 'We can ask the man. He may confess yet.'

This was met with snorts of derision from most of the office and he definitely heard one of them mutter 'Dream on'.

He wandered back to his office wondering where all the respect and optimism had gone from the police service. He made a note to ask Tom and Sophia why they hadn't picked up on a large injury to Tey's hand when they visited him at home.

'Is this a good time?' he heard someone say as he got to his desk.

'Joanna Styles, come on in,' he said to the senior CSI. 'Tell me that you've brought me some good news about the forensics on this job.'

'We've got three pounds ninety left in the budget,' she said.

He sighed. 'I'll ask for more money. Where has forty grand gone?'

'Forty? I thought it was fifty.'

'Oh, for fuck's sake. I look forward to seeing the chief with a telephone directory down my pants.'

'Is he a Mason too?'

'Very funny. What have you got for me to brighten my day, Jo?'

She settled herself in her seat and said, 'I've compared the boot marks we have from Albert Woodville's flat, particularly from the front door. As you already know, they didn't match Toby Carvell's or Leon Edwards's shoes.'

'Yeah,' said Harry. 'We've bailed them both out. The searches of their homes showed nothing new, Carvell told us where and when he parked his Ford Focus on Friday night and that checked out, even Edwards ended up with an alibi who came into the nick and vouched for him. All we've got on those two is a funny feeling that they know more than they're letting on.'

'I took their photographs in custody,' said Jo, scratching the end of her nose with her pen. 'Edwards didn't strike me as particularly bright.'

'That's another thing,' said Harry as he rubbed a hand over his stubble. 'Edwards couldn't live with the guilt of sending death threats in the post. That's why he came in here. It could be a double bluff, but I'm with you. I don't think he's got either the intelligence to plan a murder or the mental capacity to cope with the aftermath.'

'So,' said Jo, 'that leaves the two in the bin downstairs.'

'And so far—'

'I'll have to take a look at their shoes and stuff but if Jonathan Tey did throw the shoes in the sea, there's not much I can do about that. However, first look, I think that he's the wrong shoe size.'

Harry sat back and stared at her.

'So why throw your clothes in the Channel?'

'Well,' she said. 'We don't know that it was his clothes.'

'I don't know what else, other than a weapon, he would try to dispose of. The beauty of plastic cable-ties is that no one's going to call the police if they see some in a bin somewhere. A gun or a knife attracts attention. I can't rule anything out, but my money's on clothing.'

'But why?' said Jo. 'If he didn't murder Woodville, what reason could he possibly have for disposing of his clothes?'

'Let's hope the interviews shed some light,' said Harry.

Chapter 68

Toby Carvell pulled up in his Ford Focus on the opposite side of the road from Leon who sat in their company van, waiting for his friend.

Leon saw him give a small nod of his head, face in a grim expression, and get out of the car.

Things had not gone particularly well for either of them but at least they were out of the police station.

'All right?' said Leon as his friend opened the passenger door and climbed in.

'Been better, Dilly. How about you?'

In answer, he switched off the engine so that he could talk without raising his voice and turned his head towards Toby, still visible in the early evening's gloom. 'I can't believe they gave us bail conditions not to speak to each other.'

'I know. We run a business together. How can we avoid one another?'

Leon slowly blew the air out of his cheeks and said, 'Just as well we ignored them then.' He shifted his weight onto his left side and leaned against the steering wheel. 'I didn't tell them that you were there on the night Woodville died. I kept my word. I want you to know that.'

'I knew that you'd keep your word. I told them that you sent the death threats but neither of us was actually involved in killing the dirty bastard. If one of us had told them anything different, either we'd still be stuck in those bloody cells, or we'd have been charged with murder by now. We stuck to the plan, and it's working. It's why we had one.'

There was a pause as Leon thought how to phrase what he wanted to say next. After a couple of minutes of companionable silence, he said, 'Do you think about him dying much?'

'All the time, all the time.'

Toby left a short pause and then said, 'Daft question, but how about you?'

A short dry laugh followed by, 'You could say that. I don't feel bad that he's dead, just glad I don't have to worry about how I'd kill him, if that makes sense.'

'It makes perfect sense, mate,' said Toby, averting his gaze from his friend to watch the cars driving past. 'I thought for years about what I'd do if I came face to face with him. And then I did.

'It wasn't long before I started fantasizing over beautiful ways to end his life. You and me discussed it for weeks, planned it for months and waited outside his flat on all those Friday nights to watch what he did.'

Beside him, Leon nodded along, his mind in a happier place than it should have been as he allowed himself the luxury of reminiscing about all the hours he'd spent doing what he loved the most: being with his best friend. They had always been close, but no more so than when discussing how they were going to end Albert Woodville's days. Toby had been intent on doing away with him because of the pain, misery and abuse he had suffered at his hands. Leon had wanted to go through with it, partly because of his own physical abuse and mental anguish, but largely because of what he had seen Toby endure. He had wanted to help, to make things better for his friend, even if that meant plotting a murder.

'Do you reckon though,' Toby said to Leon, 'that we really could have?'

A heavy shrug from Leon. 'Don't know. How did you feel when we drove away on Friday night, knowing that the two men following him were likely to do to him what we'd been preparing for?'

'I don't know, Dilly. Part of me felt glad that we didn't have to do it ourselves, and part of me wanted to stop the car, follow them into his flat and help them kick the absolute crap out of him.'

Once again, Leon leaned against the steering wheel. He rubbed his eyes.

'But do you think,' he said, 'we would have helped them to kill him if we'd have known what they were going to do, or do you think that at the last minute we'd have stopped them and saved his life?'

The one thing that had been keeping Leon going was the belief that when push came to shove, at the final hour, he would have done the decent thing and saved a life, even if it was one as worthless as Albert Woodville's, recidivist sex offender. And because this belief had seemed like his salvation he wanted Toby to feel the same way.

'Can I ask you one thing before I answer that?' said Toby. He saw Leon nod, so carried on. 'Why did you send Mr Woodville death threats?'

This was an answer Leon struggled to formulate. He knew the reason but as so often he couldn't find the right words to express his feelings.

At last he said, 'To make him feel bad. To make him worry and wonder what was going to happen to him, like he did to us in the home. I wasn't ever going to hurt him, not with my fists.'

He cast his eyes down to his hands, massive against the steering wheel, chapped from his job and filthy from his time in the cells.

'That was always my point, Dill,' said Toby. 'I really, really wanted to kill the bloke. I was never sure that you were up to it, not in your head. You don't know how relieved I was when I saw those two fellas get out of their car and run in the direction of Woodville's flat. They'd been watching him, following him and running around in the dark dressed like that, well it was too good to be true.'

'But they killed him and we didn't tell the police what we'd seen.'

Toby reached out and put his hand on his friend's shoulder. 'They would never have believed us if we'd told them that we saw them following him to the flat. They would have wanted to know what you and me were doing there together. We were the closest they had until you dropped them a line about seeing a car. You see? Then they went looking, like good detectives, and found the car themselves. They feel better as they think they got a prisoner to talk, did some Scooby Do work and it led them further towards the actual murderers. All the while, we're off the hook.'

'We're still on bail.'

Toby let out a sigh and said, 'You're right, we are. And we're not supposed to be talking, so I'd better go. Do you feel any better now?'

Leon gave an unconvincing nod and said, 'Much. I'll do the window-cleaning round tomorrow and get you the van back for the next day.'

He watched as Toby climbed out of the van, crossed back over the road, got in his car, waved and drove off in the direction of his house.

He knew that he should feel relieved for getting it off his chest to the police, but once again, he had lied. For good reason, but nevertheless he had lied again.

When he'd told Toby the truth about Woodville's real treatment of him, he had felt purged. That was sullied again now. He couldn't afford to feel like this repeatedly, as if the troubles of the world were upon him. The one thing he knew he could never do was to confess to anyone the amount of time Toby and he had spent plotting and planning a murder. He knew that would get them into another fix with the law, and so, as agreed, he hadn't gone off script, just stuck to the plan.

Why then did he have the urge to return to the police station and tell them that it had all been a terrible mistake and he had more to tell them?

There was another thing he would never tell a soul. Toby's confession that he would have taken part in killing Woodville had sickened him to the bottom of his stomach. It was one thing to talk about taking a life, it was quite another to actually do it.

He had given Toby a chance to redeem himself, say it was no more than a big game like the games they had played in the children's home when it all became too much. But instead Toby thought he had the right to take away someone's life.

Their relationship had crossed a line and things would never be the same again.

Chapter 69

He sat alone in the dark, only his thoughts of retribution keeping him together. His mind had the ability to swing between denial and justification. If he didn't think about what he had done, he could cope. But if he allowed his mind to wander, it started to eat him up all over again. He wasn't sure if he had managed to hone that particular skill, making his mind go blank when he felt himself crumbling, falling apart.

Confusion often followed. He'd blotted out a bad memory but couldn't help trying to recall it. It was like he had seen something out of the corner of his eye, and no matter how fast he moved to focus on what was there only a moment ago, it eluded him.

He found it hard to breathe on these occasions and the only way to cope was to sit still and concentrate on nothing. A black empty space.

Gradually, it would come back to him. That was the worst part.

If he didn't think about what he had done, it was bearable. Blocking it out was more and more difficult with each day. Once he let it in, he had to deal with what it was doing to his mind.

Ian knew he couldn't block it out indefinitely. If he did, they had won after all.

Chapter 70

'Why is it,' said Harry, arms full of Chinese takeaway, 'that I'm the DI, and I had to go out and get the grub for everyone else?'

'Because you've got the job credit card,' said Sandra as she took the order from him and scanned it for her dishes.

He stood back and watched her with incredulity as she surveyed the order of twenty or so boxes, packets and bags, most of which weren't labelled, and went straight for her choice.

The incident-room door opened and Hazel, Pierre, Tom and Sophia walked in, all sniffing the air, and headed straight for the table where Harry had plonked their meal.

'There's a lot of food here for six of us,' said Pierre.

'Stop complaining,' said Sophia, 'and pass me some of that chow mein.'

'Come on then,' said Harry as he took a seat, 'what have Tey and Watson had to say for themselves?'

'Well,' said Pierre as he sat down beside his DI,

'me and Haze interviewed Jonathan Tey. He's a total stroppy twat and made no comment.'

'And me and Tom interviewed Jude Watson,' said Sophia as she poured sweet-and-sour sauce all over her plate and some down her trousers. 'Oh, for fuck's sake. Like I want to iron another pair of strides when I get home at one in the morning.'

Tom laughed and passed her a serviette.

'He spoke to us,' said Tom as he filled his own plate. 'He answered all our questions, from how he and Jonathan know each other—'

'According to Watson, their wives know one another from their children's schools,' said Sophia.

'We asked about Woodville and Watson told us what he knew about him,' said Tom as he chased a pork ball across the table, caught it with the edge of his fork before it rolled off and landed underneath the fire extinguisher.

When Sophia stopped laughing at his misfortune, she said, 'Doesn't make me feel so bad about dropping food down myself now ... He elaborated a lot in the interview about the day Eric Samuels called the meeting and how he and Jonathan stormed out. According to Jude, it was him who lost it and Jonathan who calmed things down.'

Harry listened and watched his detectives. They currently resembled a chimps' tea party, although instead of tea, they were dropping crispy duck and egg fried rice everywhere. What he did know, was that despite their terrible table manners, he trusted their judgement.

'Do you think that we've got the right two people in custody for the murder of Woodville?' Harry asked.

'No,' said Pierre. 'May not be what you want to hear, boss, but not as far as Tey's concerned. I know he's not replying to the questions but when we asked him about Dean Stillbrook and being in Sussex, he shook his head and gave a look of surprise. All we'd told his solicitor up to that point was that he was going to be further arrested for the murder of a man called Stillbrook on the eighth of May.'

'That's right,' said Hazel as she paused in attacking the food in front of her. 'Like you told us, we didn't give him a cause of death or location. I got the impression that Tey wanted to say that he'd never been to that part of Sussex, or certainly not in May at least.'

'So,' said Sandra, 'if it's not these two and it wasn't Toby Carvell and Leon Edwards with their alibi, let's hope it's third time lucky.'

That they still didn't have the right people in custody was something that Harry wasn't looking forward to explaining to DCI Barbara Venice. Even though she wasn't the sort of chief inspector to criticize the team for failing to perform, she was feeling lower than anyone else at the continued failure to charge anyone with murder.

He knew that she felt responsible and he had seen the dark circles under her eyes, noticed that her movements were that little bit slower and that she hesitated to answer the most simple question in case she said the wrong thing or went off at the deep end.

Harry himself worried about the investigation. What DI wouldn't? He didn't want an unsolved murder, and one that was connected to another in Sussex. Their situation was even worse than his own. At least his victim was a paedophile. Their victim was a man with learning disabilities who had been swept up in a young girl's panic. At the back of his mind was that at any second he might get that call to tell him there had been another murder, and sex offender or not, it was something he knew they had to prevent at all costs.

'Sir,' he heard Sophia say. 'I don't think he's listening to me. Boss, do you want some food before us greedy sods eat it all?'

He shook his head. 'Not hungry, Soph. If it's not these two in custody, Tey and Watson, the only other enquiries we've got at the moment that are taking us towards the actual suspects are the two from the café who are probably connected with the Clio. How far have we got with that, Sandra?'

Even though she was negotiating food into her mouth with one hand, Sandra still managed to push a piece of paper across to him, plucked with her other hand from the pile crammed into the box file in front of her. She found it without any effort as if she knew exactly what each of the hundreds of pieces of paper spilling out related to.

'As you know,' she said, 'the stills from outside the Co-op and from the town centre outside the café are likely to be the same two men. They're grainy but no one's completely convinced that they're Tey and

Watson. We can't see the woman's face outside the café, but the chances are it's Millie Hanson. She'll be worth another visit.

'Anyway, the car – they've narrowed it down to twenty-six and I've highlighted the most likely five, although you may choose to disagree.'

'This is great. Thank you, Sandy.'

'It's Sandra, not Sandy,' she said as she pushed the papers back into the box, stacked her plate on top of it and made to leave. 'Don't mind me. I've got work to do so I'll be in my office if you need me.'

There were times when Harry thought that he might have upset someone and perhaps should be a little more sensitive to people's needs. He didn't think this was the case at all with Sandra Beckinsale. She preferred to be on her own, and others preferred her to be on her own. Everyone was happy. He couldn't fault her work though, however frosty she could be. Most detective sergeants would have gone home some time ago.

'What's the plan then?' said Harry. 'Any more inter-views tonight?'

Pierre shook his head as he swallowed the last bite of his meal. 'No. Their solicitors were making noises about having a consultation with them and then head-ing home, ready to start in the morning.'

'OK then,' said Harry. 'I'm going to call it a night too in that case. See if the missus is still talking to me after another late finish. Call me if there are any prob-lems, or I'll see you tomorrow.'

He left them finishing their food, certain that none of them would clear it away properly and the stale smell of Chinese takeaway would assault everyone's nostrils when they came back into the office in eight hours' time.

He made a quick stop via his own office to turn off the computer and pick up his jacket and keys, and then made his way out of the building.

The chill of the night hit him as he got to the rear yard, wrapped up in the thought of that day's work. He cursed himself for not bringing a coat on a November day when his finish time could be anything from four in the afternoon to midnight. He ran the last few feet to his car, took the note off the windscreen that told him he had parked in the wrong bay and if he continued to park outside Major Crime's allocated spaces he would be banned from the car park, threw it on the passenger seat and turned the heating up full blast.

For a minute, he sat waiting for his Lexus to warm up, unsure whether to call Barbara or not. She would want to know what was happening but Harry hadn't wanted to call her from the incident room where he'd be overheard.

He hesitated and then texted her.

Jonathan T and Jude W are still in the bin. Want an update or in the morning?

By the time Harry had pulled out of his space and was driving towards the security barrier, his phone was ringing. He turned the heater down to reduce the phone's volume. The last thing he wanted was to be driving through the streets of East Rise with half the town able to hear what his DCI was talking about. On many occasions he had overheard amusing parts of other people's conversations, but allowing snatches from a murder enquiry to be blurted out at red traffic lights and give-way signs was a sure-fire way to get into trouble.

'Can the people of East Rise sleep safely in their beds tonight, Harry?' said Barbara.

'They can unless they're a convicted sex offender, or anyone suspects them of being a sex offender.'

'I take that to mean no one thinks that the two in custody actually killed him.'

He heard the start of a sigh and then it was cut short, as if she either stopped herself, or realized what she was doing and put her hand over the mouthpiece.

'Please don't tell me that you're still taking this personally, Barb. You have nothing to feel bad about. At the moment, my money's on the two Leon Edwards saw in the café being the same two who were following Woodville on the night of his murder. At the moment, we've ruled out all of the former victims from the original Woodville investigation, including Andrea Wellington who was in a mental health unit at the time of the murder. Anyone else who might have had a reason, or thought they had a reason to kill him, is probably not directly connected with him in the first place.'

He allowed that thought to sit there so they could both enjoy it: Barbara so she could stop beating herself up for something that she couldn't have known would have implications over twenty years later, and which probably had no bearing on the jury's verdict anyway, and Harry because so far they had failed to make the connection between someone in Woodville's background and his death.

'What are we missing, Harry?'

'So far, a lot of sleep. Listen, there's nothing more we can do tonight. We've got more checks and door-knocks tomorrow to find out about the Clio and hopefully, we can take that a bit further.'

'Night then,' she said, stifling a yawn.

'Get some sleep,' he said before ending the call and wondering all the way home exactly who it was who had so far escaped the incident room's radar.

He knew the answer was there somewhere, he just couldn't grasp it.

Before he knew it, Harry was pulling up on his drive-way, eyes straight to the gap in the bedroom curtains. Tonight, there was no glow from the bedside light to greet him. A feeling of relief washed over him as he realized that his wife was either asleep or pretending to be. Either way, he wouldn't have to waste energy dodging the inquisition.

He put his key in the door and pushed it open, dismay hitting him as he heard the murmur of the television from the front room. No sooner had he shut the front door, standing with his back to it, holding his breath, than the sound stopped.

He braced himself and cursed his luck for not having a few more seconds in which to gather his thoughts and be left in peace. Now the questions would start.

'Is that you?' she called.

'Yes, sweetheart. Forgot to check I've locked the car.'

He pushed himself away from the front door and went into the living room.

Harry bent to kiss her on the lips and made a point of sitting next to her. Remembering that he was still wearing his suit jacket, he emptied the pockets and stood up to take it off.

'I'll just hang this up,' he said, hoisting the jacket up by its loop, hooked over his little finger. 'Want a drink?'

'I'll have whatever you're having,' she replied.

On his way out of the room, with his back safely to her, Harry rolled his eyes. He recognized the signs of her trying to make an effort to learn about his job and delve into the day's nastiness. The problem was, he didn't want to share.

He had made a decision years ago not to talk about work to anyone who wasn't a colleague. He knew that the two worlds he lived in didn't mix at all well, and he had tried during his police service to keep details of his job strictly within professional circles.

Harry considered himself a buffer between the normal people in their ordinary lives and the deluge of death and violence that came his way in every part of his working life. He spent his career normalizing the abnormal, and he wasn't about to bring his family into any part of that torment.

It wasn't how it was supposed to be. The two should never merge.

The sad part of it was that he had never voiced this to his wife. They had been married for over twenty years and he had never told her why he refused to discuss his job.

Harry thought he was keeping her safe. Now he recognized that he was keeping her out but he didn't know how to put it right.

He came back from the kitchen with two glasses of tap water. He handed her one and said, 'Well, goodnight. I'm going to have a quick shower and I'll see you in bed.'

Once again, he bent down to kiss her and then turned away from her.

The look she gave him didn't escape his notice; he simply didn't know how to deal with it.

So he chose to walk away.

Chapter 71

Thursday 11 November

Jonathan Tey had experienced the worst night's sleep of his life. In his teens and early twenties, he'd been very used to kipping on friends' floors, in the back of cars, in the street on a couple of occasions, but nothing had come close to the banging and shouting he had heard throughout the night. The stale smell didn't help much either and, if he wasn't mistaken, there was a stench of urine coming from the metal toilet in the corner. He didn't think that it could be coming from anywhere else, unless it was leaking out of the walls.

He had tried to sleep on the ledge protruding from the wall with the thinnest mattress ever manufactured. He had been camping and slept on better, and that had been of a design that he could roll up and carry on his back all day. He had, however, known that no one with HIV or hepatitis had lain down on his bedding and presumably the stiff plastic coating of the cell mattress was all that was keeping him from a life-changing disease.

He let out a sigh and tried for the umpteenth time to stretch the scratchy blanket over his feet. They were cold. They had taken his shoes from him and his socks were not doing an adequate enough job of keeping his toes warm.

Given his size and demeanour, the last thing he wanted to do was admit that he was suffering. That would show they were getting to him. In spite of his failure to cooperate with their questions and his unwillingness to assist in any way, he felt an urge to tell them what he and Jude had done.

He stretched out on his uncomfortable mattress and closed his eyes. He remembered how carefully he and Jude had plotted what they would do to Woodville. He felt the rage build in him all over again, as it had when they'd first left the Cressy Arms and discussed what a dirty bastard Woodville was.

Jonathan felt every part of him tense as anger surged at the thought of people like Woodville being allowed out of prison to walk amongst the proper people, those without a propensity to sexually abuse and rape children. It wasn't normal and he didn't for one minute hold with the belief that they couldn't help it.

Of course they could.

How could an adult ever consider for one moment that that sort of behaviour was acceptable?

He had no regret over what he and Jude had done. They had talked very carefully about what they wanted to achieve and how they were going to go about it. Jude, the dozy bugger, wanted to write it down and make notes, even told him that he should be making a spreadsheet as he was an accountant and that was what they were good at.

Jonathan shook his head at the memory of something so ridiculous.

He kept still now as he remembered how good it had felt to go to Woodville's flat, wait in the dark until he came home and then, just out of view of the video entryphone camera, grab him and take him to the area behind the communal bins.

The management company had gone to the time and trouble to build sturdy wooden shelters to keep the rain off the wheelie bins and the people using them. The shelters also served as a very nice screen, positioned as they were away from the flats so the smell didn't cause offence and there was less chance of a pest infestation spreading to people's homes.

It meant that no one heard Woodville as they slammed his head against the wooden structure and then delivered one or two body blows, afterwards Jonathan's threat ringing in his ears: 'If we hear about you even so much as thinking of turning your fat, horrible head towards a child, we'll come back and remove it.'

Neither of them ever intended to kill him, and he was very much alive when they left him. Between them, they hadn't even hit him that hard; in fact now he came to dissect it properly with time on his hands in a police cell, Jonathan wasn't even sure that Jude had hit Woodville at all.

It had been Jonathan who had grabbed him, Jude trotting alongside to keep up. Jonathan had pushed Woodville's face up against the wooden plank that formed part of the bin shelter. That he remembered perfectly because he rubbed his face up and down, gleeful at the thought that the nonce would get a splinter. It was also him who then pushed his face to the floor, forcing his cheek into spoiled food that had rolled out from under the gap between the concrete and the bottom of the shelter. It was also Jonathan who couldn't resist giving Woodville a kick when he was on the floor, and then he remembered how Jude had grabbed his arm just as he was ready to go in for another kick.

'Enough,' Jude had hissed in his ear. 'That's enough. Just a warning this time.'

The part he recalled most vividly of all was the rush of gratitude he had felt, which Jude would never know about.

For the first time, he had wished that he'd always had a Jude in his life.

If Jonathan had had someone looking out for him, perhaps the events of twenty years ago would have been different. With a friend beside him to tell him enough was enough, he might not have put the boot in that one too many times. The eighteen-year-old student who bumped into Jonathan in the Students' Union might still be alive today instead of ending up fatally injured in the car park, all alone without his friends.

Jonathan might not have taken the beer spilt down his shirt quite as seriously as he did, aiming punch after punch at the younger man.

Jonathan might not have stamped on his head, causing a brain bleed that meant he died in hospital two days later without regaining consciousness.

At least Elaine had gone along with it and given him an alibi, telling the police that he had been at her flat from ten o'clock, an hour before the soon-to-be-brain-damaged student was seen to leave the bar.

In the last twenty years, Jonathan had learned a lot about forensics and contact traces on clothes. He would be pushed to distinguish what part of it was hobby, and what part obsession.

One thing he was fairly certain of was that as long as Jude had also stuck to the plan and told the police nothing, they would soon be free.

Chapter 72

'Well, isn't this our lucky day?' said Harry.

Barbara Venice was still looking a little under the weather and Harry couldn't help but think it was down to the investigation.

'I wouldn't use the word "lucky",' she said as she shifted uncomfortably in her chair. 'I didn't sleep very well. Haven't you got any good news for me?'

'This is good news,' he said.

She stared at him. He filled the frosty silence.

'I admit, it's not good news as far as finding out who murdered Albert Woodville goes but Cold Case are over the moon that Jonathan Tey's DNA was a match on the database for their unsolved student murder from 1996. I found it very funny that their DCI's extremely pissed off that he doesn't get to go on *Crimewatch* for the twenty-year anniversary next week.'

He was relieved to see that Barbara also saw the funny side, especially as her counterpart in Cold Case was someone she had little time for. It warmed his heart that she at least managed a smile.

'Sorry, Harry,' she said. 'Of course it's good news. A young man's family, who have been wondering for decades who killed their son and why, can finally find some peace and get justice.'

'I'm not sure that they'll ever know why. Jonathan Tey has a propensity for violence. You can call a donkey a Grand National winner, but it doesn't mean it'll win any races.'

'Did you just make that up? That's not a saying, Harry.'

'I know, but I thought I'd try it out, see if catches on. With all the management-speak bollocks out there, no one'll even notice. The chief'll be saying it before the week's out.'

She shook her head at him. 'After all these years, you're still an imbecile. Talking of catching, please don't tell me it's going to be twenty years before we get Woodville's murderers. Early retirement or not, I definitely won't still be here.'

'You're not that old, Babs.'

'I don't mean that I'll be dead, you silly old fool. I mean not here in this job.'

He laughed. 'Where's the time gone? We've known each other for so long but I don't think I've seen you look so defeated, especially over an undetected murder.'

'It's currently undetected. Let's not forget that. I haven't given up hope. We're making good progress on the EA52 number-plate enquiry. The team are working their way through everyone in the local area, including one old lady who had her plates taken off her car a few weeks ago. They've since been used in bilkings and theft from other vehicles, stuff like that.

'Whoever murdered Albert Woodville, and possibly Dean Stillbrook too, is out there somewhere. At some time they have to surface. Let's hope it's before they decide to take the law into their own hands again.'

Chapter 73

It hit Millie in one go exactly how horrendous everything had been for her and the children since Clive's death. The way she had fought a battle with herself every single day to carry on and build something of a life for them. Now, what was the point?

Millie Hanson's world had imploded. She knew that now. It was too late to change it.

She was alone with not a soul in the world to turn to. She had gone down the path too many times of trusting people and letting them into her world. That had got her nowhere.

The police had been back to see her and she didn't think she could keep her nerve for much longer.

Perhaps the children would even be better off without her? She could never contemplate suicide but perhaps she could leave them at the door of social services, or simply not pick them up from school and disappear. She wasn't sure she could be one of those mothers from the news who jetted off to Spain for a fortnight, but she could go somewhere where she'd never be found.

One day, Sian and Max would forgive her. They'd realize that she had abandoned them for their own good. Even their father's death had been her fault. If they hadn't rowed that morning before he left for work, he might not have been so angry with her, he might have seen the lorry in the distance as it started to jackknife and managed to get out of the way. In fact, now she allowed herself to think about it, he left fifteen minutes earlier that day after she called him selfish and refused to talk to him over their shared morning cup of tea.

There was no doubt in her mind that her daft attitude that day had led to his death, as if she had killed him herself.

She sat at the kitchen table, untouched tea in front of her, torturing herself all over again with the haunting thoughts of the morning Clive had walked out of the front door for the very last time.

The best way for Millie to tackle her day was to concentrate on anything else her mind could find to fixate on. This used to work, until along came Albie Woodville.

She had let her guard down completely, and a paedophile into their lives.

She disgusted herself with her own stupidity.

Millie placed her elbows on the table, put her head in her hands and wept with shame at the absolute chaos she had created for them all.

Through her tears, she convinced herself that she could see the blurry outline of her brother as he

385

stood in her kitchen a little over a week ago, and he told her that someone ought to do something about Woodville.

She shuddered at the memory of him bending down and shouting in her ear, spittle hitting the side of her face as he spat the words, 'Have you any bloody idea what a paedophile does to a child's mind?'

Her response was to shake her head, wipe his saliva from her cheek and plead with him to stop. She didn't want to hear it. She couldn't hear it.

Her children had been exposed to the worst kind of evil and she had allowed it to happen.

A shadow at the front door caught her eye. For some reason, her stomach lurched, possibly from fear, although she wasn't sure what she had to be afraid of. All the bad stuff had happened now.

The unspeakable would have been someone harming her own children, but she was careful how long she left them for in the company of anyone. Even if she was a little naïve, she was still a mother and would give her own life before allowing anything bad to happen to them. Albert was dead and in their last conversation, which was on the phone, minutes after DC Laura Ward had left her house, three long, torturous weeks ago, he had told her that he had never touched her children.

She got up and moved towards the front door, certain that someone was outside, about to knock.

Millie flung the door open and saw her brother standing on the doorstep.

'Have you been there long?' she asked, as she took in

his dishevelled clothes, several days' worth of stubble and a whiff of body odour.

'You've been crying,' he said.

Ian reached up to wipe his sister's cheek and produced a startlingly white handkerchief from his pocket, incongruous with the rest of his attire.

She took it from him and couldn't help but wonder if it was symbolic of his surrender.

They sat down on the kitchen chairs they had occupied only a couple of days before when he had made such an effort, even bringing her flowers, now wilting and dropping dried petals over the tablecloth.

'Will you please tell me what's wrong?' she said.

'Me?' He gave a wry laugh. 'You're the one who's crying. And have been for some time, I'd say, from the non-existent whites of your eyes.'

'Something's not been right with you, Ian,' she said.

'You could say that.'

'If you tell me that you didn't go round and hurt Albie, I'll believe you, or even—'

He got up from his chair, pushing it back against the wall in one movement. He put his hands over his ears. 'Fuck's sake, Mills. When are you going to see what's right in front of you?'

'Even, even if you went round there to scare him and it went wrong or he fell or something. The police wouldn't tell me how he died. Tell me you didn't do it on purpose and I'll believe you.'

She was leaning halfway across the table towards him, her hands together as if in prayer.

He stood stock-still, a measured calmness about him.

'I could tell you what you want to hear.'

She squeezed her eyes shut as if that could silence the words, or lessen their impact, for she knew what was coming, had known it all along really. It was only a matter of time before her troubled brother imploded.

'I went to his flat, kicked the door down and strangled him. I put a cable-tie around his neck and pulled and pulled until he took his last, vile, pointless breath. I took no pleasure in it but I really thought it would stop what's in my head. It didn't work. It doesn't stop when I'm sober, or awake.'

She looked up at him, fascinated and repelled at the same time.

'You couldn't have done it by yourself. The police were here asking about you and Dave. Tell me that you didn't involve Dave, too.' She was aware that her voice was near hysterical now.

'Why, Ian?'

'Do you know what Woodville said to me?' Ian said, voice at a whisper now. 'When I went round to his flat after the police first contacted you, I went to confront him. He said to me, "OK then, Max, your nephew, I'll admit I shouldn't go near him, but Sian, that's entirely different. We love each other." She's eight fucking years old!'

She felt the bile rise in her throat. This was all her fault.

'Sian,' she whispered. 'He ... he touched Sian.'

Millie had been wrong: things had been even more horrifying than she had imagined.

She had begged her brother not to do anything stupid, had even picked the phone up on more than one occasion to ask Dave to look out for Ian, as he always did, but she had done no more than shy away from the problem. If Clive had been alive, none of this would have happened.

She only had herself to blame for that too, at least that was how she rationalized it in her confused, over-tired and anxious mind.

'You killed him?' she said, unable to believe the very words she spoke. 'What are we going to do?'

She couldn't help but say 'we'. It had always been the two of them. She couldn't remember a time when Ian wasn't there to walk her home from school, help her with her homework, vet her boyfriends.

Besides, if Ian had killed someone, he had done it to protect her and her children. To protect Sian.

The terrible thing was she knew exactly what she had to do; bringing herself to do it was another thing entirely. Her heart was telling her that if she went with her conscience she really would be on her own.

The phone was in her hand before she had time to change her mind. The selfish part of her wanted to replace it in its cradle, ignore the instinct to do the right thing and sit by and do nothing.

The pull of the righteous was so very strong, even though what Ian had done had been for her sake,

Max's and Sian's. She saw the pleading in her brother's eyes. She was about to condemn herself to a life of loneliness.

'Don't, Mills,' he said, 'I'm begging you.'

'I can't do it, Ian,' she said, tears streaming down her face. The terrible truth was that she'd given in to an act of selfishness. Keeping quiet meant she could keep him here, close to her, and not have him taken away from her by the police. And he no doubt believed that she had done it for him.

The knowledge that even her act of kindness was wrought with selfishness was the only thought that filled Millie Hanson's mind as she dropped the phone and found herself in her brother's arms.

Chapter 74

'Hello again, everyone,' said Harry to his depleted staff at the morning briefing. 'I know that we've lost a couple of staff, including our DS. Sandra got called out last night to go and help Riverstone with a rape of a twenty-two-year-old woman. We've lost a couple of DCs too, plus some civilian investigators, so we're thin on the ground.'

He cast an eye over the remaining few. Less a sea of faces, more of a pond. And every one of them seemed fed up and tired. That included Gabrielle, who should have gone on another enquiry for her own sanity if nothing else, but the staff shortage forced Harry to say nothing and let her carry on.

'I know it's been a long week and whilst we've taken four people into custody and not charged any of them – well not for this murder anyway – we have at least helped to find the killer from a murder case twenty years ago through Jonathan Tey being uploaded to the DNA database.'

He paused to smile and focus on everyone in the room individually. It didn't take long, but he knew it was important for the team not to lose momentum.

'I'd like to thank you for your brilliant work so far, and stress that I know it's only a matter of time before we uncover the identities of whoever murdered our victim.

'It's been a week, and I know it's a Friday and most of you have this weekend off, but do I have any volunteers to stay on after their eight-hour shift and work until about midnight?'

Harry looked at Sophia who looked down. He glanced at Tom who made an unconvincing job of appearing to work out if he was available. He then turned his attention to Gabrielle who said, 'I can do it.'

'Me too,' said Pierre.

Hazel waved a hand at him, in more of an 'I don't want to, but I'm new so should show willing' way.

'You lot are what makes the incident room tick,' he said. He meant it, he really meant it, but he had that sinking feeling that told him that another busy weekend was about to start. The chance of there not being a sexual assault, a suspicious death or any manner of hideous crime was very unlikely. That meant his department losing staff.

Once they scattered to the four corners, they probably wouldn't all come back. He knew that some of them would become embroiled in other investigations and, like him, the senior investigating officer wouldn't want to let them go. Everyone's murder investigation was more important to them than anyone else's.

The briefing continued, each making their own contribution. Harry sat and listened, took notes when he needed to, offered advice, and buoyed them up as best he could as he ended their get-together with a heavy heart.

The most he could hope for was that come seven o'clock that evening, someone's memory might be jogged, and for new information to come to light.

Chapter 75

Early hours of Wednesday 24 November

*Two weeks and five days after Albert
Woodville's murder*

It wasn't so much that PC Karl Roundtree was bored
at 4 a.m. in the morning, it wasn't that he had any
particular reason for his eye being drawn to the silver
Renault Clio, he just had a feeling about it. Then he
remembered a briefing slide which drew all officers'
attention to a silver Clio. There had been a partial
registration number too. If he had to put money on it,
Karl would have said that it was a 52 plate.

As he sat in his marked car, partially obscured from the
road by the evergreen kerbside shrubs, but with a clear
view of anything coming up the street, Karl watched the
small car make its way towards him. It held the road well,
it didn't make any dubious manoeuvres, the driver didn't
even glance towards him as he approached the junction
where the officer had chosen to park.

With no other calls to attend, Karl thought he would drive along behind it for a while, carrying out the necessary checks as he drove, waiting to see what the driver would do.

The Clio stuck to the speed limit. The driver would have been a fool not to, although Karl had watched drivers go straight through red lights, scatter pedestrians out of the way on a pelican crossing, pull out at roundabouts, and all with him behind them in a marked car. A car marked with the purpose of making it easy to see. It amused and amazed him.

He drove at a speed to keep up, although he kept his distance. Twice he saw the driver in front look in his rear-view mirror. Karl could only see a face glance back at him, white and male. That much he could be certain of in the gloom of the car's interior and the darkness outside.

He would never be able to say what it was that initially drew his attention to the Clio; possibly it was enough that it was driving around at four o'clock in the morning and wasn't a milk float. Whatever it was, he felt his heart beat a little faster and the beginning of what he sensed was going to be a very good stop-check.

Karl waited for the result of the checks via the control room, all the while following the car, its driver now repeatedly turning his head up towards the rear-view mirror.

A lack of other early-morning checks going on meant that it wasn't long at all before Karl had the information he needed to speak to the driver.

Being single-crewed was not something that ever

concerned Karl. He had been a uniform officer for eight years and had always got the measure of people in any situation. He was a Taser-trained officer but had only had cause to use it occasionally. Not something he had ever carried out lightly and not something he would choose to do again unless his or another's life was at risk. In some situations he wouldn't have time to draw his weapon, in which case it was better to prevent any trouble than try to solve it with violence.

He knew that. The person he stopped might not.

With his lights throwing patches of blue across the town's ring road, Karl got out of his car and walked up to the driver's side of the Clio. He did so with one eye on the occupant and the other watching for movement from any other quarter. It might have seemed as if the car was only one up; it didn't mean that it was.

'Turn the engine off and step out of the car,' said Karl. From where he was standing, all the officer could see inside the vehicle was the driver and a black bag on the front seat.

The door opened suddenly in one swift movement, causing Karl to step back, mindful that he was in the road. He directed the driver, a man he estimated to be about twenty-five years old, skinny build, messy short black hair, dressed in a pair of navy jogging bottoms and a black zip-up hoodie, over to the pavement.

Karl heard the unmistakable sound of a diesel police car as it came round the ring road to join him. Despite the seriousness of this stop-check, any stop-check, he found that he was smiling at his colleagues' inability to keep away and stop themselves muscling in on what might be an interesting arrest. Although performance indicators officially no longer existed, the rest of his team were well aware that he made the most arrests in any given week. He had a reputation for finding those who were up to no good, especially in the small hours.

He watched the driver as he stood on the pavement. There was no doubt about it, there was definitely something on his mind – it was in the nervous jerk of his head, the unsteady placing of his feet, the shaking of his weedy legs inside their jogging bottoms.

Despite his size, Karl knew that a knife stuck in his side wasn't going to care that he went to the gym five times a week. The blade would cut through muscle, bone or sinew as easily as it would fat. Stab vests only covered so much and he didn't fancy another injury after only recently recovering from having a brick thrown at his shoulder.

The wimpy boy standing in front of him shaking didn't seem to be a threat, though he would rather not take the chance.

'Take your hands out of your pockets,' Karl said. 'Now stand over here under the street light.'

He could see that the driver was still uncomfortable in his presence, but by now it could as easily have been the cold causing him to hop from foot to foot.

'Whose car is this?' said Karl, poised to watch the answer as much as listen to it.

'S'mine,' came the reply. 'Had it about six months. Why did you stop me?'

'Your nearside brake light's out,' said Karl, pointing at the left-hand side of the car, eyes still on his jumpy detainee. 'My colleague's here now.'

He thumbed in the direction of the other police car which had pulled up behind his, aware that his inspector, Josh Walker, had sauntered up alongside him, and had simply uttered, 'Morning.'

As he kept an eye on the driver who gave his name as Simon Terry, Karl made to move towards the Clio.

'I've got insurance and everything,' said Simon, seemingly finding his voice.

'I know,' said Karl. 'I've already checked. If you hadn't, I'd be getting your car recovered and you'd be walking home. In the meantime, I'm having a look through your car.'

Simon opened his mouth to protest, his brain catching up with what he had been told about why he had been stopped and Karl's reasons for looking in his car.

'All right?' said Karl, rewarded with a nod from Josh.

As he turned to the Clio he could hear Josh start to make small talk with Simon Terry, a man he had nothing in common with, apart from originating from the same species.

Confident that he would find a substance, an article, an object that should not be in the car because it broke the law, Karl began methodically to search every part of the interior, starting with the black holdall.

He unzipped the bag and peered inside, disappointed when he found nothing of interest. Unperturbed, he continued in his systematic way, moving on to the glove compartment, the foot wells, between the seats and the backs. Not one thing jumped out at him or gave him the adrenalin rush he was craving, deserving, expecting.

The very last place to be searched was the boot. This, he knew, had to be it. Karl glanced over at Simon chatting away to Josh. He had his arms wrapped tightly around himself and he could see his breath as he jabbered away, making comment after comment about nothing in particular. Perhaps he had been wrong about him, perhaps he was losing his touch. If the boot failed to give him what he was looking for, he had either misjudged the entire thing or the lad was better at concealing drugs than Karl had thought.

With one hand on the boot catch and the other holding his torch, Karl popped it open.

He shone the torch into the space and initially he saw nothing whatsoever. If anything, what stuck in his mind was that it was an incredibly empty boot. There wasn't even the usual junk, empty carrier bags, tools, cans, wrappers. He spent a few seconds waving his torch over the marked carpet and then several more working in a slow arc, left to right.

A glimmer caught his eye, a bounce from the torch-light which hit the object at about the same time as a sliver of information hit his brain.

If he wasn't very much mistaken, what he was looking at was a plastic cable-tie. The very type put around Albert Woodville's neck and tightened until he took his last breath.

Chapter 76

Morning of Wednesday 24 November

'You look like absolute crap,' said Harry as he handed Josh Walker a cup of coffee.

Harry had insisted that he get Josh a drink, even though he protested that all he wanted to do was go home to bed.

'I did fast turn-around from lates to nights with only one day off, and most of that I spent with you in the pub, listening to you moaning about your marriage. I'm bollocksed and you give me coffee. That'll help me sleep, if I ever get home.'

'It's only eight a.m. The traffic'll be terrible now anyway so you may as well wait for nine. You could come to my briefing.'

'Or I could not,' said Josh, and took a sip of his coffee. 'And this is rank.'

'All right, Teddy Tired Eyes. It may not be Starbucks, but tell me again what happened.'

Josh had known Harry for far too long to think that

for one moment he wasn't going to act like a big child about to open the best early Christmas present he had ever had. He grimaced as he took another taste of the vile beverage and settled down to tell the tale all over again.

'Like I told you when I called you at five o'clock this morning, and don't pull that face, at least you've had some sleep, Karl Roundtree carried out a check on a silver Clio. I don't think that he knew the relevance of that particular make and model but he certainly knew how Albert Woodville died. It's not something that's public knowledge but he's pretty sharp when it comes to stuff like that.

'Anyway, the driver, Simon Terry, who you've now seen down in custody, seemed a bit nervy and on edge. I thought, as did Karl, that he had some drugs or something on him but it turned out that he'd done a couple of drive-outs in the car from petrol-station forecourts with false and stolen plates on, that kind of thing. He also used to lend the car out to people. That's where it got interesting.'

Harry swallowed a mouthful of his coffee and screwed his face up at the taste.

'Told you,' said Josh. 'Simon Terry was waffling on to me about people borrowing his car as Karl was searching it. There were no actual names forthcoming. At the time, it was something that he declined to tell me.'

'He'll probably change his mind now though,' said Harry. 'What with him being in custody for murder. That usually does the trick refreshing people's memories.'

It was several seconds before Josh spoke again. He scrunched up one side of his mouth and put his head on one side. 'Perhaps it's the lack of sleep but I think that his reaction to the plastic cable-tie in the boot was genuine. I mean, it's not illegal to carry or have them, is it? He gave a kind of "so what" shrug when Karl asked him if it was his and if he'd seen it before.'

Now it was Harry's turn to sit and think about his answer as he rubbed at the stubble on the side of his face. 'We've got the CSI looking over the car now for any traces of Albert Woodville's blood or DNA, and of course for traces of blood or DNA from whoever did him in. We've had four people in custody so far, who all know more than they're letting on, but not one of them was actually responsible for killing Woodville.

'After nearly three weeks, this is most definitely the break we've been looking for. Oh and Josh, before you start on about how the foundation of all good police work is the uniform stop-check, can I remind you that sooner or later we would have got a name.'

'Whatever you say,' said Josh. 'I'll talk to you another time about how a uniform patrol was responsible for stopping the Yorkshire Ripper and catching him. Not a load of suits in an office staring at paperwork.'

Harry was relieved to have grabbed back most of his staff as soon as Simon Terry was arrested. His choice of interview team was quite deliberate. He had an urge to do the interview himself but other than not wanting to hear his team's hysterical laughter at the idea of the DI leading a murder interview, it had been years since he had done one, so there was a strong chance he would make a mess of it.

Instead, he made his decision based upon his observations of how Gabrielle and Sophia had interacted with one another in the incident room over the last couple of weeks, sometimes finding himself spying out of the gap in the blinds at his window towards their desks. It was important to him to know that the team were working together well, and even if they weren't exactly friends, they needed to be able to communicate and rely on one another. They were professional people at the end of the day, and they had to behave as such.

He still found Gabrielle a little odd, and got the impression that most people did. Word had spread of the sad death of her young nephew and even if it wasn't the reason for her aloofness, it meant that the others now accepted her, where once they might have avoided her. They worked with her and tolerated her, and even knew her for what she was: a good officer with some strange views and ideas about the world. Sophia's snooping around after Gabrielle had seemed to stop as soon as he started sending them out on enquiries together, often fabricating reasons that relied on their various skills to put them in a car together. He wasn't sure they fell for it each and every time, but it at least meant that there was a bit more harmony in the office. Word had even got to him that they had spent time together outside work, although he doubted this was true.

As soon as Sophia and Gabrielle went into the inter-view room with Simon Terry, Harry took himself to the remote viewing room to see for himself how the interview progressed. He wanted to observe his two detective constables, but above all he was desperate to find out who had been driving the Renault Clio on Friday the 5th of November.

He took his seat at the point where Gabrielle had finished cautioning Terry and explaining everything he legally needed to know. She was about to ask her first question when the door beside Harry opened and Barbara Venice came in and sat beside him.

'Just starting, Babs,' he said. 'And Gabrielle is lead interview. That's good.'

He had never bothered to explain the trivia and inner workings of his investigation team to the DCI so she merely looked over at him, gave him a nod, and, like Harry, waited to see what the suspect was going to say.

If anything, Gabrielle was going to have trouble shutting him up. Terry spent the first couple of minutes explaining that he was a small-time crook, and there was no way he was involved in murder.

'Thing is,' he garbled, solicitor silent beside him, 'thing is, I let all sorts of people borrow my car. Yeah, I've done some drive-outs from petrol stations with nicked and false plates on the motor. Who hasn't?'

He gave a small laugh and then saw the look on Gabrielle's face.

'Well, you probably haven't. Your job's to nick

people like me, ain't it? What I've done, right, is I've changed the plates. I'll put my hands up to that.'

And he did put his hands up in the air to demonstrate to the two detectives how committed he was to that train of thought.

'Now, the stolen EA52 plate I've since taken off,' he continued, 'I nicked that off some old dear who parked in the next street from me. I saw her get out and go indoors, shut the curtains and I thought: I'll be back later to have them away. It was similar to mine, see. They're the sort I go for. The newer plates, they're sometimes harder to get off.'

He shook his head at this travesty that the vehicle trade was inflicting upon his livelihood.

'You were still using another set of stolen plates when you got stopped this morning,' said Gabrielle. It was in a matter-of-fact style, no accusations, not even a question. Harry liked it. He nodded his approval. He saw Barbara look over at him. He winked back at her.

'Well, I might have pushed my luck there,' Terry said, face clouding over. 'It was risky, I'll give you that. I take a chance with the old dears that they can't be bothered to go to the police station to report it as it's too far away and never open. If you've ever tried to report a crime and rung the public enquiries number, it's always busy, and old people are a lot less likely to have a computer and report it online. Thinking, see?'

He tapped the side of his head at his criminal genius.

When he could see that the two young women weren't particularly stunned by this piece of information, he continued.

'I've got a couple of different but similar sets of plates that I change over from time to time, until I think they're past their use, and then I throw them. When the officer started to follow me this morning, I was shitting it. When he stopped me and didn't arrest me straight away, I thought that I'd got away with it. Then he nicked me for murder. Fucking murder. I've never killed anyone and I don't even know who this Woodville bloke is.'

Gabrielle moved forward in her seat and pushed an A4 piece of paper with a black-and-white image on it towards him.

'That, Terry,' she said, 'was taken from the camera outside the shop where Albert Woodville was last seen alive on the evening of Friday the fifth of November. I would say this is your Renault Clio with the EA52 plate. Who was driving it?'

He bit his lip, moved in his seat and sat on his hands. At last he glanced across to his solicitor.

'My client,' she said, 'understands the seriousness of the investigation. His reluctance is due to not wanting to simply hand you a name.'

'I get that,' said Gabrielle, 'but we have your car following Albert Woodville minutes before he was murdered. Up until now, I haven't told you how he died.'

Simon Terry met her stare.

'Someone forced their way into his flat and put a plastic cable-tie around his neck.'

Terry put a hand to his own throat and lost some of the colour in his face.

Gabrielle continued. 'The exact same type, length, thickness and colour as the one PC Roundtree found in your boot this morning. If you can't give us the name of who was driving—'

'Ian,' he said in little more than a whisper. Then louder. 'Ian Hocking. He said that he and his mate, Dave, wanted to take his niece and nephew to a firework display. Give his sister a night off.'

Harry had no idea how much longer the interview continued as he and Barbara were already making their way to the incident room, making calls on their mobiles, trying to scramble an arrest team together. All the while, he was flying down the stairs, away from Simon Terry's voice, closer to the arrest he had hankered after for nineteen days, he couldn't help but wonder why he hadn't thought to examine Millie Hanson's family more closely.

He recognized the name within a second of it passing Terry's lips. It was that something that he knew he had overlooked after all.

Chapter 77

Afternoon of Wednesday 24 November

Days had gone by without Millie having to worry about her brother. He had spent a lot of time with her and the children, helped them pick out a tree and, despite her insistence that it was far too early, joined in decorating it. He even promised to come to her house early on Christmas morning and forgo his trip to the pub.

She glanced across at him as he sat on the floor with Max, helping him put some Meccano together. He caught her looking his way and smiled at her.

'Ian,' she said, 'you know that I don't want to nag you but have you taken today off? You haven't called in sick?'

'I realize it's because you worry about me,' he said, trying to find the piece he was after as his fingers sought through the array of nuts and bolts strewn over the carpet. 'I hate working at that bloody—'

'Uncle Ian,' warned Max.

He grinned at his nephew and said, 'That stupid recycling centre but until I get something else sorted in the new year, it's what's keeping a roof over my head. I haven't given up hope of that job in Sussex. I spent enough time travelling backwards and forwards down there so hopefully something'll come of it.

'Today, I booked time off to spend with you and see the kids after they got home from school. Once they break up—'

He stopped again, this time because of loud knocking at the door.

'I'll go,' said Sian from her seat on the floor. She'd been learning her spellings, her legs resting on the coffee table in front of her.

'No you won't,' said her mum. 'It could be anyone. I'll go.'

Millie got up and went to the lounge door. She stopped as she put her hand on the handle and looked back to take in the scene behind her: Sian doing her homework without a fight, Max interested in something other than kicking a ball, and her brother the happiest she had seen him in a long while.

She put one foot in front of the other on her way to the front door, her head filled with happier thoughts than she had allowed herself in a while.

There was too much noise outside her house, there were too many people and shapes blurry through the glass. This wasn't right. Panic gripped her. She knew what this was and felt the hairs on the back of her neck stand up.

Millie froze in the hallway. She started to turn, thought of hurrying back to the lounge, telling Ian to run. At the same moment that the letterbox snapped open and someone shouted through it, 'Millie, it's the police. Open the door,' she heard Sian say, 'Why is there a policeman in our garden?' Now she recognized what she was feeling perfectly: the familiar sensation of being absolutely petrified. Once again, she felt that she was about to lose everything.

Unable to resist the urge to open the front door, she felt herself pulled towards it. She saw the back of her own hand as she lifted the catch, powerless to stop the events that were in motion. There was always something about ignoring a ringing phone or someone at the front door that inevitably made her respond. She had been conditioned to behave a certain way all her life, and she wasn't about to break away from it now.

This was her fault. It if hadn't been for her and the children, the police wouldn't be here now. All the bad things that happened were her fault alone.

'Mum,' said Max from behind her in the hallway. 'What's happening?'

She turned. Her son stood a few feet from her, and directly behind him was her brother. Millie had no doubt that she had never looked at someone so in the grip of despair. Her fear for so long had been that she would lose everything. Ian's ashen face and hollow eyes told her that it had only just occurred to him, with half of East Rise police station at her front

410

door, that he was about to have all that he held dear ripped away.

'You must have known this would happen,' she said, barely audible above the rapping on the front door.

'Millie,' shouted the same voice through the letter-box. 'You'll force us to break the door down if you don't let us in.'

'I have to, Ian,' she said. 'I don't want the children to see you dragged away, kicking and screaming. Please.'

She cast an eye towards Max and said to him, 'The police want to speak to Uncle Ian. Go back in the living room with your sister.'

She was at least grateful that Ian stepped out of Max's way and slowly walked towards her.

'Do it, he said with a nod towards the front door.

The result was instant. A flood of police officers, uniform and plain-clothes, filled the downstairs of her house.

There was little to be thankful for, but Millie was hit with a surge of relief that Ian stood passively in the middle of her hallway, next to Clive's grandmother's wall clock, waiting to be handcuffed.

She heard a ripping of Velcro as the officer pulled the cuffs from a harness somewhere, listened to the ratchet of the mechanism as they were snapped on to his wrists and stood there as the tall officer, no more than twenty years old, said, 'I'm arresting you on suspicion of the murders of Albert Woodville and Dean Stillbrook. You do not have to say anything but it may harm your defence if you do not mention when questioned something you later rely on in court. Anything you do say may be given in evidence.'

She tried to take in the name Dean Stillbrook. She failed. Her mind could not contain the information. It was full to capacity with horrors that she couldn't even have begun to imagine.

Chapter 78

Harry sat at the wooden picnic table on the edge of the car park overlooking the sea. It was grey and angry. A little like his own mood. The sound of the seagulls screeching was getting on the few nerves he had left.

He checked his watch and pulled the collar of his coat up to his ears.

The noise of the waves and the gulls covered the sound of Martha's footsteps as she walked across the shingle towards him. He turned as she reached his table.

'Take a seat,' he said as he looked back at the Channel.

'We must stop meeting like this, Harry,' she said. 'Not only will people talk about us, but you're a detective inspector and this is the third time you've left the confines of the police station to talk to me. Usually it's only the lower ranks that have to speak to the likes of me.'

He looked sharply across at her.

'I'd never ask any of my team to do anything I wouldn't do myself, and that includes talking to you, as much as it pains me.'

She gave a chuckle. 'If I didn't know better, I'd say you're flirting with me.'

'Martha.' His movement as he twisted in his seat made the seat judder and brought a look of concern to her face. 'I find you despicable. You are the worst type of human being imaginable. Even so, I promised that, when this was finished, we'd talk about you and the bunch of idiots who call themselves the Volunteer Army.'

She broke eye contact with him and folded her arms, possibly against the cold, but more likely it was hostility communicated through body language.

'And don't pout,' he said. 'It'll give you lines and age you.'

'If this is all such a joke to you,' she said, 'why are you even bothering to talk to me?'

'Well, apart from the promise I made you, I want to know what's going to happen to your organization.'

'Keeping an eye on us?'

He nodded.

'We'll go from strength to strength,' she said. 'Just watch us. We're recruiting all the time. We're doing nothing illegal so you can't stop us.'

'What makes you think I want to stop you?' Harry asked. 'The one thing we share is our loathing of paedophiles, and the irony of that isn't lost on me.'

She stood up and took a step towards the car park. 'I think that we've both said all we need to say for now, except I'm sorry about the innocent ones who get swept up in all this.'

Harry knew that his face was sporting a look of incredulity at her choice of words.

'The innocents?' he asked, voice raised above the crashing of the waves.

'The man in Sussex,' she answered with a frown on her own face. 'Dean something? I understand he was an innocent victim of vigilantes.'

Harry shot up from the bench and lurched towards her, towering over her.

He spat his words at her.

'For one moment, you fucking hideous bitch, when you said "innocent", I actually credited you with giving some thought to the children of sexual abuse.'

'I—'

'Fucking shut up. You don't get to interrupt me. Let me remind you of what you did. You held your own twelve-year-old daughter down, tied her to the bed and then watched and took part whilst your boyfriend raped her. Get out of my fucking sight.'

She trembled as she took another step backwards.

'It's why I formed the VA,' she said in a cracked voice. 'To stop it happening to other women like me. So we could spot them, a support group for parents.'

Harry found himself staring down at her face once more, inches away.

'I shouldn't have met you on a cliff edge. The urge to throw you over the side is far too strong. Get in your car and fuck off before I do something we'll both regret.'

Chapter 79

Gabrielle left the crowded incident room with her empty mug in her hand on the pretence of making a drink before the briefing where everyone would congratulate one another. In truth, she wanted to get away from the noise and hum of over-excited detectives. She knew that she was supposed to feel some sort of thrill at catching a killer but it was wasted on her.

Everything in life was tinged with disappointment. She couldn't explain it to herself so she certainly wasn't going to try to spell it out for others. She accepted that she was odd, emotionless at times. Her only worry over the way she felt was that she failed to hide it. And why did police officers think everyone should be friends and know all about each other's lives? She enjoyed solitude and her own company.

She walked to the kitchen, glanced at her watch to work out how many hours it would be until she could go home and be alone, and opened the door to find Hazel already at the wall-mounted hot water tap.

'Hi,' said Hazel over her shoulder. 'Are you coming to the briefing?'

'Yes,' said Gabrielle as she rinsed her cup in the sink.

'This will be the first I've been to with the right person in custody. I expect there'll be a lot of back-slapping and good humour.'

This was the point that Gabrielle knew she was supposed to make small talk. Up until now she had had little to do with Hazel but thought that she seemed a pleasant enough person.

Gabrielle forced a smile at her as she dried her mug on the damp, stained tea-towel.

'I have to admit,' said Hazel as she reached for the milk, 'I was a bit worried about coming back to Major Crime. Things change and people move on but right now, I'm not sure why I was so worried.'

'I like Harry,' said Gabrielle, feeling her face redden.

From the corner of her eye she saw Hazel jerk and spill the milk over the side of her cup. Automatically, Gabrielle passed her the dishcloth.

'Thanks,' said Hazel. 'Yeah, he seems like an OK boss. And he's led us to the murderer. It's not been an easy few weeks but I feel as though I've settled back in.'

She paused and added, 'How about you? Do you enjoy working here?'

'There's nowhere else I'd rather be,' said Gabrielle with as much enthusiasm as she could muster, which she knew was none at all.

*

'Feels like a hollow victory,' said Harry to Barbara as they sat in his office, about to go into the briefing.

'I know what you mean,' she said. 'I've got DC Ward to interview Sian Hanson. She's a very distressed little girl and I thought that Laura would do a really good job with her.'

'In my mind,' said Harry, head in his hands, 'I pictured some sort of riled-up vigilantes, all brawn and no brains, not Ian Hocking and his old schoolfriend, Dave Lyle. No one should take the law into their own hands but . . .'

DCI Barbara Venice raised an eyebrow at him. 'But what?'

'Could you, hand on heart, say that you'd do any different?'

'I couldn't take another's life for something I felt aggrieved about.'

'He wasn't just a bit pissed off, Barbara. He'd been abused as a child and then saw the same thing happening to his niece. I'd do it for my children. You won't convince me that you wouldn't do the same.'

'We have to be better than that,' she said with a look on her face that told Harry she was trying hard to convince herself as much as him.

'The thing is,' he said, 'we're convinced that Hocking was in Sussex at the time that Dean Stillbrook's body was found, but we still have the decomposing body of Keely Kershaw that we haven't even officially linked to these two. She'd been found guilty of abusing children in a nursery under her care. My money's on that someone did her in too – it's just going to be difficult to prove.'

'And Ian Hocking's part in it?'

'Definitely not,' said Harry with a shake of his head. 'He was out of the country before she was last seen alive and returned long after the body was discovered.'

'Are you telling me that there are more people out there doing this?'

'I am, Barbara. Besides, Hocking didn't do all this alone. When we find Dave Lyle, we may have the two who murdered Woodville, but we don't stop looking there.'

He looked her straight in the eye and said, 'I've pushed my team to find whoever did this. Now I want to shake his hand and let him go.'

'That's not what we do. We gather the evidence and put it before the court. It's not our decision. This has been a very difficult investigation for all of us. I can see a little clearer now and it's definitely not the murder I want to be my lasting memory of my police career. Now I've had a chance to put things into perspective, take a breath, I'm not looking to retire just yet.'

She paused and said in softer tones, 'I know that my earlier crisis didn't go any further, and I thank you for that.'

The response was a very slight nod of the head and the words, 'Bloody glad to hear it, Babs.'

'And there's one very important thing you're forgetting about all this, Harry,' she said.

Harry sat for a second or two, chewed his bottom

lip and said, 'I think the point you're going to make is that Dean Stillbrook was a completely innocent man and died because someone took the law into their own hands.'

He rubbed a hand across the stubble on his chin and said, 'OK, my views make me an arsehole but at least I'm human with it.'

He stared at her for a few seconds, leapt from his seat and said, 'You're right, as always, Babs. Come to the briefing.'

They walked into a packed conference room. Most of the incident room were there; detective constables, detective sergeants, civilian investigators, HOLMES staff, even DI Milton Bowman who hadn't worked on the job. Harry recognized the scene before him for what it was: those who had played a tiny part in the investigation wanted to be enshrouded in its glory, plus a few hangers-on. He would have preferred to take his core staff off to the pub, but there wasn't time for that. There were other murders waiting in the wings, ready to chip away at what was left of his sanity.

It went quiet as Harry and Barbara walked in.

'Hello, everyone,' said Harry to the hushed crowd. 'On behalf of myself and Barbara, I would like to thank you all for your tireless work and dedication to finding Albert Woodville's murderer. Another arrest team are out trying to find David Lyle, Hocking's friend, and likely offender from the CCTV stills of the Clio. In the meantime, you should all be very proud of yourselves. I certainly am proud of you. Congratulations.'

Never had towing the party line for the sake of the organization stuck in Harry's throat as much as it did at that moment.

The murder of Albert Woodville would always be the lowest point in his career.

Acknowledgements

This was at times an uncomfortable book to write. Sexual abuse, especially of children, is never an easy topic.

That this novel exists at all is down to so many people for so many reasons. A fair number of them will always remain nameless but thank you so much to my wonderful agent, Cathryn Summerhayes of WME, for your enthusiasm and encouragement. Thank you to Jo Dickinson, extraordinary editor, for your insightful suggestions and help whenever I needed it. Many thanks to everyone at Simon and Schuster who has made me feel so welcome and made the entire publication process such a pleasure.

Thank you to DC Kerry Verhiest for your invaluable knowledge regarding ViSOR and the policing of sex offenders. A lengthy conversation with you made me realise your in-depth understanding of a part of policing I had only a scant idea of.

My thanks to DC Alex Hayter for making three years of my police career much easier than it would otherwise have been. There were many low points, as you'll recall, but worth every stressful moment in the end.

About a third of the novel was written in Tintagel, far too beautiful for something so grim. Nevertheless, many thanks to Tara Melton and Andrea Richards for the use of Gilbert Lodge. Cornish air, cider and clotted cream definitely brought on the inspiration.

Last, but by no means least, my husband Graham. For just about everything else.